Anything for Him

Book One in the *No Escape* Series

LK Chapman

Copyright © 2016 LK Chapman

Cover design by Books Covered

All rights reserved. No part of this publication may be reproduced, stored in a retrieval system, or transmitted in any form or by any means, electronic, mechanical, photocopy, recording or otherwise, without prior written permission of the copyright owner – except for the use of brief quotations in a book review.

The characters, events and locations in Anything for Him are fictitious and any similarity to real people, events or locations is not intended by the author.

ISBN: 978-1-8382644-0-6

This book is also available in ebook and audiobook formats.

To my husband, Ashley
For your unwavering support in everything that I do.

PART 1

Felicity

1

To begin with the shrill tones of the phone seemed like part of my dream, breaking into my sleep like a repetitive and unwelcome soundtrack. Gradually, my mind left the world of the imaginary and I realised it was the dead of night and somebody was calling me.

When I looked at the screen, I wasn't surprised to see it was Jay.

'What do you want?' I slurred into the phone, my head still fuzzy with sleep.

'Is this Felicity?'

The question cut through my grogginess. It was a woman's voice – not Jay at all – though she must be using his phone.

'Who's asking?' I said.

'Felicity, it's Georgia—'

I groaned inwardly, or maybe outwardly, I wasn't too sure.

'You need to come into town,' she continued, 'it's Jay—'

'What's he done?'

'He's drunk,' she said. She sounded on the verge of tears. 'I was trying to get him home but he won't move. He just keeps asking for you.' She let a reproachful tone slip into her voice for that last bit and I couldn't help but smile. She'd always been suspicious of me and Jay. She must be hating this. The idea put me in rather a good mood.

'Fine,' I said, doing my best to sound grudging, though in truth I was almost beginning to enjoy myself. 'Where are you?'

'In town,' she said, 'outside the old cinema—'

'All right,' I said, 'I'm coming.'

I didn't bother getting dressed. I put my coat on over the top of my pyjamas and shoved my bare feet into a pair of trainers. It was only a ten minute walk from our flat into town. You'd be able to see the old cinema quite clearly from the window in our living room in fact, were it not for the row of office blocks across the street. I walked quickly, my hands thrust into my coat pockets, beginning to shiver. This was not the best time of year for Jay to start on his drunken antics.

I heard Jay and Georgia before I saw them. They were arguing. I could hear Georgia's irritating, reedy voice carrying down the street – berating him for getting so drunk, demanding to know why he wouldn't go home unless I came to get him.

'Are you sleeping with her?' she shouted at him. 'Because if you are it's over, Jay. It's over—'

I rounded the corner and saw them illuminated by the streetlights, just in time to watch Jay cut Georgia off mid sentence by leaning forward and vomiting spectacularly onto the pavement in front of her. His sick splashed all over her tights and pink suede heels and she was so horrified that she was stunned into silence. She simply stared at her legs with her mouth open so that she looked even more stupid than she normally did. Barely a second went by before Jay was sick again, though what came out was mostly clear-ish liquid this time. Georgia stood frozen with disgust, looking from her ruined shoes to Jay's face as though she simply couldn't decide what to do with herself. The sight was so funny that I couldn't help laughing, and the sound finally alerted her to my presence.

'You,' she said quietly, as I walked towards her. 'You!'

Before I knew what was happening she flew at me, catching a fistful of my hair and twisting it in her hand, so I clawed at her face with my nails and she let go.

'Come on then!' I shouted at her, as she put her hand up to her cheek. I could see my attack had drawn blood. I gave her a hard shove, and she backed away from me, frightened. In desperation, she looked down at Jay, who was sitting cross-legged on the pavement, face oddly thoughtful as he watched us.

'Look what she did to me!' Georgia said to him. 'Look at my face.'

He did as she asked, and as his eyes rested on the nail marks his mouth twitched a little and he started to laugh.

'What the... what the hell is wrong with you?' she demanded. 'She *attacked* me!'

'Go home, Georgia,' I said.

She spun to face me again, wild and confused. I felt almost sorry for her, but at the same time, she should have seen through Jay long ago. It was painfully obvious to me that his relationship with her had been little more than a kind of sick joke.

There was a moment of silence as she considered what to do. I thought about trying to say something further, but there was no point. Nothing I could say would make things any better. With one final glance at Jay she began to walk away. 'Fine,' she mumbled, brushing past me with deliberate roughness. 'You're welcome to him.'

I watched her for a while as she stumbled along, unsteady in her ridiculous pink heels, until she rounded the corner and was gone.

...

'You proud of yourself?' I asked Jay. He was still sitting on the pavement, swaying slightly, as though to a tune only he could hear. His eyes were dull, and there was sick crusted at the corner of his mouth and on his chin, which I found strangely unnerving as I was so used to him looking immaculate. As if he could tell what I was thinking he rubbed his mouth with the sleeve of his jacket and spat on the pavement.

'I hated her,' he said vaguely.

'I know you did,' I said, feeling irritated and tired. 'You always hate them. That's how you like it, isn't it?'

Jay gazed up at me. 'Fliss,' he said.

'What?'

'Why am I on the floor?'

I managed to drag him to his feet, but instead of allowing me to lead him back home Jay made off in a different direction.

'Jay,' I called after him, 'what are you doing?'

He ignored me and continued on at a rapid pace, leaving the centre of Coalton and taking seemingly random turns. I tried to catch up with him, but when I got close he'd sprint away from me. Even in his drunken state, his frequent trips to the gym and runs along the canal meant I had little chance of catching up with him and I became increasingly confused about where we were. Although I'd lived in Coalton all my life, the housing estate we ended up in wasn't familiar to me. I had expected Jay to give up and slump down at the side of the road, maybe throw up again, but there was something of a grim purpose to the way he pressed on with his detour and I had to admit I was curious.

He slowed down when we reached a long, straight road with small cul-de-sacs and closes branching off. I tried to take his hand, but he shook me away. He was looking intently into the front gardens of the houses we were passing, as though searching for something.

'Jay, for God's sake,' I said, 'it's the middle of the night, can we go home?'

He stopped outside a house that was having some work done on its paved driveway, and bent down to pick up a brick from a pile by the pavement. 'Jay,' I said, 'what—'

He was off again before I could stop him, clutching the brick in his hand. I had no doubt in my mind that he intended to do some damage with it. Why, I had no idea. Jay was a law unto himself when he was in this sort of state. I'd had to step in many times in the past to prevent him getting in fights when we were out together.

I forced myself to run faster, and I caught him just as he stopped outside one of the houses. Half hidden behind a big fir hedge, it looked to be an eighties or nineties semi – a little bit scruffy, but otherwise unremarkable. I'd certainly never been there before, or heard Jay mention anything about who lived there. As far as I was aware, Jay didn't really know anybody in Coalton; from how he told it he'd pretty much just stuck a pin in a map and decided to come and live here. He paused for a while, as if he was thinking through his next move, then he lifted his arm, but he'd waited too long and I was able to wrestle the brick from his hand before he could throw it. I held it out of his way behind my back and he tried weakly to get it away from me, but his heart didn't seem to be in it any more, and he was in too much of a state to carry on fighting with me. He turned and started walking back the way he had come, then he paused beside a house on the corner, which had a wooden fence around its garden.

'Jay,' I said softly, as I made my way towards him, 'let's go now. Let's go home.'

He stared at me a moment, then his face contorted in anger. 'You should have let me do it!' he yelled at me, and before I could stop him he drew back his fist and slammed it into the fence, leaving a splintered hole in the wooden panel.

In my shock I let the brick fall to the ground, while Jay cried out in pain and then knelt down on the pavement clutching his hand in his lap. While Jay whimpered and swore under his breath I took a quick look up and down the street and was thankful that nobody was around. When he started making sobbing noises, I crouched down by his side and put my arms around him.

'What the hell, Jay?' I whispered into his hair.

'You should have let me do it,' he told me again.

'Do what?' I said. 'Put a brick through someone's window?'

'You don't understand.'

'Who lives there, Jay?' I asked him.

He didn't answer and I reached down to try to get him to show me his injured hand, but he'd hidden it away under his other hand in his lap.

'Let me see it,' I said.

I pulled at his wrist and he didn't budge. 'Let me see it, Jay,' I told him again.

He gave in and let me pull his hand away from his lap, and I saw he was bleeding.

'Does it hurt?' I asked him.

He shrugged. He didn't seem particularly upset any more.

'It will when you're sober,' I told him. I pulled him to his feet and put my arm around his waist. This time he didn't protest when I began to walk towards home.

2

When we got inside our flat Jay seemed, if anything, more drunk. I took him into his bedroom and deposited him on the bed, then I went to get him a glass of water. When I got back I saw that he'd made an attempt at getting undressed but hadn't quite managed it, so he was now sprawled face down on his bed with his jeans round his ankles. He looked so daft I almost laughed, until I noticed he'd managed to smear the blood from his hand all over the pristine white bed linen.

I put the glass of water down on the bedside table and tried to wake him up. 'Jay,' I said, 'you've got blood everywhere. Jay!'

He turned his face towards me and opened one eye. Then he caught sight of the blood and his face contorted with disgust.

'Need...' he said, 'need... new sheets.'

He tried to get up but I stopped him.

'Fliss,' he said, 'blood...'

'Don't look at it,' I told him. He hated the sight of blood, just as he hated any dirt and mess. Sleeping in a bed with blood on it was like a nightmare to him. But thankfully in his drunken state he managed to shrug it off, and I made him sit up to drink the water.

'I'll get something to bandage your hand,' I said.

We didn't have any actual bandages in the flat, though we did have some antiseptic cream, and I found an old tea towel which I thought would do the trick for the moment. The bleeding wasn't severe, though his hand was damaged sufficiently that I decided I'd make him go to the hospital in the morning. He was quiet while I fixed him up, watching what I was doing with bleary interest.

'I love you Flissie,' he said after a while.

'I love you too,' I said automatically.

He shook his head. 'I mean really love,' he said, 'not like how we normally mean it. I mean like I don't want to be with anyone else any more. And I don't want *you* with anyone else either.'

I finished the makeshift bandage and pulled his duvet back so he could get into bed. 'You're drunk,' I said, 'you don't know what you're saying.'

'I do know what I'm saying.' He caught hold of my wrist. 'Sleep in here with me.'

I took another look at the state of him. He'd managed to kick his jeans away from his ankles, and was now dressed in a vomit splattered t-shirt and his underwear. His sandy hair, which was normally styled to choppy, tousled perfection was a greasy mess, and he smelt of stale sweat and alcohol.

'I think you're better off on your own tonight,' I told him.

He didn't let go of my wrist. 'Please, Flissie,' he said, 'I'm not after a shag. Just sleep in here with me.'

I laughed. 'Yes, Jay,' I said, 'I understand what you want. I can see for myself that you're in no state to shag anyone.'

'I could,' he said stubbornly.

I sat down beside him and he closed his eyes. 'Jay,' I said softly, 'that house. Why were you—'

I stopped as I heard him take a deep, rattling breath. He was already fast asleep.

...

In the morning I was surprised when a knock on my bedroom door woke me. I'd assumed Jay would sleep late, but when I told him to come in I saw that he had already showered, and he was dressed in dark grey jeans and a slim-fitting white t-shirt. There was no hint of a hangover about him; he looked as fresh as if he'd had an eight hour sleep.

I sat up in bed and he came over to me. 'I had a text from Georgia,' he said, sounding puzzled, 'she called me a "fucking bastard."'

I smiled at the frown on his face. 'You don't remember, do you?'

'Did I break up with her?' he asked. Then he looked at me hopefully. 'Was I really harsh about it?'

'She realised you've been sleeping with me and then you threw up all over her feet.'

Jay grinned. 'Really?' he said. 'Did she cry?'

'Not that I saw. She went for me and grabbed my hair, so I scratched her face until she let go. I made some pretty big scratches, actually.'

'Nice,' Jay said.

'Well, no,' I said, 'it wasn't, really. In fact, I feel pretty bad about it.'

Jay considered this. 'Should I text her back, do you think?' he asked.

'And say what?'

'Dunno. Just wind her up some more.'

'I think you've done enough.'

'Maybe,' he said. He leaned in to kiss me and I turned my head away. 'Last night,' I said, 'you wanted to throw a brick through someone's window.'

Jay moved away from me and nodded.

'So you remember that?'

'Yeah.'

'Whose house was it?'

Jay's forehead wrinkled. 'It doesn't matter.'

I could see he was thinking about leaving so I grabbed his hand. 'Tell me.'

'Fliss, it was nothing.'

'Then tell me.'

'Fine,' he said with a sigh, 'the guy who lives there was being a dick about where I parked my van the other day. That's all.'

'I don't believe you.'

'I'm telling the truth,' he said. 'I just parked a tiny bit over his driveway for like two minutes while I did a delivery and he went off on one. I just wanted to teach him a lesson.'

'By throwing a brick through his window?'
'Yeah.'
'Hardly proportionate, is it?'

Jay looked away from me and I reached for his injured hand. He'd put a fresh tea-towel around it, but I wanted to see how it was looking in the light of day.

'Can I see it?' I asked him.
'No.'
'Jay, come on,' I said, 'I just want to see if you're okay.'
He still wouldn't let me, so I said, 'Does it look really bad?'
'It's pretty messed up.'
'Does it hurt?' I asked.
He nodded.
'All right,' I said, 'let me get dressed, and I'll go with you to the hospital.'

...

It was busy and noisy in the accident and emergency department. The receptionist didn't bat an eyelid when Jay explained he was there because he'd punched a fence, but I could see he was embarrassed. In fact, most of the walk to the hospital he'd tried to persuade me it wasn't necessary for him to get his hand looked at, while I quietly assured him that it was.

It was a few hours before anyone was available to see him, and when he finally came out and found me again in the waiting area he looked a bit pale and shaken, but it turned out his hand wasn't badly injured so I took him home again.

'Do you remember what you said to me last night?' I asked him as we walked.

He thought about it. 'No,' he said.
'You told me you love me.'
'I do love you. I say it all the time.'
'No, Jay. You said you *really* love me.'
I watched a smile creep across his face. 'Did I?'
'Yeah.'

'And what did you say?'

'I said you were pissed and had no idea what you were talking about.'

When we got back home, I was horrified to see Georgia standing outside, leaning against the wall and looking at her phone. She was wearing skinny jeans and a thick pink jumper that made her look like an angry marshmallow. Her hair was scraped back into a messy ponytail, so the marks I'd made on her cheek were very obvious. She scowled when she saw me with Jay.

'Oh, for God's sake,' I said, under my breath.

Jay tried to ignore her, but she took a step towards us when we reached the door so he had to look at her. 'What?' he said. 'What do you want?'

She seemed taken aback by his tone, but quickly recovered herself. 'I wanted to give you a chance to apologise,' she said.

'Why should I apologise?' Jay said. 'I never told you I *wasn't* sleeping with Felicity.'

Georgia's eyes flicked briefly over to mine, and then she turned back to Jay and gestured at her face. 'Look at me,' she said, 'look at what she did to me!'

Jay shrugged. 'So? You attacked her. What did you expect?'

Georgia gave him a long look. 'This isn't over,' she said eventually.

Back inside the flat I made myself a coffee and sat at the dining table cradling the mug in both hands. In all honesty I didn't really care what Jay had done to Georgia. I didn't exactly think it was admirable, but he was a grown man, it was up to him what he did. He sat down beside me and watched me. 'You think I went too far this time,' he said.

I looked at him. 'You can do what you want.'

I took a sip of coffee and he fiddled with the bandage on his hand.

'What do you think Georgia was talking about?' he asked. 'When she said she was giving me a chance to apologise and that it wasn't over.'

'How the hell should I know?'

'Do you think she's going to go all psycho on me?'

'Hopefully,' I said, 'it would serve you right.'

Jay watched me curiously. 'What's wrong with you?' he said. 'Why are you being like this?'

I picked my coffee up and left him at the table on his own. I suddenly couldn't bear to be around him.

3

In the afternoon Jay took himself off to the gym, and I sat down at the little desk in my room. Jay and I lived in a two bedroom flat, and while we both paid the same towards the rent, he had the big double bedroom, while I was crammed into the smaller room next to it. It didn't matter a great deal – I didn't have much stuff. But what I did have were all my tools and materials for making jewellery; the untidy jumble of metal, wire, tools and half-finished projects spread out across the small desk. I ended up losing an hour or so sat at the desk just thinking; looking through half finished jewellery projects and almost wanting to start something new, though nowadays I always found I had a mental block. In the end I just sat back in my chair and closed my eyes.

Jay arrived home shortly after and instead of heading straight for the shower like he usually did, he came into my room.

'It was two years ago today that it happened,' he announced. 'That's why you're in a mood.'

I didn't open my eyes or make any acknowledgement.

'I remembered,' he said, 'I worked it out.'

'Congratulations,' I said, 'what do you want? A medal?'

I heard him walk across to me and he put his hands on my shoulders. 'Talk to me about it, Fliss.'

I opened my eyes and looked up at him over my shoulder. 'You want to hear about it, do you? Really?'

'Well… yeah,' he said slowly.

'No, you don't.'

He let go of me. 'Fine,' he said, 'if that's how you want to be. I'm having a shower.'

I sat on my own a little longer, then I wandered into the bathroom to join him. He hated using the communal changing rooms at the gym and always came home to wash. I knew he was sensitive even about me seeing how he did it, but I'd grown used to the way he'd clean each part of himself at least twice before moving on, how he didn't like it if any part of him aside from his hands and feet accidentally touched the bath, tiled walls or shower screen, and how he hated any sort of time limit or pressure being put on his strict routine. The more stressed or unsettled he felt, the longer the whole thing would go on for. Not that he ever admitted to feeling either of those emotions, but I knew that he did.

'What do you want?' he asked me as I sat on the end of the bath, occasional sprays of water misting my face.

'Look... I'm... I'm sorry I snapped at you,' I said. 'I know you were trying to help.'

'You just don't believe I really want to.'

'Jay, you don't have to pretend that you care. I didn't start spending time with you, or move in with you because you cared. I did those things because you *didn't*. You just treated me exactly like I was anyone else. That was all I wanted. That's what I *still* want.'

'It's not though, is it?' Jay said. 'Or you wouldn't still get so down about it.'

To my surprise, he turned the shower off and stepped out of the bath so he could sit on the edge of it beside me with a towel around his waist.

'Fliss, I do get it, you know,' he said. 'After all, my mum killed my dad. What happened to you is the same but just the other way—'

I slammed my hand so hard on the side of the bath that Jay flinched. 'Your mum did not *kill* your dad!' I said. 'Your dad died of cancer. You can't *give* people cancer. My dad burned himself and my mum alive in what was supposed to be our family home. Does that sound like the same thing to you?'

'All right,' Jay said. 'Look, I'm not good at this. And you're right, when I first met you I really didn't care, but... I do now.'

'If you say so.'

'Fliss, at least he waited until you were out,' Jay said at length, 'I mean, you hear about it on the news, don't you? Guys who get in debt like your dad and then kill their whole family, their kids and everything.'

I could have laughed, his attempt to console me was so ridiculous.

'I'm serious,' he said, 'it really could have been worse. Your mum and dad were pretty old anyway. The real tragedy would have been if you had died when you'd only just started really living.'

'Jay, they were my parents.'

'Yeah. I know.'

'My dad could have asked me for help. It's not like I was a little kid, I was working—'

'It's pride, isn't it?' Jay said. 'He wouldn't have wanted to take money off of you.'

'Yeah,' I said bitterly, 'because what he did instead was so much better.'

Jay touched my arm briefly. 'Look, how about I cook something for you later? Take your mind off it. Would that help?'

I shrugged. Dinner obviously wouldn't help, but at least it couldn't make it any worse.

I actually did feel a bit better as it reached evening, and while Jay went to the little shop across the street to buy some wine and some ingredients, I curled up on the sofa with my eyes closed waiting for him to get back. About twenty minutes later I heard his key in the door, but when he burst inside he was incoherently angry, yelling and swearing before I even reached the hallway.

'Jay,' I said, 'what on earth has—'

I stopped as soon as I saw him. His lip was bloody and swollen, and he had a graze down one arm like he'd fallen.

'Oh my God,' I said, 'did someone do this to you?'

I reached towards him but he ignored me, pacing the hall, face white with rage.

'Fucking Georgia's brother and some other fucking prick,' he said, gesturing towards our front door, 'they jumped me. Right outside the building.'

I tried to put my arm around him and steer him towards the living room, but he twisted away from me, going instead into the bathroom. I followed him inside and he spat into the basin, splattering the gleaming white porcelain with blood, and recoiling slightly when he saw it.

'So you know who it was?' I said. 'In that case we should call the police. Georgia obviously told them to do this, she can't—'

'No,' he said, 'no... I'll fucking... I'll fucking deal with it myself.'

He started towards the front door so I stood in his way.

'Don't even think about it,' I said.

He shoved me out of the way. 'I'm going round there,' he said.

'Jay, no!' I said. 'You're being ridiculous. You're going to get yourself arrested.'

I ran after him all the way out of the building to the car park.

'Jay, please, please, don't do this,' I said. 'You're going to make it worse.'

He got inside his van so I stood behind it, shaking with fear and adrenalin as he started the engine.

'No!' I screamed at him uselessly. 'This is crazy!'

He started to reverse towards me and I had no choice but to step aside, but I knew something terrible would happen if Jay got involved with Georgia's family while he was feeling like this and I had to stop him.

'Jay!' I shouted again, as he made it out of the parking space in a screech of tyres and started speeding towards the road. At the very last second he stopped, and I ran towards the van. But he hadn't given up on his plan, he'd just decided to let me come with him, and he swung the passenger door open so I could get inside.

I begged and begged him not to do anything. He was driving like a lunatic, and I thought he'd end up wrecking the van, or even killing somebody.

'Just let me call the police,' I said for probably the twentieth time. 'Please Jay, don't go round there.'

'Shut up.'

'Jay, listen to me. This is what she wants. She's angry about what you've done, and she wants a reaction! Either she wants you to go to over there so they can beat you up even worse, or they'll wait for you to do something to them and call the police. Surely you can see that?'

'I don't care.'

'Please,' I said, 'Jay, please, please, don't let her win. Just let it go.'

All of a sudden Jay swerved to the side of the road and slammed on the brakes, throwing us both forward in our seats.

'Jay?' I said.

'All right,' he said flatly.

'All right what?'

'I won't go round there.'

I tried to reach across to him but he moved out of the way. After a second or two, he looked round at the road to check nothing was coming and pulled away from the curb. I thought he'd drive us home again, but instead I realised we were making our way towards the housing estate from the night before.

'Jay,' I said, 'why—'

'I'll tell you when we get there.'

I stayed silent until he pulled up opposite the house he'd wanted to vandalise the night before. I'd never believed his crap about going there to settle a score over where he'd parked his van, and I could see from his expression as he looked at the house that I'd been right to doubt him. There was no way a dispute about parking could create the level of hatred I saw in his face.

'Jay,' I said slowly, 'who lives here?'

'Mark,' he said. 'Mark Hutchington.'

4

It wasn't a name I was familiar with.

'I don't understand,' I said, 'who is Mark Hutchington?'

Jay wiped his busted lip with the back of his hand, then he opened the door and spat some blood onto the street outside. 'He used to be my friend,' he said.

'Okay.'

Jay closed the door again and seemed to consider how best to start explaining.

'You know I was sort of homeless for a bit?'

'Yeah.'

'I asked him for help. I went to him when he was at university, and I begged him to help me. Do you know what he did?'

'No.'

Jay looked at me grimly. 'He threw me out,' he said, 'he threw me out onto the fucking street.'

'Why didn't you go home?'

'Home?' he said. 'You mean with my *mum*?'

'Yeah.'

Jay shook his head in disbelief.

'So,' I said, 'I still don't get it. If Mark was your friend, why wouldn't he let you stay?'

'Because he doesn't want to be associated with me.'

'Perhaps... perhaps he didn't understand how bad things were for you,' I suggested.

'Oh, he understood,' Jay said, giving the house across the street a dirty look. 'He understood all right.'

'So, then, why...'

'Because I wasn't good enough for him any more,' Jay said. 'Not when he had all his posh new friends to impress. And it would be exactly the same now. He's got it made, and he doesn't want to be reminded that he fucked up my entire life.'

I was quiet for a while. 'Jay,' I said gently, 'all he did was refuse to let you stay. How can you say he messed up your whole life—'

Jay slammed his hand against the steering wheel. 'Because he did!' he said. 'Everything that's gone wrong for me is because of him. He doesn't even know what he's done. He just sits there with his fancy job, and his degree, and his car and his flat, and his family who actually care about him, and what do I have? I don't even own my fucking *van*.'

I reached out for Jay's leg and gave it a gentle squeeze. 'You have a flat,' I said, 'and you have a job. And you have... me.'

Jay glanced round at me briefly. 'He *owns* his flat,' he said. 'It's the ground floor part of that house. And that's his car.' Jay pointed to a blue Fiesta.

'And his family?' I asked. 'Does he have a girlfriend... or a wife?'

Jay laughed. 'Fuck, no,' he said. 'I've been coming here for years and I've never seen a woman with him. In fact, he never goes anywhere. I don't think he even has any *friends*.'

'I thought you said he has a great life,' I said.

Jay made a noise of exasperation. 'It's better than mine.'

I looked across the street at the house where this Mark Hutchington apparently lived. 'You said you've been coming here for years?' I said.

'Yeah. I like to see what he's doing.'

'Why?'

'So I can work out how to teach him a lesson.'

I struggled to take it all in. Was Jay actually being serious? Did he really blame some old friend for all his own troubles?

'We'd been friends almost forever,' Jay said. 'Since my parents moved to Tatchley just before I started school. That's the village where I grew up,' he explained. 'Tiny little place. He was the only other kid my age who lived there. For a long time, anyway.'

I nodded. Jay didn't often talk about his past in any detail, and although he had mentioned his parents and the little village to me briefly before, I had certainly never heard of Mark, or much else about his childhood.

'I... I didn't have a very good time when I was younger,' he said. 'I got a lot of stick at school. People always making digs about... stuff. Mark... Mark kind of stood up for me.'

'I'm glad someone did,' I said.

Jay wiped some fresh blood from his lip with the back of his hand. 'Yeah,' he said, 'well, it only makes what he did to me even worse.'

'And what was that?'

Jay gazed out of the window. I could see a light was on in one of the downstairs rooms of the flat, though most of the ground floor was hidden behind the fir hedge. I waited a long time for Jay to answer, and when he did, it wasn't what I expected. 'He slept with my girlfriend,' he said.

'And that...' I said slowly, '...that *ruined* your life?'

'Yeah,' he said. 'I loved her. But right from the start he wasn't having it. He did everything he could to turn us against each other, stirring things up, making me and her fall out with each other. He kept on and on and on, driving a wedge between us, and then I found out he was sleeping with her.'

My mind was reeling. For one thing, it was extraordinary to me to think that Jay ever cared about a girl enough that this would have any impact on him, but even more remarkable was the fact his pain about it barely seemed to have faded. He was angry. He was *still* angry.

'When... when was this?'

Jay worked it out. 'Eleven years ago.'

'So it was when you were... what... *sixteen*?' I asked, astounded.

'Yeah.'

'She was your first girlfriend?'

'Yeah. She moved to the village with her parents when she was fifteen, and I... we started seeing each other. Her name... her name was Sammie.'

I took a deep breath and let it out slowly. 'I don't understand this,' I said. 'You're telling me that you're still so upset about something that happened between your best friend and your girlfriend when you were kids that you actually want to get *revenge?*'

Jay didn't answer.

'Jay, teenagers do stupid stuff. I did stupid stuff when I was that age. I doubt Mark ever meant to hurt you.'

'He did.'

'Jay—'

'You don't understand,' Jay snapped. 'Mark *knew* how much it meant to me, being with a girl who loved me like she did. He *knew* what losing her would do to me.'

'Sometimes...' I said gently, 'sometimes all that isn't enough. When you really want to be with somebody... friendship, it just goes out the window. Sex is a far stronger drive than loyalty. There's no two ways about it. I'm sure Mark never meant to take her away from you, but in the heat of the moment he made a stupid decision.'

'No,' Jay said.

I began to get irritated. 'So what are you going to do, then? Are you going to keep hanging around his house like some sort of stalker? Do you think that's you not letting him win, spending all your life figuring out how to get revenge on him for something he can probably barely remember?'

Jay turned to me. 'Oh, I've figured out how to get revenge,' he said.

'How?'

'Simple,' he said, 'you're going to do it for me.'

...

I stared at him. 'What?'

'I thought of it just a few minutes ago. After you said if I went round to Georgia's I'd be letting her win. Something just clicked in my mind.'

'I'm not getting involved in this.'

'It wouldn't take long,' he said. 'I just want to do to him what he did to me.'

'Which is?' I said, though I had a feeling I knew.

'I want to sleep with his girlfriend.'

I closed my eyes and rubbed my forehead. 'But he doesn't have a girlfriend,' I said. The pieces were all coming together in my mind now, and I spoke the rest of what I guessed his plan to be with horror. 'You want *me* to be his girlfriend,' I said, 'don't you? So that you can take me away from him.'

Jay grinned as though he was very proud of himself.

'Jay,' I said, 'no.'

Sammie

5

Sammie waited a while before speaking to the two boys. Not for lack of confidence, she had plenty of that. It was because it took a few weeks for her to believe they really were going to stay in this ridiculous little village – her parents weren't suddenly going to hold up their hands, realise it was all a terrible mistake and take her back to Kent where she belonged.

She'd seen the boys a few times, sometimes with their families, sometimes on their own, sometimes just the two of them together; one tall and lanky with a disastrous heap of unruly black hair, thick and curly like a dog's; the other a scrawny, angry looking boy with a hard face and an arrogant stride. It was the latter Sammie found the most appealing, though to be fair, some fun could definitely be had with either of them.

The village was so small that she knew their names, even without speaking to them. The scrawny one was called Jay, and it was his mum who had sold her parents the house. Not because the house was originally hers – she lived in a little two bedroom terraced cottage in the centre of Tatchley – if a church, a tiny corner shop and a pub could be called a "centre". No, she was the estate agent that her parents had dealt with, and she'd told them about her son Jay, and the other boy Mark, who would both be in Sammie's year at school.

Sammie had been bothered by thoughts of her new school on and off all of the summer holidays, but now the start of term was drawing close they'd become particularly troublesome, so she decided to take a walk through the woods late one overcast summer afternoon to try to take her mind off of it. She'd tired of her usual pursuits – even her most recent favourite, which was sunbathing topless, or occasionally completely nude, in the generous and very private garden that had come with her new house. If anything, the garden was actually a little *too* private for her liking. She'd thought it would be funny to one day startle the postman or a neighbour, but had realised eventually that this would be almost impossible. The postman didn't even have to walk up to the house, the drive was so long they had a mail box at the end of it rather than a letterbox in the front door, and everyone knew her parents were away working in London all day, so nobody came. It had become too cold for sunbathing now, anyway. In fact, as she wandered through the dank, shady trees she wished she'd worn something a little warmer than the shorts and t-shirt she had on.

When she caught sight of the two boys they were crouched on the ground in a little clearing in the woods and they appeared to be building something out of branches, which struck her as remarkably childish, considering they were fifteen like her. She stood silently, watching them. They were intent on what they were doing and didn't notice her straight away, so she stayed half-hidden behind a tree trunk and took a good, long look at them. The tall one, Mark, was apparently in charge of whatever was taking place, talking in an authoritative but low voice that she couldn't quite catch, and occasionally gesturing with his lanky arms while the other boy, Jay, listened closely. She took a step forwards, and even though this brought her out of her hiding place behind the tree she got the impression they were so used to being undisturbed that it didn't even occur to them that anyone would be around. She took a couple more steps into the clearing, and now they finally heard her, dropping what they were doing and staring up at her in surprise.

'Hello,' she said.

Both boys practically fell over themselves to stand up. Mark gave her something of a reluctant smile and brushed the mud from his jeans, while Jay cocked his head a little to one side and made no attempt to hide the fact he was checking her out, looking her up and down with careful interest.

'I'm Samantha,' she said, meeting Jay's observation of her by giving him a thorough visual appraisal herself. 'Most people call me Sammie.'

'Mark,' said Mark.

'I'm Jay,' said Jay.

'I know,' she said, 'I've already heard about you both.'

Mark nodded, running a hand through his disastrous black hair. 'Yeah, we already knew your name as well,' he said. 'You're from London, aren't you?'

'Kent,' she said. They looked blank. 'Below London,' she explained.

There was a small silence, and Sammie noticed that there was a huge contrast in how the two boys were dressed. Jay was wearing dark, acid-washed jeans with bright yellow stitching and his t-shirt was grey and slim-fitting, while Mark's jeans were slightly too short, in an unfashionable shade of simple, clean blue denim and his t-shirt hung from his shoulders like a flapping green tent.

'So, you live in that massive house,' Jay said, filling the silence. 'My mum said that place was *well* expensive.'

'Mm,' Sammie agreed. She doubted that Jay's mum had actually used the term "well expensive" but she let that slide.

'Your parents must be loaded,' Jay continued.

'Yeah,' she said, 'I guess they must be.'

He looked at her a little strangely. 'Don't you like it?' he asked. 'I'd love to be rich.'

Sammie laughed. 'It's kind of embarrassing,' she said.

There was a big, dead tree in the clearing and they sat down on it, the two boys at one end and her at the other.

'What were you doing?' she asked them.

'Nothing much,' Jay said.

Sammie raised an eyebrow. 'Sounds fun,' she said. 'So, does anything ever happen in this place?'

They looked at each other and both answered at once, Mark describing the village as "pretty dead" and Jay not mincing his words with a verdict of "pretty shit".

'There's usually a big bonfire in November,' Mark said, 'and sometimes a barbeque in the summer.'

'Is that as good as it gets?'

'It's a good opportunity to nick some alcohol,' Mark explained, 'nobody pays much attention to what we're doing.'

Sammie smiled. 'Oh, well, that's something,' she said.

They carried on sitting for a while, talking about nothing much. Sammie noticed that Jay continued to look at her a lot. In particular, she noticed he kept stealing glances at her chest, which was admittedly quite well displayed in her little pink t-shirt. When she thought neither of the boys were looking she pulled her top down a bit to give Jay more to look at, and she was sure she saw his eyes widen when he noticed.

'How do you feel about starting a new school?' Mark asked her.

Sammie shrugged. 'I don't care,' she said, 'exams are a waste of time anyway.'

He looked surprised, which was about what she'd expect. He looked the type to be into schoolwork.

'It's okay at Rangewood,' he said, 'and besides, you know *us* now.'

Sammie made a non-committal noise. She wanted to forget about school.

'What was your old school like?' Jay asked her.

'Shit,' she said. 'What are any of them like? They're all the same.'

Mark was clearly turned off by her attitude, which was a shame, but not the end of the world as Jay was quite obviously fascinated by her. In any case, Mark didn't stay for much longer. He muttered something about needing to go home and left, though not before giving her and Jay a long look which she found hard to read. She forgot about it soon enough and focussed all her attention on Jay, just as he had made no secret of doing to her, and her heart fluttered in her chest. He really was quite nice. He looked even better close up than the times she'd seen him across the street. She shuffled closer to him on the dead tree trunk. She didn't say anything, but slowly, very carefully, she let one of her hands come to rest next to his. And then, without a word, she touched his little finger with hers, and when their skin met, she felt herself practically fizzle with electricity.

Felicity

6

Jay spent most of the evening trying to persuade me to agree to his plan. He drove back home, but he carried on talking about it all through dinner and when I could tell he really wasn't going to quit I finally snapped and said 'Jay, just stop will you? I'm not going to whore myself out to another man for you, and if you care about me at all you won't ask me again.'

This finally stunned him into silence. He stared at me a few seconds, before saying, 'Is that what you think?'

'What?'

'That I'm "whoring you out?"'

I sighed and turned away from him. I was exhausted by what had happened over the weekend and felt I'd had about as much as I could take.

'You're asking me to have sex with another man for you,' I explained to him. 'And I'm not doing that.'

Jay frowned, seemingly still mystified. 'We pick people out for each other all the time,' he said. 'That's what we've been doing the past couple of years, isn't it? Going out and spotting new partners for each other.'

I searched his face. 'And this is still that, is it? You're saying this is the same thing?'

'No!' he said. 'It's nothing like the same. I used... I used to like seeing you with other guys.'

'But not any more?'

'No. Not any more. I want to stop all this.'

'Then why are you asking me to do it again?'

'Fliss,' Jay said slowly, 'this is the last time. Don't you see? I just want to make Mark suffer, then we can be together—'

I stood up. 'I'm not sure I want to be with you.' I wanted to walk away, but something about him made me stop. His eyes were fixed on my face, and there was something of a sincerity about him that I didn't see too often. I sat back down by his side.

'Jay, even if I did agree… which I'm not,' I added quickly, 'would it really make you happy? Do you think getting revenge is going to change anything?'

'Yes.'

I sighed. 'It probably wouldn't even work. You know that, don't you? What are the chances, really, that Mark would even like me?'

'He would. I know he would.'

'Jay, no matter what you say, the answer is still no. I can't be his girlfriend. If it was only sex, then maybe… maybe that would *theoretically* be doable, but you're asking me to pretend I really like him. I'd have to spend huge amounts of time with him, and be affectionate with him and let him into my life. I can't do that on your say so, with some man I've never even met.'

Jay was quiet for a time. 'I know,' he said finally. 'I'm sorry, Felicity.'

To his credit, Jay didn't mention it again for the whole of the next week. He was polite and careful around me, letting me have my space. I could see he wanted to talk to me, but I made it obvious I wasn't receptive to any conversation about Mark or about the direction of our relationship and he respected that.

I didn't relent and let him tell me anything further about it until the following week, when I had the morning off and decided I'd go along with him in his van while he did his deliveries. I wasn't sure whether it was by coincidence or design, but mid-morning his route took him near to the area where Mark lived, and I found myself asking more questions.

'What was she like?' I asked abruptly.

'Who?' he asked.

'Your girlfriend. The one Mark—'

'Sammie,' he said.

'Yeah, Sammie.'

Jay thought about it while he drove. 'She was blonde, like you,' he said slowly. 'But skinny. Like, not really many curves. She had long legs, and pale blue eyes.'

He paused as though expecting me to tell him whether this was the correct answer. 'Jay,' I said, 'I kind of meant what was she like as a person, not what she looked like.'

'Oh,' he said. 'I don't know. She was just… normal. Although, sometimes she did things that were kind of weird, I guess. She didn't get on that well with her parents. They pretty much ignored her.'

'Did she love you?' I asked.

I waited for him to answer for so long I thought he'd forgotten I'd asked a question. 'Jay,' I said, 'did she—'

'I heard what you asked.'

'So… did she?'

'Yes,' he said, 'I believe that she did.'

'And you loved her?'

'Yeah. More than anything.'

I left it there until a little later when we stopped for lunch. It was starting to rain, and we sat inside the van in a lay-by while cars rushed past by our side. I sat cross-legged in my seat, watching the raindrops slither down the window.

Jay largely shunned any sort of fast food, or even any sort of "normal" food. He'd made both of us a bean salad, full of lots of fresh herbs and vegetables. Jay had always nagged me to eat more healthily, and often cooked dinner for me to try to encourage me. I was grateful to him for doing it – it made my life easier – though I quickly became fed up of too much health food so he knew not to push it too hard.

'How long were you together for?' I asked as we ate.

Jay stopped chewing for a second. 'Why do you want to know all this?' he asked. 'If it's not going to change how you feel about what I asked you to do with Mark.'

'It's not,' I said. 'But I'm curious.'

'We were together for around... eight or nine months.'

'Where is she now?' I asked casually.

Jay gave me a sharp look. 'How should I know?' he said.

'So you completely lost touch? You're not friends with her online, or—'

'No,' Jay said.

'Did she... did she ever say anything to you about what happened with Mark?'

Jay had a forkful of salad halfway to his mouth, and he lowered it again.

'She wouldn't have meant to have had sex with him,' he said. 'He must have talked her into it. She was... she was kind of... vulnerable. I wasn't always there for her like I should have been, but part of that was because Mark kept causing trouble. If I'd been better at telling her how I felt she would never have turned to him.'

'That's very understanding of you,' I said.

Jay raised his fork to his mouth again and chewed silently for a while. 'I understand *her*,' he said at length, 'I didn't to start with, but I've had a lot of time to think about it, and I get it now. The person... the person I can't understand is *him*.'

Sammie

7

Sammie asked the boys to her house the next day. It was a Friday and only three more days of the summer holiday remained. After the weekend, she'd start her new school. Unfortunately, her mum had decided that the day Sammie invited the boys round would be a good day to work from home, so when they came inside her mum was there at the kitchen table with a mug of coffee, reading through some lengthy document with a blue biro in hand.

'I said I'd give Mark and Jay a tour of the house,' Sammie told her.

Her mum looked up, first at her, then at Mark and Jay. Sammie thought she looked old and tired. She was like a piece of paper that had been screwed up then stretched out flat again but had never really recovered, and her hair, which had always used to be a mass of thick, blonde curls, was looking decidedly thin and washed out. Sammie hated the way her mum looked now, because it was as though she'd given up. It took slightly too long before her mum spoke, a drawn out moment while the boys stood awkwardly, eyes exploring the enormous, shiny white kitchen, and her mum thought about whatever it was she was thinking about. 'Okay,' her mum said at last. 'Just... keep it down. I need to finish this.'

Sammie wandered through the downstairs of the house, the boys traipsing after her. Her home wasn't a great source of interest or pride to her. It had been designed by an architect for the previous owners, who as far as Sammie was concerned must have had more money than sense, because to her the vast open spaces felt cold and lifeless; the white walls clinical, and the rigid expanses of glass unfriendly and uncompromising, looming over her like threatening transparent giants. However, she understood the house was a source of curiosity and admiration for other people so she dutifully showed the boys the sitting room – with its log-burner, pile of Country Living magazines on the coffee table, and a massive vase of lilies on the sideboard; the TV room, with a couple of squashy sofas and heaps of furry cushions; and then the utility room, where a lot of the yet to be unpacked boxes were being stored.

'This is bigger than the whole kitchen in my house,' Mark said, as he took it all in.

'Really?' she said, although in truth she wasn't surprised.

'How come your parents have so much money?' Jay asked, which made Mark eye his friend disapprovingly, though Sammie didn't particularly mind the question.

'My dad has his own business.'

Jay nodded as though this explained everything.

'What does your mum do?' Mark asked.

'She works in my dad's company. She used to translate books into English from German, or vice versa, before the business took off.' She paused a moment, then added, 'She was happier when she was doing that.'

Now it was Mark's turn to nod, and Sammie noticed that Jay's attention had fallen to reading what was written on top of some of the boxes, and he had stopped on one that said *Sammie's trophies*.

'What's in that one?' he asked.

She knelt down to open it while Jay and Mark watched in silence. The box was taped shut and she had to pick at the end of the tape with her nail for a while before she could grab it and peel it away. The boys crouched down by her side as she started taking things out – medals, framed photographs, and the trophies. She laid them out on the floor and the boys obediently looked at them.

'Most of them are for gymnastics,' she explained, 'and a few from dance competitions.'

'Woah,' Mark said, 'there's a lot. If one of my sisters had won these they wouldn't be sitting in a box. They'd probably have been the first thing to get unpacked. My mum would have had them up on the mantelpiece and invited all the neighbours round to see them within about half an hour of moving in.'

He laughed and Sammie giggled, though she felt a bit sad. Her parents obviously had no interest in looking at them, otherwise wouldn't they have done as Mark said – put them all up, and showed them off to people?

'Will you still carry on with it?' Jay asked. 'Now you've moved here?'

'No,' Sammie said, 'I gave it all up ages ago.'

'Why?' Mark asked.

'Couldn't be arsed,' she said.

She started putting everything away again, because she didn't feel like looking at it. 'You should have carried on,' Jay said, 'you could have been in the Olympics or something.'

Sammie laughed without much humour. 'Yeah,' she said, 'maybe.'

'How often did you have to practice?'

'As often as I could. When my brother wasn't in hospital.'

'You have a brother?' Mark asked, looking around the room as though her mysterious brother might suddenly jump out from behind the boxes.

'Did have,' Sammie said, 'he's dead now.'

The boys didn't know what to say. 'What did... what did he die of?' Mark asked finally.

'He had a rare genetic disorder. The doctors originally said he wouldn't make it to his second birthday. But he made it for ten years.'

'My dad's dead,' Jay said.

Sammie stopped putting the trophies away. 'Oh,' she said.

'Yeah. He had cancer. It was really quick. It meant my mum had to come back and look after me again.'

'What do you mean?' Sammie asked.

'She left,' Jay said, 'she fucked off when I was six. I think she's still well pissed off that dad died and she had to come back and deal with me again.'

Sammie frowned down at the remaining pictures and trophies for a while. She wasn't really sure what to say. Then the door opened.

'Sammie,' her mum said, 'what are you doing in here? I told you to leave all this stuff alone—' she stopped talking when she saw which box Sammie had opened. 'You're showing them those,' she said.

'Yeah.'

'Oh… well. Okay.' There was a strange expression on her mum's face, and Sammie realised she'd forgotten that the trophies were in there. 'Well… put them all away again when you're done,' she said, 'I haven't decided where we're going to put them yet.'

She left the room again and Sammie thought – yeah, and you never will.

…

After that, Sammie continued the tour upstairs, where she showed Mark and Jay her dad's study, and the room where her parents still kept some of Alfie's stuff – not on display, but in boxes on the floor, as though he was away somewhere and they were waiting for him to come back and unpack his belongings himself. She showed them the family bathroom with its big claw-footed bath in front of the window, and then she made a bit of a mistake. She showed them her parents' bedroom – not in detail, she just opened the door enough that they could peek inside, then she showed them one of the two guest bedrooms, where it was quite obvious somebody had recently slept.

'Is someone staying with you?' Mark asked.

'N-No,' Sammie said, 'it's…' she struggled to think how to explain the fact that her parents didn't always sleep in the same room. 'My dad sometimes works until quite late,' she said, clutching at straws, 'and he sleeps in here so he doesn't disturb my mum when he comes to bed.'

The two boys looked at each other, but she could see they hadn't really grasped the significance, and soon they were distracted as she took them into her own bedroom, with its vast vaulted ceiling, massive king size bed, and a multitude of colourful rugs on polished wooden floorboards.

'Fuck me,' Jay exclaimed, and Mark mumbled something about how he shared a room with his brother.

'This is awesome,' Jay said, heading straight to the window, which looked out over the garden.

'Yeah,' Sammie mumbled.

'Your garden goes right down to the woods, doesn't it?' Jay asked.

'Mm.'

'That's one of the best bits of the woods,' he said, 'where we were hanging out the other day, near your garden. Hardly anyone else comes down there.'

'I don't like the woods,' Sammie said, 'they freak me out.'

'Really?' Jay said. 'How come?'

'I can hear animals at night,' she said, 'they come up into our garden. It's kind of weird.'

Jay watched her for a moment, and then he grinned. 'You know what you need,' he said, 'you need someone else in that massive bed with you. Stop you getting frightened.'

They chatted a while longer, then Mark had to go home because it was his sister's birthday. It turned out he had quite a few siblings – three sisters and a brother – and he was the middle child, with his brother and one sister older than him, and the other two sisters younger. Sammie showed him out, while Jay stayed upstairs in her bedroom.

'You know he likes you,' Mark said as Sammie opened the front door for him.

Sammie felt her cheeks go a little pink. 'He told you that?'

'Yeah,' Mark said.

Sammie smiled and Mark watched her closely. 'You should…

you should be careful,' he said.

'Why?'

'He won't treat you very well.'

'What do you mean?' she asked.

Mark pulled his hand through his hair and looked over his shoulder at the drive, anxious to be away. 'I mean...' he said, 'I just mean... he doesn't care about you.'

'I wouldn't expect him to, yet,' Sammie said, 'he's only just met me.'

At this, words seemed to fail Mark, and he gave up on the conversation with the excuse that he needed to get going. But Sammie stayed in the doorway for a while, staring after him, wondering what on earth he'd really been trying to say to her.

Felicity

8

I continued to hold off on making any commitment to either Jay, or his revenge plan for some time longer. Occasionally what he was proposing almost made a crazy kind of sense, but then I'd think about what was involved, and the way he so casually asked me to do it, and my mind would be set against it.

It was the most unlikely thing that made me reconsider; a meeting with my best friend Leanne, who had long been Jay's biggest critic.

I met up with her on a Saturday night, on a weekend when three other friends from our schooldays – Grace, Hannah and Becky, were back in Coalton visiting their families. We met in Leanne's flat – a small, cosy place on the lower ground floor of a big old Victorian house, where light from the already inadequate windows was blocked out by billowing red, purple and pink voiles, turning whole rooms the colour of Leanne's own resplendent hair. I never quite got used to the way the pavement was above our heads, preferring the airiness of mine and Jay's modern top floor flat, but it was perfect for Leanne and her daughter Kayleigh. The whole place felt like some sort of magical, fairy grotto. Everyone else was already there by the time I arrived, and we sat around drinking cheap rosé wine from plastic wineglasses in the living-cum-dining-cum-play room on a sagging sofa and a couple of bean bags.

My friends were all full of positive news about jobs, holidays and boyfriends, and to start with most of the conversation centred around Grace's plans for her wedding to her childhood sweetheart, and what we'd do for her hen party. I began to feel like one big elephant in the room as I considered the mess of my own life, and right on cue Leanne turned and said, 'So, how's your flatmates-who-fuck thing going with Jay?'

Becky, Hannah and Grace all snorted with laugher and I glanced at Leanne — sitting on the arm of the sofa she looked majestic, like a queen looking down on her subjects — and she was dressed in her usual esoteric manner; jeans and a purple corset, with a string of big, black beads looped around her neck.

'Actually, I've kind of got an announcement to make about that,' I said.

Leanne opened her mouth in an expression of comical horror. 'Oh my God, you're not *pregnant*, are you?' she asked, and then pealed with laughter.

'No,' I said, 'but you don't have to sound so horrified by the idea.' I averted my eyes from hers for a moment and mumbled the rest staring down at the floor. 'We're thinking about making a go of things.'

Leanne drew in her breath. She hadn't expected that. The others in the room were forgotten as she fixed her eyes on me, and reluctantly I met them with my own.

'Really?' she said. 'You and him, an actual couple?'

'Yeah,' I said, 'what's so wrong with that?'

Leanne looked around the room, as though she was struggling with where to start.

'Didn't you say before that you'd never want anything serious with Jay?' Grace asked me. 'You said you weren't sure you could ever trust him.'

I sighed. Already I felt under attack. All of them were looking at me now and I knew that I would continue to get the third degree about Jay until I somehow nipped it in the bud. I tried to give a satisfying explanation, but what came out sounded rather limp. 'Things change,' I told them.

'Jay doesn't change though,' Leanne said, 'seriously, Fliss. I mean, fair enough even *I* probably wouldn't kick him out of bed, but when it comes down to it, the guy's a dick.'

I stared at her, outraged, then I got up and went out to the kitchen. Leanne followed me, but the others stayed in the lounge, where I could already hear laughter again.

'Is it too much to ask for you to be happy for me?' I asked Leanne.

'No – but, Fliss, not with him.'

She pulled herself up onto the kitchen worktop, and sat watching me. 'I'm not trying to upset you,' she said.

'Oh right. By calling Jay names.'

She laughed. 'Okay, look, you know what I'm like, Fliss. I have no filter. But it's coming from a good place. Listen to me. It's not just the string of other girls, it's *him*. There's something not right about him, Felicity, you must be able to see that—'

I shook my head. 'He's had a hard life, he was on the—'

'—streets,' she finished my sentence. 'Yes, I know. You've told me enough times. And why did he end up homeless? You don't really know, do you? The temper on him I'm not surprised he fell out with his family. Aside from you no one else would ever be crazy enough to take him on, and talking about getting *serious* with him—'

I glared at her, and then I picked up my glass of wine and dumped it in the sink.

'I'm going home,' I said.

'Fliss,' she said, 'come on, don't be like that.'

I started towards the door, and angry tears stung at my eyes. I heard Leanne jump down from the worktop and I let her take my arm.

'Oh, Fliss,' she said, giving my arm a little squeeze. 'You're in love with him, aren't you?'

She steered me over to the tiny kitchen table in the corner and gave me a fresh glass of wine.

'Flissie,' she said, 'how long have we known each other?'

'Forever,' I said.

'Then listen to me. I know you, and I'm telling you you've changed.'

'Wouldn't you have done?'

'What happened to your parents was the worst thing,' she

said, 'and none of us can blame you for losing the plot for a while. But men like Jay...' she paused for a moment. I could see that being tactful was proving a challenge for her. 'You met Jay so soon after it all happened,' she said, 'and I'm sure he was a great distraction. The thing is... he uses you.'

'No he doesn't.'

'He does. He goes back to you when he's bored with whoever his latest fling is. You're just... I don't like to say this, but you're easy for him Felicity. He doesn't have to put any effort in, you're always just *there*.'

I put my head in my hands. 'I'm not stupid,' I said.

Leanne reached out and touched my hand briefly. 'I know that,' she said. She paused for a while. 'You know what one of the worst things is for me, when I look at you now?'

'What?'

'You don't make jewellery any more.'

'I try to,' I said, 'but my heart's not in it. It has nothing to do with him.'

'Doesn't it?'

I thought about it. Jay had never encouraged me to carry on trying to do it, but he certainly never stopped me. What I did in my spare time wasn't really much to do with him, just like all his time at the gym and out running wasn't much to do with me.

'Fliss,' Leanne said, 'I'm not trying to upset you. But surely you can see that a random guy you met one week after you lost both your parents might not be the best person for you long term. You weren't thinking straight—'

'And you still think I'm not?' I snapped. 'I am *able* to make decisions myself. I don't need you to tell me what to do.'

'Fine,' Leanne said harshly, 'you do what you want. But I don't think you've ever even grieved properly, have you?'

I didn't answer and she carried on. 'And I think that Jay realises that and that he knows exactly what he's doing. Fliss, he's a nasty piece of work. He saw straight away that you're vulnerable and he's using it to do whatever the hell he wants—'

'How dare you?' I said suddenly. 'How dare you talk to me

like that? I am not *vulnerable* and I'm no pushover.'

'Then why are you contemplating getting with a man who treats you like shit?'

I stood up. 'I really am going,' I said.

'Okay, Fliss,' Leanne said, 'walk out as soon as I start saying something you don't want to hear.'

I spun to face her. 'What's that supposed to mean?'

'You are *better* than him.'

'What?' I said. 'What the hell does that even mean? You don't know him.'

I left the room and Leanne called after me, 'The Felicity I used to know had some self-respect!'

...

When I got home Jay was surprised to see me back so early.

'What's going on?' he asked. 'I thought you were going to be at Leanne's all evening.'

'Change of plan.'

He must have been able to hear in my voice that something had happened. 'She's been talking about me again, hasn't she?' he said.

'Can we arrange for me to meet him?' I asked abruptly.

Jay frowned, and then his eyes widened as he understood.

Sammie

9

With Mark out of the way, Sammie's heart began to flutter as she made her way back to Jay. She glanced quickly into the kitchen, where her mum was still hunched over the report she was reading, and then she ran up the stairs two at a time.

Jay turned as she came in the door, and she couldn't help but smile at the sight of him sitting there, silhouetted against the bright light from her bedroom window. She closed the door behind her very gently until it shut with a soft click, and then joined him on the bed.

'I was thinking,' Jay said, 'if your parents are so rich, how come you're not in a private school?'

Sammie moved a little closer to him on the bed, and although he didn't react, she saw in his face that he understood something was going to happen between them, and that he was excited.

'Are you glad that I'm not?' she asked him.

'Yeah,' he said.

They kissed for a long time, the sun streaming through the window warming their bodies, nothing but the sound of their breathing and, for Sammie, a kind of roaring in her ears. When they broke apart Jay smiled at her, then wiped his mouth with the back of his hand like it was no big deal.

'You didn't answer me,' he said.

'What?'

'About the school.'

'Oh,' Sammie said, and she paused to consider her explanation. 'My parents haven't always had so much money,' she told him, 'it was only when my dad's company took off, about five years ago. They thought about putting me in private school but I wanted to stay with all my friends. Then my brother got really bad and after he died they weren't really interested in any of it any more.'

Also, she thought to herself, around the same time they stopped being interested was when her "staying with friends" argument stopped being true. After Alfie died somehow all her friends had drifted off. She couldn't remember quite how it had happened. It had been gradual, she supposed, like sand through an hourglass – they hadn't all turned against her, but the friendships had just eroded away, until one day she'd realised she actually didn't have any friends, not any more.

'So,' Jay said, 'are your parents all weird about your brother now? Do they freak out if you talk about him?'

'No,' she said, 'they don't freak out. They go a bit silent and distant. They don't like talking about him, if that's what you mean.' She put her hand on top of his. 'What about your mum?' she asked. 'Does she freak out if you mention your dad?'

'No,' Jay said, 'she says I can talk about him if I ever need to.'

'Do you ever need to?'

'No,' he said, 'what's the point?' He looked round at her. 'Do you ever need to talk about your brother?'

'No,' Sammie said, meeting his eyes, 'what's the point?'

They talked a while longer undisturbed, and Sammie thought her mum must have assumed both boys had gone home, because she was sure if her mum had any inkling she'd been up in here in her bedroom with one of the boys for this long she'd have come upstairs to interrupt them.

'Why did your mum leave?' Sammie asked Jay.

'I don't really know,' he said. 'My dad used to tell me that my mum had gone away to find herself and that she must be well hidden because it was taking a long time. Then he used to laugh like he'd said something really funny. I didn't understand what he meant because I was only a little kid, so I took it literally and started telling a teacher that my mum had got lost and that's why she wasn't at home any more. I think the school told my dad because after that he explained it to me properly.'

'And what did he say?'

'He said that she was a selfish, lazy bitch who'd rather go off travelling than deal with her responsibilities.'

'Really?' Sammie said. 'He said that to you?'

'Yeah,' Jay said, 'and when he got ill he used to say "that fucking bitch gave me cancer."'

Sammie took a deep breath. 'That's messed up,' she said.

Jay shrugged. 'It's true though,' he said, 'it was hard for him to look after me on his own. Really hard. The stress made him ill.'

Sammie couldn't think how to answer and they briefly fell into silence, until she suddenly remembered her conversation with Mark. 'Hey,' she said, 'before Mark left, he said some strange things about you.'

'Did he? What did he say?'

'He said you like me.'

'Well, that's true,' he said, and Sammie felt herself blush a little.

'Then he said you won't treat me well and you don't care about me.'

Jay stared at her. 'He said *what?*'

'I know,' Sammie said, 'weird or what?'

'I don't... understand why he would say that.'

'Neither do I.'

Jay thought about it for a long time, brow furrowed. Sammie watched him silently. His face was nice when he was thinking; he looked brooding, melancholy.

All of a sudden Jay seemed to figure it out. 'I bet I know what it is,' he said.

'Yeah?'

He grinned lopsidedly. 'Before I met you yesterday, when we'd just seen you around in the village, I used to... say stuff about you.'

'What kind of stuff?'

'You know,' he said, 'about what you look like. About your—'

he held his hands up to his chest, cupping them like he was holding a pair of boobs. Sammie giggled. 'The thing is,' Jay continued, 'Mark's family are all really old-fashioned and stuff. Like, they don't even have the *internet* at his house, and he had to really fight before they let him have a phone. I guess he probably thinks you go straight to hell or something if you look at a girl's tits. His parents don't even let him have sex education at school.'

'Really?' Sammie asked. She'd never known anyone whose parents had done that.

'Yeah, he has to, like, go somewhere else for an hour while they're teaching it. Him and his sisters are pretty much the only kids in school who aren't allowed.'

'Does he... does he not know *anything* about it?' Sammie asked, with a kind of wonder.

'Nah,' Jay said, 'he knows about it. I mean, you can't really not, can you?'

Sammie took it all in for a moment. 'That's so weird.'

'Yeah. But I guess that's why he said that stuff to you. Maybe he thinks I shouldn't look at a girl like that unless we're like, *married* or something.'

Sammie glanced down at her chest, hidden underneath a cotton t-shirt. Her breasts weren't very big, and she often thought they were a weird shape – pointy and almost triangular when she wanted them to be firm and round. But she liked that Jay was excited by them – excited enough that he'd even made comments to Mark about it.

'Do you want to see them?' she asked.

Jay's eyes searched her face. She could tell he wasn't sure he had entirely understood her. 'See what?' he asked.

She laughed. 'My *boobs*, you idiot.'

Sammie loved watching his face as she took off her t-shirt and bra. He obviously couldn't believe his luck, and he didn't take his eyes from her chest as he slowly lifted up one of his hands to touch her.

'What do you think?' she asked him, once he'd cupped one of her breasts in his hand.

He looked from her chest up to her face, then down again. 'I...' he said. He didn't seem able to speak, so Sammie kissed him.

Felicity

10

Jay and I spent the rest of the evening talking it through, working out how a meeting with Mark could be arranged.

'It needs to be something quick and simple,' I said, 'I need to get talking to him, fast. Does he... does he have any interests or anything? Some way it would seem like we had something in common?'

'I don't know,' Jay said, 'not that I know of. I told you before that he doesn't really do anything much, not as far as I can tell.'

I closed my eyes for a second, thinking. 'I don't know,' I said, 'I can't think of any way of meeting him that won't seem weird.'

Jay tapped his fist against his chin. 'Okay,' he said at length, 'what if you have to go to his flat for help? Like, you need to use a phone or something.'

'When on earth does that ever happen nowadays?'

'Well,' he said, 'if you didn't have your phone because... you'd been mugged.'

I stared at him. It sounded crazy, but actually, it might just work.

'It would have to be convincing,' I said, 'I couldn't just turn up at his door, I'd need to look hurt and shaken. I... I'd have to be injured somehow.'

'You mean... you want me to hit you?'

'I... I don't know. I guess... I...' I trailed off, and then an idea occurred to me. 'How about this,' I said, 'we go over there, check his lights are on and he's definitely in, and then we could figure something out about making me look injured on the spur of the moment.'

'I don't know,' Jay said, 'I can't... you don't want me to do anything to you in the van or in the street – someone might see me. I can drive over there, check he's in and then come back and pick you up.'

'No,' I said, 'I might have changed my mind by then. I'm coming with you.'

Jay gave me a long, hard look. 'All right,' he said, 'fine. Let's go then.'

It was a very strange drive over to Mark's flat. We cruised down the street past the house, checking for signs of life, and sure enough a light was on in one of the downstairs windows. Seeing that, Jay pulled up a safe distance away in case Mark should look out.

'Now, do you definitely understand what you're doing?' Jay asked me.

'Yes.'

'Go over it again for me.'

'Okay,' I said, 'I knock on the door, say I've been mugged and I need to use his phone. I tell him it'll be a little while before my flatmate can pick me up, giving me a good few minutes to talk to him and suss him out. Then I say you're probably waiting and I leave.'

Jay nodded, satisfied that I'd got it. 'And what name will you use for me if it comes up in conversation?' he asked.

'Jason,' I said, 'because if I start saying Jay it gives me a chance to recover it. Are you... when are you going to hit me?'

'Not yet,' he said, 'come on.'

We both got out of the van, and he gave me a hug, before taking my hands in his. 'I love you, Fliss,' he said, 'and I'm so grateful to you for doing this.'

I started to say I loved him too, but I was beginning to feel nervous and before I got the words out he'd let go of my hands, got hold of my head, and smashed my face as hard as he could against the side of the van.

I cried out in pain and shock, but before the noise could alert anyone he clapped his hand over my mouth and we both sunk to our knees while he inspected his handiwork.

'Right,' he said, as I sobbed against the palm of his hand, a warm trickle of blood seeping from my nose and running over his fingers. 'I'm happy with that.'

I continued to cry, and he held me close. 'Fliss, I'm so sorry,' he whispered into my hair.

'I need...' I said, 'I need... to go.'

He didn't let me out of his arms straight away. 'I love you,' he said again. 'I couldn't do it while you were expecting it. If you'd been looking at me waiting for me to hit you in the face I wouldn't have been able to.'

'Let me go,' I said, pushing him away, 'let me go and do this.'

I practically held my breath all the way to Mark's front door, following Jay's instructions about going round the side of the building to the door to Flat A. My head was pounding, blood was dripping from my nose unchecked, and I didn't know how I could possibly keep up any kind of pretence the way I was feeling. I even considered giving up and going back to Jay in the van, but as though he guessed what I was thinking I heard the engine start, and watched helplessly as he drove away. With nothing else for it, I took a deep breath and stopped at Mark's front door. Then I knocked on it.

Sammie

11

By the time Sammie started her new school on Monday, her and Jay were undeniably an item. She had seen the boys again at the weekend – they'd met in the little clearing in the woods near her garden, and sat on the dead tree. But she and Jay had spent most of the time making out, until Mark got fed up and went home. In fact, it surprised her how much Jay was willing to do in front of his friend, because as well as kissing her, he put his hand up her top to feel her breasts again. In fact, only when his hand dropped down to the fastening of her jeans and she whispered, 'Not yet,' did he seem to remember Mark was there at all, and the boys exchanged a look with each other, one that Sammie didn't really understand.

On the morning of her first day, Sammie's mum announced that she would work from home, so that she could drive Sammie into school and pick her up at the end of the day. Although Sammie supposed the gesture was well meant, she didn't want to miss the opportunity of seeing Jay on the bus, and besides, however well meant it was she knew her mum's gesture was ultimately an empty one. By tomorrow she'd be gone again, not getting home until nine or ten at night. Sammie was beginning to understand the routine by now. For all their talk of a new start in the country, her parents didn't want to be there. To make a new start you had to try, and all her parents tried to do was bury themselves in work.

She told her mum she'd catch the bus, and although she was happy that this meant she could sit next to Jay for a while, the rest of the day didn't work out quite the way she hoped. Once she got to Rangewood School she discovered that not only were the two boys not in the same form group as her, but that her and Jay were in almost none of the same classes. She was in all the top sets, with Mark, but Jay was not, and so she only managed to see him during break times.

...

It was a weird day. The school was smaller than the one she'd gone to before, and it was scruffier. Her old school had been new and smart – while this one had been built in the sixties or seventies – it was boxy and somehow flimsy looking; an ugly mishmash of red panelling and red brick. The teachers tried half-heartedly to settle her in, but she was in her final year, and she felt they weren't that interested in a new arrival so late in the day. As if this wasn't bad enough, she immediately fell into the role of being the strange new outsider, with boys staring at her and girls seeming to dislike her instinctively; especially after she spent the whole of break time entwined with Jay, giving everyone the impression she was some sort of slag.

'They think you only met him today,' Mark said to her quietly in double maths.

'I don't care what they think,' she whispered back.

By the time the day was almost over, she felt completely drained. The worst lesson of all was the final one: History. Neither of the boys were in her class and so she ended up having to sit on her own at the back of the room, the other kids stealing the occasional glance at her. Even though proper teaching hadn't really begun yet – the lessons on the first day were mostly about getting organised and talking about the year ahead – Sammie already felt unsettled and out of her depth and thought she would struggle to stay afloat. The more enthusiastic of her teachers told her she could go to them if she needed extra help, but Sammie doubted whether she would bother. She tried, but she just couldn't seem to think of the exams as being that important. The most important thing to her now was Jay, and the next time she would get to be alone with him again.

When the bell rang and it was finally home time, Sammie practically ran to the road at the front of the school to get to the bus stop. She hoped that Jay might already be there, but he wasn't, and she felt lost in the crush of people she didn't know. She noticed one group of boys staring at her, and eventually lost her temper.

'What?' she said. 'What do you want?'

The largest boy in the group — a horrible, greasy-looking slab of a human being — turned to her and said, 'Get them out then.'

To begin with she simply didn't understand. Then a bolt of shock went through her. Surely Jay hadn't told them?

One of the other boys joined in, removing any shadow of a doubt that they knew. 'Go on, new girl, show us your tits.'

They burst out laughing at her look of shock. But she wasn't going to let them win that easily. She started unbuttoning her school shirt. 'There you go,' she said, flashing them her bra. 'Happy now?'

They all stared at her, amazed, then they burst out laughing again while Sammie did her shirt back up, feeling ashamed. She wasn't quite sure who had won out of that exchange, them or her. But one thing was for sure — Jay had really let her down. Far from making her first day easier, he'd turned her into a laughing stock.

She ignored Jay the whole of the bus ride back to Tatchley, much to his confusion.

'What is *wrong* with you?' he asked her, taking hold of her shoulder from his seat behind her.

'Nothing,' she said, wriggling away from him.

Jay leaned closer. 'Why are you being such a bitch then?' he hissed at her.

Sammie spun round. 'Because you *told* everyone!' she said. 'You told everyone I showed you...' she lowered her voice, although only a couple of other kids remained on the bus; an unhealthy looking boy a couple of years older than them, and Mark's two younger sisters, who sat as far away from their brother as possible, giggling and whispering together. Sammie met Jay's eyes. 'You told everyone I showed you my breasts.'

'I didn't tell anyone anything!' Jay said. 'What are you on about?'

Sammie glared at him. 'Then why were there boys at the bus stop asking me to show them my tits?'

Jay frowned. 'I didn't tell anyone,' he said. 'I swear. The only person who knows is...' his eyes slipped across to Mark, who was sitting quietly on the other side of the aisle, making a show of being interested in the fields rolling by outside the window.

'Hey,' Jay said to him. Mark looked round slowly. 'Why've you been telling everyone about me and Sammie?'

Mark couldn't give a satisfying answer, and when they reached Tatchley his sisters made off without a backwards glance, and Mark looked nervous as both Jay and Sammie took a step towards him.

'Why'd you do it, Mark?' Jay asked him. 'You jealous or something?'

Mark looked down at the ground. 'No,' he said quietly.

'You are,' Jay said, 'you're jealous of me and Sammie. Just because *you* haven't even seen a pair of tits before.'

Mark met Jay's eyes, and Sammie saw he'd gone a bit red. 'Of course I've *seen* tits before,' he said.

'Oh,' Jay said, 'what? Your *mummy's*, when you were a baby?'

Mark turned away again and Sammie couldn't help but let out a little giggle, even though her insides twisted uncomfortably at the way Jay was taunting his friend. She was angry with Mark for what he'd done, but with what Jay had told her about Mark's old-fashioned family, she could see that what Jay was saying was a little too close to the truth.

'Leave him, Jay,' she said, 'he's not worth it. Let's go to the woods or something.'

'I've got a better idea,' he said to her, making a point of Mark overhearing, 'my mum's still at work, why don't you come back to mine?'

Sammie let her gaze slip across to Mark, and she noticed his eyes were shiny, like he was almost in tears. She took Jay's hand, but before they'd taken a single step Mark said, 'You know he only wants you to go home with him so he… so he…' he stammered to a halt and gave up.

'What?' Jay said nastily. 'So that I can what?'

Mark looked so uncomfortable and the tears in his eyes were so visible that Sammie was scared he actually would cry. 'Come on,' she said to Jay, 'let's go.'

'No,' Jay said, 'if he's got something to say let him say it. Go on, Mark.'

Mark opened his mouth, but he couldn't get any words out.

'Say it,' Jay said, 'say what you were going to say.'

Mark tried again, stammering to Sammie, 'He only wants you to go to his house so he can…' he almost gave up again, then in a final desperate attempt he said, 'so he can… so he can have *sex* with you!'

Sammie couldn't help but burst out laughing at the ridiculously earnest and naive way he said it, as though he thought it was his duty to warn her. She put her arm around Jay and said, 'Yes, Mark. I know.'

Felicity

12

Mark clearly had no idea what to make of me and even less idea what to do. His eyes went straight to the blood dripping from my nose, and he kept his hand on the door handle as though he was half considering shutting the door in my face. I could barely keep myself together enough to even look at him properly; all that registered to me was that he was tall and skinny with a big mop of unruly dark hair.

'Could I... could I please use your phone?' I asked. 'I was.... mugged. Just then, out there—' I gestured towards the road. 'They took my phone. I just want to call my flatmate to come and get me—'

Mark quickly moved aside. 'Yeah,' he said, 'yeah...um... come in.'

I stepped into his flat, finding myself in a narrow, drab hallway with doors along one wall.

'Here,' he said, 'come through.'

I followed him down the hall, and he looked back at me a couple of times, at my injured face. I held my hand up under my nose to try to catch the blood and I noticed that we were walking on a pale cream carpet. He was probably worried I'd get bloodstains on it.

At the end of the hall was a cramped living room stuffed with a lot of dowdy furniture, and he led me into a little alcove around the corner that served as his kitchen. He pointed vaguely towards the sink, where there was a washing up bowl full of soapy water and a couple of pots and pans. He'd obviously been in the middle of clearing up after his dinner. He picked up the bowl and placed it on the floor, steering me towards the sink where I bent forwards and held the top of my nose.

'What... happened?' he asked. 'Are you all right?'

He hovered by my side, not too close to me, but close enough that I could tell he was genuinely concerned.

'It was a couple of teenagers,' I said, 'I just... want to go home.'

He picked up his phone from the kitchen work top. 'Would you like me to call your flatmate for you? Or the police?'

'No,' I said, a little too quickly. 'No,' I said again, 'thank you. I... don't want to call the police.'

He waited a while and the flow of blood from my nose began to ease.

'It looks like you've had a nasty whack on your forehead as well,' Mark said, 'do you want some frozen peas to put on it?'

'Yes,' I said, 'thank you.' I worried in the back of my mind that Mark might doubt my story about my injuries – that he'd somehow know they'd been caused by being smashed into a solid object rather than being punched or hit in the face, but I quickly calmed myself down. He had no reason to doubt my story, and I'd given no explanation as to how the teenagers had attacked me. All he'd see was the blood, and my shock, and he'd have no reason not to take me at face value.

'Could I... could I use your phone now?' I asked him.

'Sure,' he said, 'here you go.'

He held it out to me, and I took it. 'Thank you,' I said, yet again, 'and sorry... about this.'

'It's fine,' he said. I realised I was just staring down at his phone in my hand, and he helped me. 'You just... you know,' he said, bringing up the call screen.

'Yeah,' I said, 'sorry.'

I started dialling Jay's number.

'Let me get you those peas,' Mark said.

I finished typing the number while Mark rummaged in a little freezer. On initial impressions – which had been very short and admittedly under bizarre circumstances – he seemed all right. I thought I could probably have sex with him, if it came to that. He didn't seem strange, or creepy. I stole glances at him while I waited for Jay to pick up and concluded that Mark seemed quite timid, if anything, with soft brown eyes and a pale, pointed face that gave him an unusual, gentle quality.

Jay took a little while to answer.

'Jason,' I said, using the name we'd agreed on.

'Yeah?' he played along.

'I need you to come and pick me up.'

I carried on explaining, very aware that Mark was listening. It was so hard to act correctly, to continue to sound shaken when I was almost beginning to congratulate myself. I kept thinking that Mark would see straight through me, but once I'd made a show of explaining to "Jason" where I was and what had happened, he seemed convinced.

'He's going to be about fifteen minutes,' I said.

'Here,' Mark said, handing me the bag of peas. 'Can I get you anything else? Painkillers? Tea? It must have been a shock—'

'Yes,' I said, 'thanks.'

He stood still for a moment, looking muddled. 'Uh... yes to which thing?' he asked.

'Oh.... both, please.'

He encouraged me to sit down and gave me a handful of tissues to dab at my nose, then he filled the kettle and went off in search of some painkillers.

'Are you sure you don't want to call the police?' he said when he came back. 'If they took your phone—'

'No,' I said, 'I... I'd rather not. They were just kids, I feel a bit silly to be honest.'

I pressed the peas against my face and closed my eyes for a second.

'Does it hurt a lot?' Mark asked. He handed me a pack of painkillers. 'Here, I'll get you some water.'

I popped two pills out of the pack and swallowed them with

a little water. For a minute or two he busied himself in the kitchen making tea, then he sat down on the other end of the sofa, placing one mug on the coffee table in front of me, and one in front of himself. Then he immediately got up again. 'I've got biscuits,' he said, 'custard creams.'

He went and got them and handed me the packet. 'You should eat something,' he said, 'isn't that what you're supposed to do when you've had a shock?'

I took one and tried my best to give him a small smile, then figured I should probably say something else about the mugging.

'I had a feeling something was going to happen as soon as I saw them,' I said, 'but I told myself I was being stupid. Just because they're teenagers doesn't mean they're criminals, right? Look where that got me.'

Mark took a sip of his tea. 'It's usually quiet round here,' he said, 'you must have been really unlucky.'

I gave what I hoped sounded like a nervous laugh. 'No shit,' I said.

We sat in silence for a little while, waiting until it was time for me to be picked up by "Jason", who in reality was probably just sitting in his van, mere metres from Mark's flat. Then I noticed Mark was looking at me – at my wrist to be precise.

'Sorry,' he said. 'I was just looking at that bracelet. It's really unusual.'

'Thanks,' I said, holding it out so he could look at it better. 'I made it myself.'

'Really?' he sounded genuinely amazed, and I felt a stab of pride. It was quite a simple piece of jewellery really – a silver cuff bracelet, very honest, and raw – almost masculine in appearance, with decorative rivets and a simple stippled effect.

'Is that what you do, then?' he asked.

'No,' I said, 'God, no. I wish. I'm a receptionist. At Treacle Street Surgery, in town, by the—'

'Yeah, I know it,' Mark said. 'Well, not the surgery, but I know the street.'

'Oh,' I said. 'Yeah. Kind of a weird name, isn't it? Talking of which… I don't even know *your* name, and I'm sitting in your flat spoiling your evening.'

'It's Mark,' he said.

'I'm Felicity,' I told him. I took another biscuit, and then picked up the peas to press against my head again.

'I think you might get a nasty bruise,' he said.

'Yeah.'

'Look, I know you don't want to, but you should call the police,' Mark said. 'People shouldn't get away with attacking you in the street like that. I really would be happy to call them for you—'

'No, Mark, please,' I said, 'you've been very kind. But I just want to get home and go to bed. They really were just kids, after they'd done it they looked as scared as I was.' I looked at my watch. 'You know, I should probably go and wait outside, my flatmate will be here any second.'

'Let me wait with you.'

'No,' I said, 'it's all right. I've taken up enough of your time.' I handed him the bag of peas. 'I really appreciate this,' I said, 'thank you.'

…

Jay could barely contain himself when I got back into the van. He was parked some distance down the road, well away from Mark's flat where he might potentially have been spotted.

'What happened?' he asked. 'How did it go?'

Before I answered him, I looked him right in the eye and then gave him a slap.

'Fliss,' he said, recoiling, 'what?'

'That's for what you did to my face,' I told him.

He sat with his hand on his cheek for a while, watching me.

'It went well, Jay,' I said, 'it went really well.'

He lowered his hand and gazed at me in astonishment. 'You mean… you're going to *carry on with it?*'

'Yes,' I said, 'yes, Jay. I must be losing my mind, but...I'll carry on with it.'

Sammie

13

Sammie felt nervous as she stepped inside Jay's house. The cottage was quite small, and quirky – tastefully decorated in blues and whites, a collection of shells on the little windowsill by the front door. Jay asked if she wanted something to drink but she said she didn't, so they stood awkwardly in the hall until he said, 'Do you want to come upstairs?'

Once they reached Jay's room, Sammie found it a big surprise. Not that she'd been in a large amount of boys' bedrooms before, apart from her brother Alfie's – though he'd been a lot younger – but even so, Jay's room struck her as decidedly unusual. The bed was immaculately made – a plain and pristine pale blue duvet, tucked neatly down the side where the bed was against the wall; a small white desk where Jay had a computer but little else apart from some pens and pencils in size order next to the keyboard, and a few books neatly arranged in colour order on a shelf. There was a wardrobe as well, and a chest of drawers, both closed neatly – nothing over-flowing, and not so much as a stray sock on the carpet. It was the tidiest room Sammie had ever seen.

'Your room is... nice,' Sammie said.

'Thanks.'

Jay sat down on the end of the bed and she sat beside him.

'I'm sorry,' Jay told her, 'about what happened to you at the bus stop. I shouldn't have told Mark about what happened between us, but I didn't think he'd start telling other people.'

'It's okay,' she said. 'I know it wasn't your fault.'

'Who was it?' Jay asked. 'Who was giving you all the hassle?'

'I don't know their names,' Sammie said, 'but...' she looked at Jay shyly. 'I got so annoyed I flashed my bra to get them to shut up.'

'Did you?'

'Yeah,' Sammie said, 'it was stupid. I'll have made things worse. Mark says everyone already hates me because they think I only met you today, and they saw us together at break time. They think I'm a slag.'

'It'll be all right,' Jay said. 'If anyone gives you any trouble, just come to me.'

Sammie made a little noise of agreement, but inside she wasn't so sure that going to Jay would help. From what little time she'd spent at the school, she'd understood a few things. Firstly, that Jay was not generally liked or respected. Secondly, that as a newcomer she didn't have the right to start going out with someone at Rangewood straight away, even if it was someone so unpopular. It wasn't what she did that made her a slag, Sammie knew well enough from her previous school that having sex or doing sexual things gained you admiration whether you were a boy or a girl, but the way she'd gone about things with Jay even in the space of one day seemed to have broken all manner of unspoken rules. If Jay started getting involved and defending her, it would probably make things worse.

Jay put his arm around her and Sammie snuggled against him. 'Jay,' she said, 'why do you think Mark told everyone?'

'Isn't it obvious?' Jay said. 'He's jealous. He fancies you as well.'

Sammie looked at Jay in astonishment. *'Really?'*

'Yeah,' Jay said. 'He told me in the summer, before we met you properly. I told him I thought you were hot, and he said he thought so too.'

Sammie considered it. It did make a lot of sense. Mark obviously wasn't happy she was going out with Jay, and that would certainly explain why. Instead of talking further about it, she turned and kissed Jay, and this time when his hand slipped down to the waistband of her skirt, she didn't tell him to stop.

They spent the rest of the afternoon in bed together, gradually becoming comfortable enough to take all of their clothes off. Sammie showed Jay how to touch her, placing her hand over the back of his and guiding him, and in turn he showed her how to touch him. The only difficult moment was when Jay began to try to push her onto her back, and she realised he meant to get on top of her. To begin with she thought she should let him. After all, when Mark had made his stupid attempt at warning her what Jay wanted her to go home with him for she'd implied she was okay with it, but her heart started pounding and she whispered, 'No. No, Jay. Not yet.'

'I thought you said—'

'I know,' Sammie said, 'but I'm not ready. I'm sorry.'

Jay stopped what he was doing and stroked her face. 'Are you sure you don't want to?' he asked.

'Yeah,' Sammie said, 'not today. I don't want to go any further today.'

Jay lay down at her side and propped himself up on his elbow. 'You're not trying to wait 'til you're sixteen, are you?' he said. 'When's your birthday?'

'May,' Sammie said.

'Oh,' Jay said, 'so you haven't even been *fifteen* that long.'

Sammie nodded. She was always one of the youngest in her year at school.

'Man,' Jay said, 'I definitely can't wait until next *May*.'

Sammie smiled. 'It's all right,' she said, 'I'm not trying to wait until I'm sixteen. I just… I need a bit longer, that's all.' She met his eyes. 'I enjoyed what we did, though.'

Jay smiled back at her and kissed her briefly. 'So did I,' he said.

...

Sammie had to leave at about five-thirty, so that she'd be gone well before Jay's mum got home from work at six. She walked home thinking about what had happened with Jay, and could barely stop herself from grinning. She didn't particularly like being back in her empty house – her mum had decided to go in to work after all when Sammie had refused the offer of a lift to school – but not even that could get her down today. If she closed her eyes she could still feel the sensation of Jay touching her, and she was full of so many different emotions she felt she might burst.

She went upstairs to her bedroom, where she thought she would lay on her bed for a bit and think about the wonderful afternoon, when her phone vibrated in her pocket. She took it out, assuming it would be a text from Jay, but she was surprised to see it was from Mark.

Sorry about wot i said earlier. I just dont want u 2 get hurt when jay gets bored of u.

Sammie stared at the words for a long time. Then she tried to put them out of her mind. Like Jay said, Mark was jealous. Perhaps she'd tell Jay about the message tomorrow, or perhaps not, but for the moment, she didn't want anything to spoil her happiness.

Felicity

14

I went to see Mark again on a Wednesday evening, a few days after my initial turning up at his door. I'd taken a couple of days off work to "recover" after our first meeting, because as Jay pointed out I needed some explanation for the state of my face, and he thought the easiest solution was to carry the mugging story through to my work as well. I felt a little bit guilty about doing this but soon put it aside when I did return to work and received only the most cursory expression of sympathy from my co-workers. I was well aware that two years of regularly turning up late or hung-over had pushed their regard for me to a record low, and dead parents or not, I had come to be seen as something of an irritation. And a liability.

Mark was almost as surprised when he opened the door to me again as he had been the first time I showed up. He took in the sight of my face, where the bruise had turned an angry greyish-purple, and looked out to the street behind my back as though he was concerned something else might have happened to me.

'How are you?' he asked finally.

'I'm okay,' I said.

He waited for a moment, and I realised he was expecting me to explain why I was at his door.

'I… I just came here to say thank you,' I said, 'you were very kind, and I'm sorry I spoiled your evening. I feel a bit silly about the whole thing now—'

'Don't,' he said. He reached out his hand for my arm, and

then stopped halfway as though he wasn't sure what he was doing. He let his arm drop to his side again. 'Don't feel silly, I mean,' he said. 'I'm glad that I *was* here, so that I could help.'

I smiled, and he smiled back, but awkwardly.

'So, here's the thing,' I said, 'I was wondering, would you let me buy you a coffee or something, sometime? To say thank you properly.'

'There's no need,' he said.

I took a moment to try to work out whether he was genuinely or deliberately misunderstanding me. In normal circumstances I would have walked away, but I couldn't. Of course there was a good chance that he just didn't want to see me again, but I needed to put that thought out of my mind. I *had* to get him to go out with me, and if he perhaps couldn't recognise when he was being asked out then I'd have to make it clearer to him.

'There may not be any need,' I said, 'but I'd like to, anyway.'

He was taken aback. 'Oh...' he said, as it finally clicked. 'Okay, well... yeah. I guess. That'd be... nice.'

We arranged the time and place and there was a difficult moment when we exchanged numbers and without thinking I took out my phone, completely forgetting that he thought my phone had been stolen.

'You got a new phone?' he asked.

We both looked down at the phone in my hand, which was quite clearly not new, and for a second I was consumed with panic until I managed to stammer out a story about a friend giving me their old phone. I was convinced for a moment that I'd blown it, but he accepted my story without question. I felt relieved, and almost proud as I hurried home to Jay, but when I got inside he didn't seem too happy. He was waiting in the hall as I came in, with a face like a smacked bum.

'What's wrong?' I asked him. 'Has something happened?'

He inclined his head towards the living room door as I put my coat and shoes away in the cupboard, and I saw the cause of his distress myself when I noticed a pair of big, lace-up black boots on the floor in the hall.

'Is Leanne here?' I asked.

He nodded.

'Oh, God,' I said quietly.

Jay stepped up close to me and spoke quietly, his breath on my neck making my hairs stand on end. 'Give me some good news,' he whispered, 'what happened with Mark?'

I turned and smiled at him. 'It's on,' I said.

As soon as I walked into the living room Leanne took one look at my face and let out what I can only describe as a shriek when she saw the bruising. 'Did you do that?' she asked Jay. 'Is that why you were so reluctant to let me in to wait for her?'

Jay rolled his eyes and leant against the wall with his arms folded.

'Answer me!' Leanne said. She got up from where she'd been sitting on Jay's spotless leather sofa to confront him, and it struck me how ridiculously out of place she looked in our clean, white, sterile flat. She was like a tornado of colour, purple hair flying, a richly embroidered skirt swishing around her ankles. Next to her Jay looked small, diminished, like a common garden bird next to peacock. But he certainly wasn't intimidated by her.

'What if I did?' he said. 'What are you going to do?'

Leanne was so taken aback by his response that she froze for a moment, then she gave him a slap so hard it made me gasp.

I rushed over to them, but the damage was already done. Jay fixed his eyes on Leanne. 'You fucking bitch,' he said.

'Stop,' I shouted, pulling them away from each other, 'the pair of you, stop it.'

Jay carried on glaring at Leanne, but she turned towards me. 'What the hell are you still doing here?' she asked. 'Why didn't you walk out the second he did this?'

'Because he didn't do it!' I said. 'I was mugged, on Saturday night, after I was round at yours. They took my phone. It was nothing to do with Jay.'

'Bullshit,' she said. She gestured towards Jay, who still had a mark on his lip from his fight with Georgia's brother. Plus, it was clear from the state of his hand that he'd hit *something* recently. The bandage was off now, but his hand still looked sore and scabbed from the night he punched the fence.

I grabbed Leanne's arm and pulled her out into the hallway. 'Look,' I said, 'Jay hasn't done anything to me. He's had a rough few weeks and he got in a fight.'

'I don't believe you,' she said, 'not about any of it.'

'That's fine,' I snapped, 'but you've got no right to come round here and accuse Jay of something he didn't do.'

Leanne didn't reply straight away. I could tell she was far from convinced. Finally, she took my arm, gently. 'I had to come and see you,' she said, 'I know that something isn't right here.'

'Lee—'

'No. Listen to me,' she said. 'I'm telling you, there is something wrong with him.' She gestured around the square, empty hall. 'This isn't normal,' she said, 'this isn't how normal people live.'

'I like it like this,' I said, 'what's wrong with being tidy?'

'There's tidy, and there's downright weird,' she said, 'apart from in your room there isn't a speck of your personality in this place. It is *all* him. What if you wanted to leave your shoes out? Or leave the dishes until the next morning? Does that earn you one of those?' She pointed at my face.

I sighed in exasperation. She was being ridiculous, but I didn't know how to explain, and before I could, Jay came out and joined us.

'I can hear what you're saying,' he told Leanne.

'Good,' she said, 'then you'll know I'm not going to let you get away with this.'

'What?' he said. 'Get away with what? You think I'm abusing her, is that it?'

He turned to me. 'Am I abusing you Felicity? Go on, you can tell her the truth.'

I looked from one of them to the other. 'This is stupid,' I said. 'I hate this. I hate the two of you fighting over me.'

'No,' Jay said, 'give her an answer. She wants to know, so tell her.'

Leanne shook her head and laughed without humour. 'I don't need her to answer me,' she said. 'You think I'd believe a word that comes out of her mouth when you're standing over her? And you *really* didn't want me here when I turned up, did you Jay? Were you scared of me seeing her face, or do you just not like her having friends of her own?'

I could see Jay was getting angry again. Wanting to avoid another scene like the one we'd had in the living room I tried to calm things down.

'Lee, was there something else you wanted?' I asked.

She gave Jay a dirty look and then turned to me. 'I was going to remind you to reply to Grace about her hen party,' she said. 'She's emailed you a few times and you haven't got back to her.' She looked me up and down. 'I can see why now,' she said. 'You've obviously had other things on your mind.'

I raised an eyebrow. I'd seen the messages, but I hadn't been able to face thinking about it. 'It's two months away yet,' I said, 'how much notice does she need to organise a piss-up in Coalton?'

Jay smirked and Leanne turned away towards the door with a swish of her skirts. 'I can't see any point in talking to you while *he's* here,' she said. 'You call me, okay? Any time.'

She bent down to pull her boots on, and I noticed as she fiddled with the laces that two of the several silver bangles jangling around her wrist were ones I'd made for her. I felt a pang. She'd always been a huge supporter of my jewellery, and at any given time up to fifty percent of the generous array of metalwork adorning her body had been designed and made by me.

'I've got to go and pick Kayleigh up,' she said.

''Bye then,' I said.

She gave me a long look.

'You can come with me,' she said meaningfully.

'Why on earth would I do that?'

She studied me again and I thought she was going to speak,

but then her eyes moved to something behind me – a big mirror by the door.

'What's up?' I said.

She walked over to the mirror, while Jay and I watched her in confusion.

'Here you go, Jay,' she said, placing her fingers on the glass and giving him a pointed look. 'Time to learn that nothing is perfect.'

With that, she drew her fingertips down in a swift motion, making four blurry smears on the glass. 'Oh, and Fliss,' she said, 'if you want to make up stories about being mugged, don't leave your phone in full view.'

I followed her gaze to my handbag, which was on the floor in the hall as I'd been too distracted to put it straight into the cupboard like I usually would. The zip was undone, and right there, sat on top of all the other contents, was my phone.

'You come to me if you need to, Fliss,' she said, 'day or night. I mean it. You don't have to stay here with this creep.'

Sammie

15

The next day at school Sammie did end up having to deal with a fair bit of stick about flashing her bra at the bus stop, but it didn't bother her as much as she had originally thought it might. If anything it seemed like Jay got more hassle over it than she did, and at break time she thought he might actually get in a fight with one boy, until Mark pulled Jay away and calmed him down.

'Are you happy with what you've done?' Mark asked Sammie later on, following her as she nipped to her locker between their Maths and English classes.

'What do you mean?'

'Jay almost got in a fight because of you.'

'He cares about me,' Sammie said, 'I can't help that.'

'He'll act like he cares about you for now,' Mark said, 'until he's got you into bed. That's... that's all he wants.'

Sammie slammed her locker closed. 'He's got me into bed,' she said, 'I was in bed with him yesterday after school.'

Mark looked disgusted and shocked and Sammie knew he assumed her and Jay had lost their virginity together. But the words she had used were not inaccurate and she was in no rush to enlighten him about the details of what her and Jay had actually done while they were in bed.

'So... so you... you actually did—' he stopped. 'Jay would have told me,' he said, and then he didn't seem able to say anything further.

Sammie felt triumphant for the next few hours, and it wasn't until the last lesson that Mark spoke to her again, obviously having cleared the matter up with Jay.

'He told me... what happened,' he whispered to her at the beginning of class while everyone was settling down.

She turned to him. 'Don't you think it's a bit weird to be this fascinated with mine and Jay's love life?' she said.

Mark's face turned red and his eyes glittered with anger, or perhaps it was hurt. 'I'm *not*,' he said, 'I just think the two of you are rushing things.'

'Yeah?' she said. 'What, compared to *you*, you mean?'

Mark stopped looking at her to take a pen and pad of paper out of his bag, and he slapped them down on the desk.

'I'm sorry you've got a crush on me, Mark,' she said, 'but I—'

'Who told you that?'

'Jay did,' she said, 'he said you fancy me.'

Mark looked as though he was going to argue, but apparently thought better of it.

'Just because *you've* never even kissed anyone before,' Sammie said, though she felt guilty and ashamed as the words came out of her mouth.

'How do you know?' he said. 'You don't know anything about me.'

'Oh,' she said, 'so you have then, have you?'

Mark glared at her with real hatred, and something else in his eyes that she couldn't quite understand. Then, before either of them could say anything else the teacher told them all to quieten down and they took it to heart, keeping up a stony silence for the entire fifty minutes, until the bell rang for the end of the day.

On the bus home, Sammie found a text from her mum that had been sent a couple of hours earlier, saying that tonight her parents would take her out for dinner to celebrate her starting her new school, and that they'd leave work in the next ten minutes or so. Sammie worked it out and realised this meant her parents would be back not long after she got home herself, so although she had been planning to spend another afternoon with Jay, she had to call it off.

Inside the house she plonked herself down in the TV room

to channel surf for a while. Jay text her and said he was thinking about what they would be doing right now, if she'd been able to come round, so on a whim she lifted her top up, took a picture of herself and sent it to him. His reply was very quick.

Oh man i want 2 touch u so bad, i want 2 see the rest of u.

With a quick glance around the room, even though she knew she was alone in the house, Sammie pulled her jeans down to her ankles. Then she hooked one finger into the elastic at the top of her knickers, pulling them down just enough for her pubic hair to begin to show, and took another picture of herself. She liked the effect when she looked at it, it seemed cheeky and sexy without showing him everything, and although her heart began to race and her cheeks felt hot, she quickly hit send. She smiled and threw the phone down on the sofa beside her, lying on her side in a little nest of cushions. Her parents should be getting back any time now.

She must have ended up falling quite deeply asleep, because when her phone rang it was quite some time later, and it woke her with a start. The TV was still on so she grabbed the remote and turned it off before answering the call, which she wasn't surprised to see was from her mum, and even less surprised to hear that the reason for the call was that the meal was off.

'Something came up,' her mum explained, 'we still haven't left. We're going to grab dinner on the way home.'

'Oh,' Sammie said.

'I'm sorry, Sammie,' her mum said, 'but it's just one of those things.'

Sammie didn't answer.

'There's a ham and pineapple pizza in the freezer I think,' her mum said, 'if you want to have that.'

'Yeah,' Sammie said, 'I might do. When will you be home?'

There was the sound of a low murmur of conversation between her mum and dad.

'Not until at least ten,' her mum said. 'It might be after you've gone to bed.'

Sammie made a noise to show she understood. Inside, she felt kind of strange. She didn't particularly like being in the house on her own during the day, but she *hated* it in the evening. It sounded silly, but the big expanses of glass in the house scared her in the dark – the big, yawning blackness felt menacing to her. She usually spent evenings in her room, with her music turned up to cover the disconcerting quiet and occasional weird and creepy sounds of the countryside. Her mum ended the call without any further discussion, and Sammie thought about the fact that her parents were also pretty deluded if they thought she went to sleep not long after ten. In fact, she was usually still awake until midnight or so, and was more than aware of her parent's hushed arguments that usually ended with her mum in tears.

She uncurled herself from the sofa in the TV room and padded into the kitchen. She couldn't be bothered with the pizza, and instead chose a tin of tomato soup she found at the back of the cupboard. She heated it up and ate about half, then tipped the rest down the sink and put the bowl in the dishwasher. Then she went up to her room, drew the curtains, sat on her bed and wondered what to do. She had hoped she might get another text from Jay, but he had fallen silent since she sent him the second photo, and she supposed that now he had finished thinking about what they would have done together he had probably moved on to some other thing.

She found it strange, though. She would have thought he'd be really excited about her showing him so much of her body in a photo, and she'd half expected him to ask to see even more, though she wasn't sure she'd have been willing to do that. Curious to check it had reached him, she opened her sent messages, and froze. She had no idea how she'd done it, and she was so horrified that she felt cold all over.

She hadn't sent the second picture to Jay. In her flustered excitement her finger must have slipped, and sent the message not to Jay, but to Mark.

Felicity

16

'Stupid, interfering bitch,' Jay said as soon as Leanne had left the flat. His eyes rested on the finger marks she'd made on the hall mirror. 'And what the hell was all *that* about?' he asked.

'Jay, I'm sorry,' I said, 'she shouldn't have started accusing you of things. But she's my friend, so please don't call her a bitch.'

'You're defending her?' Jay said, incredulous. 'You're defending her after the way she spoke to me?'

I didn't answer, and Jay brushed his fingers very gently over the bruise on my forehead.

'I can't believe she thought I'd do this to you,' he said.

'You... you did do it to me.'

Jay gave me a funny look. 'Yes, but not in *anger*.' He put his arms around me. 'It frightened you, didn't it?' he said.

I made a noise into his t-shirt and he kissed my hair. 'What I did to you made me feel sick,' he said, 'but the injuries had to be convincing. They had to look bad enough that Mark—'

I pulled away from him a little. 'I understand, Jay. But... you did it so... smoothly. Like you knew exactly what you were doing.'

'Because I'd spent the whole drive thinking about how to do it!' he said. 'What are you saying? That you think I'm so used to hitting women that it's like second nature to me?'

'No,' I said. 'No, of course not.'

Jay eyed me suspiciously. 'I wish you didn't spend so much time with Leanne,' he said, 'she puts ideas in your head about me.'

For the next fifteen minutes or so Jay cleaned the marks on

the mirror laboriously with soapy water. He washed the entire mirror, including the frame, then went and got a clean tea towel to dry it. As if that wasn't enough, he then went over the whole thing again with a duster and furniture polish.

'Jay, I think it's done,' I said, when he wouldn't stop polishing it.

He carried on for a couple more minutes, then he finally decided it was satisfactory and went back to the kitchen to put the cleaning things away.

'You know, she might not like the way I am with you,' Jay said, 'but I don't exactly think *she* treats you with that much respect either.'

'What do you mean?'

'She came round here, telling you what to do, having a go at you about not replying to some stupid email about Grace's hen party, saying I'm no good. She talks down to you.'

I shook my head. 'It's just her way.'

'Well, I don't like it. You shouldn't let her bully you.'

'I don't, Jay,' I told him. 'I don't let anyone bully me.'

Later on, when we went to bed, I decided to ask him about something that had been troubling me.

'Jay, you told me that Mark stood up for you when kids at school were giving you a hard time?'

'Yeah,' he said, 'well, kind of. I could handle it myself. All he did was try and get me away from situations before I got so wound up I ended up getting myself expelled or something.'

'Right,' I said, 'what I don't get is that you made it sound like Mark went out of his way to sleep with Sammie because he knew it would hurt you. If he cared about you, why would he want to hurt you?'

'Jealousy,' Jay said, 'or maybe he did it out of sheer spite. He liked it better when I was miserable; it made him feel like I actually needed him.'

'He's not like I expected,' I said at length.

'Mark?'

'Mm.'

'Why?' Jay asked. 'What did you expect?'

'Well, the way you described him, I thought he'd be a bit more... a bit more... a bit *less* nice.'

'Nice?' Jay said.

'Well, yeah. I mean... I don't really know him. But he just doesn't seem the type to—'

'Don't be taken in,' Jay said. 'Mark's manipulative. He can act all sweet and innocent when he wants to, but believe me, he's just out for what he can get.'

I didn't question him further. I closed my eyes, and as I drifted off to sleep I considered Jay's words, and how at odds they seemed with the shy, quiet man that I'd met.

I met Mark on Sunday, in a little cafe called The Apple Tree. It was painted lime green on the outside, with a carefully crafted air of eccentric carelessness on the inside; mismatching tables and chairs, antique frames containing photos of various animals in tiaras and an extensive menu of coffees and loose leaf teas. It was one of Leanne's favourite places, though when I arrived I wondered why on earth I'd suggested meeting Mark there. He'd arrived before me, and looked rather out of place at one of the window tables on his own, sipping coffee from an oversized yellow tea cup. When he caught sight of me he stood up to greet me, then seeming not to know what to do with himself he clumsily sat back down again.

'I said *I* was going to get the coffee,' I said.

He grinned sheepishly, and showed me his half-empty cup. 'I massively over-estimated how long it would take to get here.'

I laughed. 'You haven't been here before then?'

'No.'

I sat down opposite him. 'I forgot how... trendy this place is,' I said, 'we can go somewhere where the tea comes in bags if you'd rather.'

'No, it's cool,' he said. 'I like it here.'

I went and got myself a coffee, wondering how I was actually going to do this. I wasn't prepared for how nervous I felt. One wrong move and he could discover I knew Jay, and not to mention the whole plan being ruined, he'd think I was crazy into the bargain.

When I sat back down, Mark looked at the bruising on my face.

'It's looking much better,' he said.

'I've put makeup over it.'

'Oh,' he said.

I struggled to think of something to say, but my mind was blank, and we spent an uncomfortable minute or two in silence.

'I was surprised you came back to see me the other day,' he said eventually. 'I thought you wouldn't want to go back to... where it happened.' He paused a moment. 'I'm glad you did, though.'

'Well, you can't spend your whole life being scared,' I said. 'If I didn't go out any more, they'd have won.'

'That's easy to say,' he told me, 'but I'd understand if you felt frightened. *I* would be. I think you were very... brave... to come back just to thank me.' He looked a little flustered. 'Sorry,' he said, 'that came out sounding really stupid. I meant it as a compliment.'

'I know what you meant,' I said, 'and thank you. That was a nice thing to say.'

We fell into silence again for a while. I could see Mark was finding it difficult to relax, and to be honest, I wasn't finding it much easier. It began to dawn on me that to achieve what Jay wanted was going to take weeks, months. I couldn't believe Mark had been taken in when I asked him out, God knows how I was going to keep this up for long enough that he would really open up to me, have *feelings* for me.

'Did you make that, too?' Mark asked me, pointing at my necklace.

'I did,' I said. I'd purposely worn a piece of my own jewellery as it had interested him before, and I held the necklace out to him so that he could look at it.

I watched his face while he examined it more closely. It was a luxuriously wide metal necklace, looping round my neck like a collar, and he took quite a bit of time to really study it.

'I like how the fastening is part of the design,' he said, which took me aback. He was right – I'd deliberately put the clasp at the front, tried to make it look interesting, but I wouldn't have expected him to notice. Leanne sometimes said things that suggested she had given my creations more than a cursory glance, and my dad had always been interested in my jewellery, but nobody else was really that bothered. They'd say it was cool, sometimes, but Mark had really looked at it, and actually thought about it.

'Yeah,' I said, 'I like to try to do that. I think the whole thing should look interesting, not just one part of it. It's kind of fun to take the bit that most people would think of as ugly and then make it... like... the star, I guess.'

'Yeah,' Mark said, 'I totally get that. I...um... I take photos of old industrial stuff sometimes. You know, like old factories, or weird old bits of machinery.' He let out a nervous laugh. 'It's not as pretentious as it sounds.'

I laughed too. 'You'll have to show me sometime,' I said.

...

It ended up being a lot more fun than I expected, talking to Mark. He knew a little bit about all sorts of different things, and when I spoke he really engaged with me – asking me questions, wanting to know more. He told me that he worked in IT support, which he found boring. He had a degree in IT and business, and he even mentioned briefly about the village he grew up in – Tatchley. I felt a shiver through my body when he said it – as it confirmed in my mind beyond doubt that he really did know Jay; that he had grown up with him, spent his childhood with him, in the tiny little village.

'How did you get into making jewellery?' he asked me once we were both on our second cup of coffee.

'It was because of my dad, I think,' I told him. 'When I was growing up he was always mending stuff and making things in his little workshop at the bottom of the garden. I loved how he could take some old thing apart and fix it, and put it back together again. He started teaching me about what he was doing, and I think it was when he taught me how to solder that I realised I really loved working with metal, so I started making things out of it. Usually jewellery, but I'll try and make anything, really. Whatever takes my fancy.'

'So you're self-taught?' he said. 'You've never done a course or anything?'

'No. I don't think I'd want to. I don't really do it much now, anyway.'

'How come?'

I stirred my coffee absently. 'I don't know,' I said. 'I got a job, my own place to live. Things just kind of, overtook it.'

'Mm,' he said. 'I think you've got a real talent though.'

I laughed. 'Mark, please—'

'I mean it.'

'It would be nice if there was some money in it,' I said, part joking, part serious. I'd thought about trying to make a bit of money from it in the past, but it had never seemed feasible, and since my parents had died I'd given up on the idea completely.

Mark sat up, suddenly particularly interested. 'You're trying to make a business out of it?' he asked me.

'Not... not really a business, no.' I started to feel embarrassed. It seemed silly to talk about my jewellery as an actual business. 'I just used to sell it online occasionally,' I explained, 'mainly to justify making more, if I'm honest. I.... there was a time I considered trying to get more serious, have a website and stuff – make myself a kind of brand, but... it never really happened.'

Mark considered this for a while. 'Well, if you want a website, I can help you make a website,' he said, 'any online stuff, I'm happy to get involved with. I can help you have a think about how to promote it as well, if that would be useful.'

I stared at him, astonished. 'Really?'

'It's not that big a deal,' he said casually. 'In fact... would you need photos as well? Of the jewellery?'

I nodded.

'Well then,' he said, 'you've come to the right place.' He grinned, and I couldn't help smiling back as he excitedly counted off his relevant skills on his fingers. 'Websites, business, marketing, photography,' he said, 'I'm pretty happy to get my teeth into any of those, and you've brought me an excuse to do all four.'

I laughed. 'Mark, that's so kind, but I can't ask you to do that. Besides, I really don't do it much any more. I've still got all the stuff but...'

'Just have a think about it,' Mark said, 'the offer still stands.'

'Mark... I... I can't afford to pay you, or anything—'

'I'm not asking you to. I'd enjoy doing it. It feels like a long time since I've had an interesting challenge.'

'Is that what you like? Challenges?'

'Yes and no,' he said, 'but getting an income from something *you've* made, what could be better than that? I'd love to start my own business, I'm just waiting for the right idea to come along.'

'Yeah?' I said. 'Well, look, I will give it some thought. It's... it's really exciting.'

Sammie

17

Most of the night Sammie worried about the picture she'd mistakenly sent to Mark. A couple of times she almost contacted him, but she couldn't think what to say, and resolved that she would get up early and talk to him at the bus stop. He was nearly always the first one there, while Jay was generally the last, so it should give her at least a few minutes to explain her error to him.

Sure enough, when she got there Mark was already inside, sitting on the bench with his back against the wall, reading a book. His two sisters sat the other side of the shelter to him, giggling over something together. Sammie plonked herself down next to Mark, glad to be out of the drizzling rain. The bus shelter was rather more elaborate than the usual transparent, plastic affairs full of adverts that you got elsewhere. It was a proper little three-sided building, with a pitched roof and a wooden bench inside, which helped it blend in with the rather more *select* surroundings of Tatchley.

Mark glanced at her, and she could see he wasn't happy. He closed his book and shoved it into his school bag. Then he turned to his two sisters. 'Could you leave us alone for a minute?' he said. 'I want to talk to Sammie.'

The two girls stared at Sammie, their dark eyes wide.

'But it's *raining*,' one of them said.

Mark sighed in exasperation. 'Go and stand under that big tree down the road,' he told them.

Reluctantly the two girls stood up, and after another curious look at Sammie, they wandered off. As soon as they were out of earshot, Mark fixed Sammie with a piercing glare.

'Why did you send me that?' he asked.

'It was an accident,' Sammie said, 'it was meant for Jay. I don't know what happened—'

Mark narrowed his eyes. 'I don't believe you Sammie. I think if *I* was sending *pornographic* pictures of myself, I'd be pretty careful who I sent them to. I don't think I'd send them to just anyone by mistake.'

'What are you talking about?' Sammie said. 'It wasn't *pornographic*, it was just a laugh.'

'That's not how it looked to me.'

'What would you know about it?' she snapped.

'Is that what he's getting you to do now? Send him stuff like that?'

'No,' Sammie said.

'You know there's nothing to stop him showing it round the school, don't you? Or putting it online.'

Sammie's stomach clenched. Even though the only picture Jay had was just of her in her bra, she'd been using her arms to push her breasts together and give herself better cleavage, and the picture she'd ended up with could hardly be described as anything except sexual. 'He wouldn't do that.'

'You'd better hope not.'

She looked up at the road as a car went past, throwing up a spray of mucky grey-brown water that landed not far from their feet. 'You're being ridiculous,' she told Mark, 'it was *just* a laugh, why are you making such a big deal out of it?'

Although she was desperate to ask Mark whether he'd tell Jay about the message, she couldn't bring herself to, and all day she was on edge. But Mark simply avoided both her and Jay, and spent time with some of his other friends – a luxury he had that her and Jay didn't.

After school, Sammie went to Jay's house again and they spent another couple of hours in bed, playing and exploring each other. Jay didn't try to push her to have sex, but it was obvious he wanted to and she was glad that he was so keen.

ANYTHING FOR HIM

'I loved the picture you sent me,' he told her.

Sammie tried to smile, but the thought of her conversation with Mark made it difficult. Jay didn't seem to notice though.

'Why didn't you send me more?' he asked.

'I... my mum phoned me,' Sammie said quickly, 'about the meal we were supposed to be going out for. Then it felt a bit weird after I'd just spoken to my parents.'

Jay laughed. 'Fair enough,' he said. 'Send me one later, though. Once you've gone home and I'm missing you.'

'Maybe,' Sammie said.

'I spent ages looking at the one last night,' Jay said.

'Yeah?'

'It really turned me on.'

Sammie finally managed to smile properly. 'You might get one later,' she told him playfully, 'if I think you deserve it.'

When she got home she didn't immediately do as he asked, she waited until she was going to bed, and sent him a couple of pictures as she got changed out of her clothes.

Im not goin 2 b able 2 sleep now, Jay text her back.

Sammie giggled to herself, and quickly typed a reply.

I wish i cld come and sleep in bed with u, she told him.

So do i. Ur makin me really want 2 hav sex wiv u. i cant stop thinkin about it.

Sammie looked at the words for a long time. She still felt a bit frightened, but a sort of boldness had come over her after sending the photos. *At the weekend,* she told him, *while your mum is at work. We can do it then.*

The next day at school the plan became a little more elaborate. Sammie suggested that they could meet up and go into town on the bus on Saturday, where they could hang out for a bit and have a sort of date together, and then after that they'd go back to his and have sex. She could see Jay didn't understand why she wanted to make it more complicated, but he was happy enough to go along with it. The real reason behind her suggestion was that she wanted to go into town with him to buy some condoms, but she was scared if she told Jay the truth he might try to talk her out of it or say it wasn't necessary. He'd never mentioned anything about contraception before, and it was pretty obvious to her that he had no anxieties about having sex with her without being careful.

The whole morning at school they were filled with excitement about their plans, and Mark was largely ignored as they spent all of break time entwined with each other, whispering about the weekend.

The day seemed like it could hardly go any better, until towards the end of lunch when they were walking back to the school building, and a couple of the boys from the bus stop who'd teased Sammie started making comments again. Sammie wasn't on her own this time, and walking hand-in-hand with Jay, while Mark tagged along behind, she didn't feel all that bothered about what the boys were saying. It was stupid, playground stuff, and with Jay's hand in hers Sammie could hardly care less. She thought Jay felt the same, but she couldn't have been more wrong.

The fight started before she really understood what was happening. All she knew was that one second they were walking along ignoring the taunts, then in a flash Jay went for one of the boys, taking him so much by surprise that even though he was larger than Jay, Jay had him sprawled out on the ground in a second. Mark quickly stepped in to try to break it up, but not before the boy's nose had been bloodied, and other kids formed a circle around the pair, the chant, 'Fight, fight, fight!' filling the playground and drawing everyone towards them. Sammie held her hand over her mouth as she watched what was going on. Jay was so intent on causing more injuries that Mark could barely hold him back, and the look on his face frightened her. She'd seen something similar once in her parents after Alfie had died, when they used to scream at each other. A look like they weren't in control any more – like whatever normally kept them together, held all their feelings in, had gone, and she had no idea what they would be capable of.

The fight was over in just a few short minutes. Jay was pulled away from the other boy by a teacher, and even though for a while he still struggled and swore, he thankfully realised that the game was up for him and calmed down a little. The boy on the ground, whose name was Dean, got unsteadily to his feet. There was blood all down his shirt, and he looked at Jay and said, 'He's fucking mental. He needs locking up.'

For the next hour or so lessons were off for Mark and Sammie, as they found themselves explaining, along with some of the other kids, what they had witnessed, so that appropriate punishments could be doled out.

Sammie had never particularly been involved in school discipline procedures before. She'd rarely got in trouble herself at her old school, and she was surprised how official everything was. She had to give a statement about what she'd seen Jay do as though she was being interviewed by the police. She tried to play it down and emphasise Jay had been standing up for her, explaining, a little shyly, 'He's my boyfriend.'

When it was finally over she went back to her Biology class with Mark, who scowled at her. 'Nice going, Sammie,' he said, 'you know he's probably going to get excluded.'

'I didn't do anything,' Sammie said.

'You're the one who flashed your bra at Dean and the others. Jay just got himself in a ton of trouble sticking up for you.'

'I didn't ask him to!'

Mark looked her up and down. 'I wish you'd never moved here,' he told her, 'you should have stayed in Kent.'

Mark and Sammie tried to go and see Jay after school, but his mum answered the door. She was clearly stressed and upset, and

Sammie looked at her with interest. She'd never seen more than a quick glimpse of Jay's mum before, and she was surprised to see she was really quite a young woman, so young that she must have had Jay when she was only a teenager herself. She was dressed in navy blue suit trousers, a white blouse, and had a little scarf round her neck that reminded Sammie of an air hostess uniform, except she knew Jay's mum was an estate agent. Her makeup was really subtle and unusual, her lipstick lighter than her natural lip colour so that her mouth was the palest pink, and her eyelids were coloured almost white with shimmering eye shadow, showing off long, feathery eyelashes.

'Mark, Sammie,' Jay's mum said, 'I'm sorry, but Jay is grounded and I don't want him seeing anyone right now.'

'Please,' Mark said, 'we want to see if he's okay.' He said the word "we" with just the tiniest hint of contempt, that Jay's mum would almost certainly miss but Sammie heard loud and clear.

'He's okay,' Jay's mum told them, 'but he's been excluded for a week.'

She didn't seem to want to speak to them any further, so Mark and Sammie began to walk towards their respective homes. Before arriving at the place that they would go in separate directions, Mark said, 'I told you he'd get excluded.'

'I don't know why he kicked off like that,' Sammie said, 'why did he get so angry?'

'Because that's what he does.'

'He… he's done this before?'

'Yeah. Lots of times. It's because of what happened with his mum and dad.'

'Is it?'

'Yeah,' Mark said, as though it was obvious. 'It's affected him. People don't understand him.'

Sammie realised that he included her in that statement. 'I think I understand him,' she said.

'No, you don't,' he said, sounding disgusted. 'Not even close.'

He started to walk away, then he looked back at her.

'Don't go thinking it's romantic, that he got in a fight over you. Jay is always spoiling for a fight. It doesn't mean anything.'

He left and Sammie stood still for a while, staring after him. Then she slowly made her way towards home, wondering what on earth was going on.

Felicity

18

Although I tried to fight it, to my surprise my head was soon buzzing with thoughts of starting jewellery making again. Jay was somewhat less enthused when I outlined the main bullet points of my date with Mark while we sat at the dining table with mugs of tea. He listened closely to all the cues that indicated Mark might like me, and laughed out loud when I told him Mark had said I was talented at making jewellery.

'Oh my God,' he said, 'could he be any more obvious?'

'What do you mean?'

Jay raised an eyebrow. 'Come on, Fliss,' he said, 'he doesn't like your jewellery, does he? He wants a shag.'

I drank some of my tea, a little ball of pain and anger beginning to bloom inside me.

'I think he was being genuine,' I said.

Jay stared at me. 'Don't be so stupid, Fliss,' he said, 'what's more interesting? This—' he reached out and touched my necklace, 'or this—' he said, squeezing one of my breasts. I moved out of his reach.

'Is that what *you* think, then?' I asked him. 'My jewellery is how I express myself. Just because you clearly have no interest in that, is it so hard to believe another man does?'

Jay's mouth dropped open. 'Fliss,' he said, as I stood up, 'Fliss, come on, I didn't mean it like that.'

I ignored him and his words followed me as I walked away. 'Fliss,' he said, 'you're being ridiculous.'

Inside my old room I sat at my desk and took some of my old

projects out from the drawer where I'd dumped them. My feelings were mixed as I looked at the little collection of rings, bracelets and necklaces. I knew it was a silly dream to think I could ever give up my job to work on it, but maybe with Mark's help I *could* make a little bit of money. When Jay knocked on the door a few minutes later I didn't answer, but he came inside anyway and sat on the end of my bed.

'Fliss,' he said, 'what I said just then, it didn't come out right.'

I made a noise of disgust and dropped the jewellery back into the drawer.

'I don't want you to get taken in by him,' Jay went on. 'He's giving you all these ideas about starting up making jewellery again, but is that really what you want? Your jewellery... it reminds you of your dad, doesn't it? And it makes you unhappy.'

'I don't know.'

Jay stood up and came to put his arms around me. 'Fliss, people will say things they don't mean sometimes. Mark... well, as far as I can tell he hasn't had a girlfriend in years. He's trying to flatter you, but he doesn't really know you.'

'I thought that's what you want? For him to like me?'

Jay kissed the top of my head. 'It is,' he said, 'but I don't want you to get hurt. Your... your jewellery is very clever, but... let's face it, people aren't really going to *buy* it. I don't want you to get your hopes up and be disappointed, when you're already... well, you're already a bit fragile, aren't you?'

I touched the necklace around my neck and Jay let go of me to pick up the mirror I had on the windowsill. He brought it over and held it in front of me so I could look at myself.

'You're so beautiful,' he said, 'but when you wear things like that necklace, it just looks... it looks homemade and cheap. It's not... it's not as pretty as you are. It brings you down. You understand what I'm saying, don't you?'

I looked closely, and I had to admit I could see what he meant. I'd always thought my jewellery looked unusual and quirky, but actually, in a way, it did look kind of naff. I reached up and undid it.

'The thing is,' Jay said, taking the necklace from me and putting it in the drawer with my other discarded creations, 'it threw me a bit, the idea that you might start making jewellery again, because I'd had some thoughts about what we could use this room for.'

'What's that?' I asked. I expected him to say something silly, trivial — a gym or something, as that's where he spent half his life. But when he did make his suggestion, I was so shocked it took my breath away.

'I thought... I thought it would make a nice nursery.'

...

That evening I got a call from Leanne, trying to make peace with me about her disastrous visit to the flat. We talked for half an hour or so, but it was obvious she was still determined to turn me against Jay and by the end of the call I was on even worse terms with her than before. Jay had gone out for a run, but once he'd come back and had a shower I went to talk to him in his room, suddenly feeling curious to know more about the girl who had inspired his plan with Mark.

'Do you have any pictures of Sammie?' I asked.

He frowned. 'Yeah,' he said, 'a couple. Why?'

'Can I see them?'

He seemed reluctant, but eventually he asked me to leave him alone for a minute while he tried to find them. I didn't really understand why I couldn't stay in the room as he looked for the pictures, and could only assume that once he started going through his wardrobe he thought there might be something in there I wouldn't want to see. I didn't think much of it. Having stumbled upon his search history on more than one occasion, I couldn't imagine he'd have anything in his wardrobe that could shock me. He finally came and joined me at the dining table, where he plonked down an old cardboard shoebox with a small amount of sentimental items in it — photos, a few certificates from his school days, a couple of Valentine's cards.

'I don't have much,' he said, 'only what I took with me when I left home.'

He picked through the small pile, where there were some loose photographs from school trips, some from when Jay was only a child, with fluffy hair and a surprisingly round face. In these old pictures he was invariably with Mark; the taller, dark-haired boy appearing somehow very serious and responsible beside the mischievous looking Jay. There seemed to be only one picture of Sammie, and it featured Mark and Jay as well, and all three were in school uniform.

I took the picture from his hand, and looked at the three faces in it. Jay and Sammie were both grinning, and I looked at her face; her pale skin and cool blue eyes, her lips a light, delicate pink. I thought that beside the two boys she appeared almost a little posh or superior, but the way she was smiling was genuine, and Jay looked happy too; happier than I'd ever seen him.

'You look like you were very in love with her,' I said.

'I was,' he said. 'Do you think it looks like she loved me?'

I examined the picture again. Jay had his arm tightly around Sammie's shoulders, and there was no doubt she was comfortable being there with him. But it wasn't Jay and Sammie who drew my attention. I mumbled to Jay that Sammie did look like she was in love with him, but my eyes were fixed on Mark's face. It was hard to draw any conclusions from a picture – perhaps he had been caught with a strange expression, maybe a second later he'd have been smiling too – but he certainly wasn't smiling in that moment. He was staring at Sammie and Jay. And if I wasn't mistaken, he looked like he absolutely hated them.

Sammie

19

Mark and Sammie obediently stayed away from Jay for the next few days while he was grounded. Sammie spent a lot of time texting him, and he often moaned about how fed up he was and asked her to send him something to brighten up his days. His appreciation and excitement over her ever more daring photos inspired her to keep sending more, until it made her blush to think about the little collection of images he had of her. She longed to see him in person, but it seemed like his mum was around more often than usual, and their plans to go into town and then sleep together at the weekend had to be put on hold.

By Tuesday the following week Jay told her for about the hundredth time that he was going mad from boredom. His mum had returned to work as normal, so after school Sammie decided to go and see him. Unfortunately, she couldn't stop Mark tagging along, and when Jay opened the door to them he was visibly delighted to see her, but less impressed to see Mark in tow. But Mark seemed oblivious to the fact he was unwelcome, so for half an hour or so Sammie sat bored on Jay's bed watching the two boys playing videogames.

'Mark,' Jay said eventually, 'do you think you could...'

'Could what?' Mark asked stupidly.

Jay rolled his eyes. 'For Gods' sake,' he said, 'we want you to give us some space, Mark. We want to be *alone* together.'

Sammie giggled and Mark glared at them both. 'Fine,' he said, as he strode out of the room.

Jay and Sammie waited until they heard the front door close, then they quickly shed their clothes and got under the covers together. Jay started touching her straight away, but she said, 'Wait a minute, Jay. Can we just lie here for a while?'

He groaned. '*Sammie...*'

'Just for a minute,' she said.

He stopped touching her and let her lie quietly in his arms, and her body gradually became more relaxed, more used to the sensation of his skin against hers. She liked being naked with him, and she began to feel safe, and close to him. 'Is your mum still angry with you?' she asked softly. 'About the fight?'

'Sammie, I don't want to talk now,' he said, 'let's talk after.'

'After what?'

'After we have sex!' Jay said. 'That's what you came here for, isn't it?'

Sammie opened her mouth and then closed it again. 'Jay,' she said firmly, 'not today, I—'

'We were supposed to do it at the weekend,' he said, 'that's what you told me.'

'I know,' Sammie said, 'but... we don't have... we don't have any condoms. I was thinking we could get them when we went into town, unless... unless you... have some?'

He shook his head. His eyes were still fixed on her. 'I got excluded from school for you.'

Sammie didn't know how to answer and she began to feel nervous.

'I'm on my final chance,' he continued, 'if I go back and get in a fight or anything again, I'll get kicked out.'

'Jay, I'm sorry—'

'I beat up Dean because he was talking shit about you,' he said. 'He was practically calling you a slut, and I stood up for you.'

Sammie pulled away from him. 'Don't pressure me,' she said, 'I'm not going to do it at all if you pressure me.'

At this, Jay softened, or pretended to. 'Sammie,' he said quietly, 'I'm not trying to pressure you.' He touched her face. 'You don't realise what it's been doing to me, though. All these conversations we've had, all the things you've sent me... you knew what you were doing.'

Sammie smiled, just a little. 'Have I been winding you up?'

'Just a bit!' Jay said. 'And I've had nothing else to think about, here in the house all day.'

Sammie giggled, and Jay kissed her.

'I want to do it,' she told him, 'but we should get some condoms.'

Jay watched her closely. 'Come on,' he said, 'you're not going to get pregnant your first time.'

'You...' Sammie said incredulously, 'are you being serious?'

Jay smirked as if to say he thought it had been worth a go.

'Look, how about this,' he said, 'I won't... finish... inside you. I'll only do it for a little while. I just want to feel what it's like.'

'Jay...' Sammie said.

'Just five minutes,' Jay said, 'let me have five minutes.'

'No—'

'Three.'

'Jay—'

'Two minutes,' he said. 'One minute. Thirty seconds.'

Sammie laughed, partly out of amazement at his persistence, partly out of nerves, because she knew she was going to give in.

'Is that a yes?' Jay asked. 'Was that a yes to thirty seconds, Sammie?'

She carried on laughing, until her nerves returned when Jay began to gently push her down onto her back.

She wasn't sure how long it had been, thirty seconds, or two minutes, or five, but they were startled rudely from their lovemaking when there was a knock on the bedroom door, and with barely a pause, it opened. Sammie let out a little cry, and her and Jay struggled to pull the covers over their bodies. Jay's mum stood in the doorway, too surprised even to look away to begin with, she just said, 'Oh God, oh my God,' then she averted her eyes and spoke to the carpet, but Sammie could see her body was rigid with anger. 'Jay,' she said, in a deceptively calm voice, 'I want you to get dressed and then come downstairs and talk to me in the kitchen.'

She left the room and Jay threw his clothes back on as quickly as he could, while Sammie stayed in bed, wrapped up in the duvet.

'Jay,' she said, 'what's she going to say?'

Jay kissed her reassuringly. 'It's all right,' he said, 'don't worry. I can handle her.'

Sammie watched as he left, and he closed the bedroom door behind him. Despite his words, he looked worried and angry. She stayed in bed a little while longer, listening to the sound of him going downstairs, and the kitchen door closing. Briefly there was silence, and then she heard raised voices. Slowly, she got out of bed and started putting her clothes back on. Her legs were shaking a little, and her insides were very sore and tender. She wished that she hadn't been left on her own. She wanted to talk to Jay about what they'd just done; about how she felt about it, but with him gone she felt confused and uncertain, and suddenly, overwhelmingly, alone.

The shouting downstairs went on for five, maybe ten minutes, before Sammie grew curious and opened Jay's bedroom door a crack in the hope she might overhear something. Gradually, she became bold enough that she stepped out into the hallway and crouched at the banister, where she could see the top half of the kitchen door. She'd barely been there a second when the door downstairs opened and Jay burst out.

'Jay, come back and finish talking to me,' his mum said.

Sammie assumed that at worst he'd walk off and ignore her, or maybe argue back, but what he actually did was much more extreme. Casually, as though he'd said and done this sort of thing many times before, he said, 'Oh, fuck off,' and slammed the door in his mum's face.

Sammie darted back inside his room as quickly as she could before he came upstairs, and settled herself on the bed as though she'd been there the whole time.

Jay slammed the door when he came to join her, then he threw himself down on the bed next to her. Sammie thought he'd say something, but to her surprise he started kissing her, and pulling at her clothes.

'Jay!' she said. 'What are you doing?'

'Let's carry on,' he told her, and he pulled harder at her top, trying to get her to take it off.

'Jay, no,' Sammie said, 'your mum's downstairs, what—'

'I don't care.'

Sammie pushed him away firmly. 'Well, I do,' she said, 'what's wrong with you?'

Jay finally let go of her. He stood up and paced to the other side of the room, and Sammie thought he was calming down. Then, to her astonishment, he made a loud noise of anger and frustration, and slammed his fist into the wall.

For a while there was silence. Sammie was so shocked she didn't know what to say or do, and Jay seemed even to have surprised himself a bit. But then he started swearing at the pain in his hand, and Sammie looked at the wall by his bedroom door, where he'd damaged the plasterboard.

'It's okay,' she said, rushing over to him and trying to put her arms around him. 'It's all right, it doesn't matter that much, does it?'

Jay carried on swearing and pushed her away, and she started to cry because she was so confused and shaken. 'Jay,' she said, 'Jay, you're frightening me.'

'I wanted it to be special for you,' he said.

'It was,' Sammie told him, wiping her tears away, 'it *was* special. I... I really liked it.'

Sammie thought Jay was beginning to calm down, but out in the hall she could hear his mum coming up the stairs. Seconds later she burst into Jay's room, and Sammie stepped back well away from her, even though the slim woman in a ruffled blue blouse and a pencil skirt was hardly a formidable sight. Jay's mum took one look at the hole in the wall and for a second

Sammie thought she was going to flip. But instead, she said in a very quiet and restrained voice, 'Jay, I want you to walk Sammie home now. Then you are going to come straight back here, and you and me are going to have a conversation. A *long* conversation.'

...

On the walk home, Jay was still fuming about what had happened, and as they reached her front door Sammie said, 'Why was she even back so early? I thought she worked 'til nearly six. It was only just gone five.'

Jay kicked out moodily at the doorstep. 'One of the fucking neighbours,' he said, 'apparently one of them phoned up mum's work. They didn't even speak to my mum, they just left a message with someone else there saying I'd been playing loud music for hours on end.'

Sammie frowned. 'But... we weren't.'

'I know,' Jay said, 'it's fucking stupid. They've got it in for me. Everyone fucking has it in for me.'

Sammie carried on thinking about it, while Jay muttered angrily to himself. It made no sense to her at all. Her and Jay hadn't had any music on, let alone loudly, and even when Mark had been there earlier and him and Jay had been playing games, it hadn't been *loud*.

'I don't get it,' she said.

'It ruined everything.'

Sammie touched his arm. 'It didn't ruin it,' she said gently, 'not for me. I... I'm upset your mum found us, but it doesn't change what happened before that, does it?'

'Doesn't it?'

'Well, didn't you enjoy it?' she asked. 'Was it... was it how you thought it would be?'

'No,' he said, 'I didn't think we'd get walked in on.'

Sammie sighed inwardly, and decided she'd tell him how she felt about it anyway, even if he wasn't interested. 'It was... it was even more painful than I thought it would be,' she said, 'but I didn't mind, because it was so wonderful, and I was so happy it was happening.'

Finally, Jay calmed down and looked at her. 'Did it really hurt a lot?' he asked.

'Yeah,' she said, 'I think... I think it might be one of the most painful things I've ever done.'

Jay touched her face. 'I really liked it, Sammie,' he said. 'It was... it was more, sort of... difficult, than I expected. But it was amazing.' His face clouded over again. 'I just can't believe it ended like that,' he said, 'if I find out which neighbour it was—'

'Jay, don't,' Sammie said, 'don't get upset about it again. I'm sure other people have had even weirder first times. I mean, it didn't even seem like it could happen at all to begin with, did it? With Mark not wanting to take the hint and leave us—' She stopped suddenly as the memory of Mark's face flashed into her mind. He'd looked so angry, and upset, and *jealous*, when Jay had told him to go.

'Jay,' she said slowly, 'this call to your mum's work. You don't... you don't think it could have been *Mark*, do you?'

Felicity

20

Although Jay remained sceptical about me trying to sell my jewellery – and a part of me was inclined to agree with him – I found that ideas began to trickle in anyway, until I thought to hell with it, and sat down at my desk. To begin with I felt oddly self-conscious. I couldn't switch off and focus on what I was doing, and I nearly gave up. Finally I took a deep breath. It was now or never, I decided. I had loads of new ideas, but if I couldn't put them into action now, I had to accept I probably never would. With that decided, I laid out all the sketches I'd hastily done over the past few days, and tried to get myself back into the zone.

I surfaced a couple of hours later, when Jay told me he'd made dinner.

'Tell me about what you've made,' he said as we sat together eating salmon with steamed vegetables.

'I thought you weren't interested?'

Jay shrugged. 'You know how I feel about it,' he said, 'but if it's important to you, then it's important to me, and I want to hear about it.'

I started to tell him, then I went and grabbed what I'd done so far to help me explain better, holding the necklace I'd been working on up to me to show him how it would sit against the skin. He listened carefully as I explained my idea – the way the metal would eventually form an elegant silver loop around the neck and then plunge down into a luxurious spiral just below the throat, but he couldn't hide the glazed look that crept into his eyes.

When we'd finished eating he said, 'You should call Mark.'

Suddenly, I understood. 'That's why you've come round to the idea, isn't it?' I said. 'It's not because it's important to me, it's because it will help with the plan for Mark!'

Jay watched me in silence. 'Fine,' he said at last. 'Fliss, I'm not interested in it. In fact, I think it's really stupid, and a complete waste of time. But Mark likes it and I want Mark to like you. Is that what you wanted to hear?'

'I really don't like you much sometimes,' I said.

'Would you rather I lied?'

I picked up my phone. 'Okay,' I said, 'I'll call him.' I stood up to go and talk to Mark in private but Jay stopped me. 'No,' he said, 'in here.'

He started clearing away our plates and I dialled Mark's number. To begin with I was reserved, stung by what Jay had said about my jewellery, but before long I was babbling away with excitement over the new collection I was going to put together and eventually told him I'd like to take him up on the offer of some help making a website. He sounded thrilled, suggesting we meet up one night to talk about it, so I arranged to go to his flat for dinner the very next day. Although Jay pretended to be intent on clearing up in the kitchen, I knew he was listening to every word.

'Jay,' I said afterwards, 'next time I have to call him, could you let me have some space?'

'Why?'

'Because it's weird having you in the room with me judging every word I say. It's hard enough doing all this pretending, without you reminding me of it.'

'You didn't sound like you were pretending,' Jay said, with a sideways glance at me.

'Well, good,' I said, 'that's the idea.'

Jay continued being suspicious of me all evening. He wouldn't talk to me and was clearly having a sulk. Since he was acting that way anyway I decided to continue work on the necklace, and before long Jay came in and sat on the end of the bed in my room, watching me work.

'Jay, why don't you leave me to it?' I said. 'I need to concentrate.'

'Are you going to be doing this every night now?'

'Not every night,' I said, 'but I want to get a fair bit done this week.'

'So when you're here you're going to be doing that, and then the rest of the time you'll be out with him,' Jay said, as if the reality of his plan had only just occurred to him. 'When are we going to talk about what I said the other day? About us maybe trying for a baby?'

I sighed. 'Jay,' I said, 'we are a long way off that conversation.'

...

When I got to Mark's the next day, I was confronted with a kitchen full of food. He'd said he was going to make pizza, but every surface seemed to be covered in ingredients – from mozzarella to parmesan, olives to tinned pineapple, ham to chorizo. There was even a big bowl of salad, and garlic bread.

'I didn't know what you like,' he said, 'so I got everything.'

I laughed. 'You're not kidding,' I said.

'Yeah,' he said, 'I guess I went a bit overboard.'

The pizzas were delicious. I ate more than I thought I'd be able to, but when I looked round at the kitchen there was still a lot left.

'You're going to be eating the rest of this stuff for a week,' I said.

'Yeah,' he said, 'well, I'm just pleased that you liked it.'

I helped him take our plates and things into the kitchen, and offered to help him wash up but he wouldn't let me.

'I'll do it later,' he said, 'tell me about what you've been working on.'

I didn't take much persuading. We sat on the sofa and he listened to me pouring out my ideas.

'I'll make some simpler pieces as well,' I explained. 'Probably things people can get personalised with names or initials or whatever, so they can get something unique but not actually that expensive or time consuming for me to make.'

'Yeah, that makes sense,' Mark said, 'a small number of unique, expensive things and then a lot of cheaper, simpler ones.'

I stretched my legs out and sighed contentedly. I felt very full, and very relaxed. Mark's flat might be poky, and the furniture that had come with it from the previous owners was a bit grotty, and ugly, but it was a cosy place to be. The sofa was so big that it closed off the corner of the room we were in like a little nest, and Mark was an easy person to be with.

'Are you enjoying getting back into it again?' Mark asked me.

'Yes, and no,' I said.

'Why no?'

'Oh... I don't know,' I said. 'It's fun to pretend I'm doing something good with my jewellery, but how good is any of what I'm making, really? I wonder whether I'm just kidding myself.'

'Fliss, it's good.'

'Really?'

'Yeah. Honestly, I wouldn't say it was if it wasn't. I don't lie.'

I smiled and laid my head back on the sofa, gazing up at the ceiling. My hand was resting next to me on the cushions, and suddenly I felt Mark touch it. My initial instinct was to snatch it away, but I didn't, and after a minute or two I found that I didn't mind it so much.

We talked all evening. He told me about his family, and his brothers and sisters. He had three sisters, one older than him and the other two younger. Two of them had families of their own. He also had a brother who was a couple of years older, and doing a PhD in something Mark didn't seem to understand well enough to be able to explain to me.

'Do you see your family much?' I asked him.

'No,' he said after a brief pause, 'I don't really... go back home much.'

'How come?'

He thought about it, almost seeming to weigh me up. 'I've

got… some bad memories back at home,' he said.

I wanted to ask him more, but I could see he wasn't ready to discuss it, so reluctantly I held back.

'What about you?' he asked. 'Do you see your family much?'

I hesitated before answering. In the past, straight after it had happened, I had told people the truth about my family. But more recently I'd changed my tactics. I didn't like dealing with people's reactions, and I'd come up with a convenient alternative.

'My parents both died in a car crash,' I said.

Mark stared at me. 'Oh,' he said, 'oh… God. I'm sorry. When? How—'

'It was about two years ago. Please don't feel sorry for me. It's just… you know. What's happened has happened. I don't dwell on it.'

'Well, yeah, but… I feel bad for saying I don't go home much now.'

'Why?'

'Because I… well, I can. But I choose not to, whereas you…' he trailed off awkwardly. I could see he was searching for another topic to divert attention away from himself and his flustered feelings, so I put him out of his misery. 'So you're definitely up for helping me make a website?' I said.

'Yes!' he said in relief. 'I'd love to. I'm free at the weekend, if you want to—'

'Yeah,' I said, 'that'd be great.'

Mark drove me home at the end of the night, and kissed me before I got out of the car. I could see he still felt a bit weird over what he'd heard about my parents, and I was glad I hadn't told him the whole truth because God knows what a state he'd have got himself into if I'd come out with all of that.

Jay was still awake doing some cleaning, and when I got inside he looked me up and down. 'You're not staying over with him then,' he said.

'No,' I said, 'it doesn't look like it.' I examined his face closely. 'Are you… disappointed?'

'No,' he said, 'and yes. I want... I want to get it done.'

'He kissed me,' I told him.

'What, properly?'

'Yes, properly.'

All of a sudden Jay's mood transformed, and he stopped cleaning the kitchen sink to give me a hug. 'Well done, Fliss,' he said.

'Don't say well done.'

He pulled away from me. 'What should I say? Thank you?'

'No,' I said. 'You don't have to say anything. We both know what I'm doing and why I'm doing it. But I'd rather you didn't remind me.'

PART 2

Sammie

21

To Sammie's surprise and delight, the months after Jay's exclusion from school and getting caught in bed with him were some of the happiest of her life. Despite how angry she'd been with Jay about everything, Jay's mum seemed keen to get to know Sammie and said she could come for dinner pretty much whenever she wanted, so she'd go round there three or four times each week. She enjoyed being part of a family, where there was a proper adult there in the evening making food and giving structure to the otherwise blurry, boring hours. She liked Jay's mum's cooking too – she made nice simple things like sausages with buttery mash, or fish fingers, or cottage pie with peas and sweetcorn on the side. Sometimes after dinner she'd give Sammie and Jay some money and tell them to go and get icecreams from the little village shop and they'd sit in the cottage's cosy lounge and eat them in front of the TV.

If her parents realised that she was going out with Jay they never said, and so she never told them. She supposed they must suspect something when she kept going round to his for dinner, and she started to think that they were glad of the arrangement, because it meant she was out from under their feet.

After his sixteenth birthday at the beginning of November, Jay got a part time job in the kitchen of the village pub, and with his first few weeks pay he bought Sammie a necklace – a lovely little sapphire pendant on a silver chain. Sammie enthused over how beautiful it was and how happy he'd made her, and Jay smiled. 'I love you, Sammie,' he said.

It was after this that things changed. Gradually at first, so that it was hard to even be sure. Jay would be incredibly, almost excessively nice to her one moment; saying that he loved her more than anything in the world, telling her she was beautiful, saying he wanted to be with her forever, then in the next breath it was like he used these declarations of love to punish her – saying she didn't love him as much as he loved her, accusing her of having feelings for other boys at school, and expecting an explanation if she didn't answer a call or text from him straight away. He became strange about sex as well; pushy and stifling, expecting her to do whatever he wanted whenever he wanted her to, and he was more and more demanding about what she sent to him in photos. Before long he had built up quite a collection of pictures, including some of her doing things to him, or him doing things to her. Sometimes she felt so scared and uncomfortable about the images that she struggled to sleep. She wasn't sure how to talk to him about it, so she didn't. She soon learnt that to stay in harmony with him she had to consistently be what he considered "a good shag", to not complain too much when he sometimes refused flatly to use the condoms she bought, and to not say no to him – because when she said no he would argue with her, tell her she was "frigid" or being a bitch, accuse her of not loving him or threaten to split up with her.

Sammie had never thought, when she'd considered things like this in the past, that she'd let someone pressure her the way Jay did. But his arguments made a twisted kind of sense after a while. Perhaps he really did get so excited sometimes that it was physically impossible for him to stop and put a condom on. Maybe she was unreasonable to ever say she didn't want to have sex after she'd made him want it so badly through something she said or did, and perhaps not wanting to do things that were unfamiliar or made her nervous really did mean that she was cold, and prudish and unkind, because after all Jay loved her, and she loved him, and you were supposed to make sacrifices for the people you love.

...

It was at the beginning of December that he first hurt her. They were in bed, as they nearly always were, and she felt his hand on her hair. She thought he was going to stroke it – not that he did things like that often – but sometimes he did, when he was happy. Instead she felt him start pulling one particular strand, making a sharp little pinprick of pain.

'Jay,' she said, 'what are you doing? That hurts.'

He ignored her and carried on pulling, until it came free from her head. That done, he laid the blonde strand on the pillow in front of her, practically beneath her nose, and went back for another. Sammie let him continue as two, three, four strands were added to the little pile and then she tried to move out of his way.

'What are you doing?' she said. 'That really hurts.'

Instead of answering, Jay reached out towards her bare arm, pinching a little fold of skin between his nails until the pain made her eyes fill with tears.

'Stop it!' she said. 'Jay, stop it.'

She pushed him away from her and stared in horror at the spots of blood rising from his nail marks on her arm.

'What's wrong with you?' she said. 'I'm bleeding!'

She got out of bed and started walking towards the little en suite bathroom in the corner of her room.

'I'm bored of you,' he said.

She turned round. 'Stop it, Jay,' she said, 'I don't know why you're trying to hurt me—'

'It's because I don't like you,' he said, 'and I don't like the way you look. I thought you were pretty, when we first started going out, but when I look at you now I don't know how I could have thought that.'

Sammie went inside her little bathroom, slammed the door shut, and locked it. The bloody mark on her arm still hurt and her heart was beginning to race with anger and shock.

She heard Jay's footsteps and when he knocked on the door she ignored him.

'Sammie,' he said, 'come on. Let me in.'

'Leave me alone. You said you don't like me, and I don't like you, either. Not when you're being like this.'

Jay knocked on the door a little longer, until she got sick of it and turned the lock to let him in.

'I'm not going to sit and listen to you being nasty to me,' Sammie said.

'I was only saying,' he said. 'I'm sorry, but... I'm just fed up of looking at you.'

'Why are you being like this?' she asked. 'What's wrong with you?'

Instead of answering, he took hold of her by her head, and deliberately whacked it into the tiled wall. She gasped in pain, and started crying, but Jay just walked away, and when she came out of the bathroom again she found that he'd gone.

22

When her parents got home from work later that evening, Sammie wanted to say something. The injuries Jay had done to her weren't visible – the place he'd hit her head was underneath her hair, and the place he'd pinched her was completely hidden under a winter jumper, so they'd never guess what had happened. All through dinner, she felt like she wanted to say it, but in the stony silence around the dining table, she couldn't find a way.

She waited until later, when her mum was filling the dishwasher, and her dad had gone to do more work stuff in the study upstairs. But the words still wouldn't come, so she just hovered around in the kitchen with her secret simmering away inside her.

'We thought we'd keep things pretty simple at Christmas this year,' her mum said as she finished putting the last few plates in the dishwasher. 'Just get something nice and simple to cook, have a relaxing day.'

'Okay,' Sammie said. She knew what this meant. Her mum had said something similar every year since Alfie died. It meant she'd buy a few bits and bobs of readymade food from the supermarket, drink too much wine, and pretend to be enjoying herself when she actually kept disappearing upstairs to have a little cry. Sammie didn't particularly care about Christmas. She hated it now. It had been fun when Alfie had been alive, even though he was ill they still enjoyed themselves – making it almost over-the-top special. Now he was dead, nobody wanted to make anything special any more. If Sammie suggested doing anything – playing a game, watching a film, going for a walk, her parents would look pained and mumble some excuse, until Sammie learned it was better not to ask.

'I just...' her mum said, 'I just can't be bothered with it all, you know? All the... fuss.'

'Yeah,' Sammie said, 'that's okay.'

Sammie watched her mum pop a dishwasher tablet into the machine and close it up. It was difficult to know where to start. Before she could even get to the issue she'd have to explain that Jay was her boyfriend, and that seemed hard enough.

'Mum... I... could I talk to you?' she said.

Her mum turned round. 'Can it wait?' she said. 'I feel like I haven't stopped since six o'clock this morning. I just want to sit down.'

'Yeah,' Sammie said, 'I just—'

Her mum must have realised it was something fairly serious because her face softened a little.

'What is it, Sammie?' she said.

'It's just... I... you know Jay?'

Her mum looked at her for a moment and then smiled. 'Is he your boyfriend?' she asked.

Sammie blinked. 'Um... yeah,' she said, 'he—'

'I thought he was,' her mum said. 'I *have* noticed how much time you spend with him.'

Sammie tried to smile and her mum looked at her carefully. 'Have you had an argument with him or something?'

With relief, Sammie nodded. Her mum seemed to get it so far, perhaps it wouldn't be impossible to tell her the rest.

'Sammie, life is too short to worry about arguing with boys,' her mum said, 'there'll be plenty of time for that when you're older.'

'I... really like him, mum,' Sammie said, with difficulty.

Her mum frowned. 'Sammie, he doesn't come round here when we're at work, does he?'

'No,' Sammie lied.

'Are you sure?'

'Yeah.'

Her mum narrowed her eyes and Sammie knew she didn't believe a word of it. She also knew that the question wasn't really – does he come round here? It was – are you having sex? But there was no chance her mum was going to come straight out and ask her that. But then her mum's next question surprised, and offended her.

'Oh my God,' her mum said, 'you're not *pregnant* are you, Sammie?'

Sammie stared at her. How could she possibly have thought she could open up to her mum about her relationship, about Jay hurting her, about any of it, when she just came out and accused her of things like that?

'Of course I'm not!' she shouted. 'I'm not *stupid*!'

Furiously, she ran out of the kitchen and up the stairs to her bedroom, slamming the door so hard the sound reverberated all round the house. She heard her mum's feet on the stairs after her, but instead of coming into her bedroom she heard her parent's voices in the study. They talked for maybe five minutes, and then the door to her room opened and her dad came in.

'Sammie,' he said, 'what's this about you bringing boys back here when we're out?'

'I *don't*,' Sammie said, 'I told mum—'

He strode towards her and Sammie edged back on the bed where she'd been sitting to get further away from him. Her dad was frightening when he got angry.

'You are *fifteen*,' he said, 'if I find out you've been bringing that boy here—'

'He's not "that boy,"' Sammie said. 'His name is Jay.'

For a moment her dad's face was almost white with anger, and then all of a sudden it was like a light went off. Instead of arguing with her, he just seemed to decide that he actually didn't care any more, and he turned and walked away.

Her parents argued that night, in their bedroom next door to hers. They were trying to do it quietly, and she couldn't make out the words, but she could hear their hushed, angry voices. Sammie didn't feel at all guilty about having Jay round, or going round to his. What they did was just a natural thing to do, no matter what her parents said or did they could never stop her having sex with him and Sammie thought it was wrong of them to even bother trying. But that wasn't the main issue. The main issue was that they'd been so angry with her. How could she talk to them about what was happening to her if they were angry? She couldn't say what Jay had done to her if he was never supposed to have been in the house, and even if she did, what would happen? They'd be so shocked. They'd be horrified. Sammie didn't want to watch them being shocked, and she certainly didn't want to risk them finding out about anything else, like the photos Jay had of her. But before she fell asleep, she did think, with a twisted kind of joy, that if Jay ever beat her up so badly she was in hospital, or even better if he *killed* her, that maybe everyone would think how bad her parents were to not have realised, and they'd feel guilty, and they'd wish they hadn't treated her like this.

Around midnight, her phone vibrated and she saw she had a text from Jay:

Im really sorry about earlier i hope ur ok. Id had a argument with my mum n i was feelin pissed off but shldnt hav taken it out on u. I love u

Sammie replied instantly, almost without thinking.

Its ok. My parents are arseholes as well. I love u 2.

Felicity

23

As time went on I carried on seeing Mark and working on my jewellery business, and before long I'd built up quite a good jewellery collection consisting of several different necklaces, earrings and bracelets, some of which were more expensive one-offs, some simpler designs that I could make relatively quickly and easily, and a few customisable items where people could specify names or initials they wanted incorporated into the pieces. Mark created a wonderful photo gallery of my work on the website he made for me, and we started thinking about other sites I could sell my jewellery through, and how I could try to promote myself. I thought of a name for my business – Steel Rose, and although Jay made no secret of the fact he found my new enterprise ridiculous, he tolerated it as he could see it was a good way for me to carry on spending time with Mark. In fact, for a while I found myself in a routine where I was able to manage my relationships with Mark and with Jay fairly well. Mark came back to the flat a few times when Jay was out, but we largely met at his and Mark didn't seem to notice or care that he never met my mysterious flatmate. And although it took a little while, Jay was delighted when Mark and I started sleeping together, which he thought would mean Mark would soon tell me he loved me so that he could finish his plan, but this didn't prove to be the case. In fact, although Mark seemed to enjoy spending time with me I was surprised how disinterested he was in sex, seeming to find far more passion for my fledgling jewellery business than for spending time in bed with me.

Inevitably, this fact became apparent to Jay, and instead of being pleased with me about how much work I put into his plan, he began to make barbed comments to me, hinting that he thought I enjoyed spending time with Mark and that I wanted the whole thing to drag on, and suggesting that I wasn't trying hard enough. It was usually easy enough to nip these sorts of arguments in the bud by reminding him how lucky he was that I was prepared to involve myself in his crazy revenge plan at all. I thought that that was the end of it and he'd be reasonable, but I could hardly have been more wrong.

It was the night of Grace's hen party that everything changed. Jay told me he didn't want me to go, and didn't hold back at throwing every manner of insult and accusation at me – telling me how disgusting he thought my dress was, how selfish I was to go out when I hardly spent any time with him as it was, and how disloyal it was to go out with my friends when they were so vocal in their dislike of him. In all honesty, my relationship with Leanne and the others was hardly good. I'd barely spoken to any of them since Leanne came to the flat, and I was pretty sure she had been at work turning all the others against me – at least for as long as I stayed with Jay. He made one final attempt to stop me going out when I wandered into the living room to say goodbye to him before I left and he looked me up and down.

'I can't believe you're really going to wear that,' he said as he took in my minidress and heels.

'The dress code is slutty dresses,' I explained. 'I'm not the biggest fan of it either, but it's what Grace wants.'

'Mm,' Jay said, 'well, I'm about to cook us dinner.'

I stared at him. 'Jay, I'm going out. You know I'm going out.'

'It's risotto,' he said, 'your favourite.'

I shook my head. 'Jay, stop it. I'm not going to let you make me feel guilty about this.'

He slammed the pan he'd just got out of the cupboard down on the hob so hard that it made me jump. 'Fine,' he said, 'go out then. And wear that dress if it's so important to you.'

'Thanks,' I said sarcastically, 'I will.'

Jay turned to me. 'Good,' he said, 'I hope you get raped.'

...

The party ended up much as I expected. I was already fuming about what Jay had said to me, and on top of that Leanne was decidedly cool with me, and although Becky, Hannah and Grace tried to act normally, they didn't keep it up for long and the consensus to ignore me spread to the rest of Grace's friends. I ended up following them around listlessly, getting progressively so drunk that far from caring I began to find the whole thing almost amusing.

I stumbled home to Jay in the early hours of the morning, where I went into the living room thinking I would drink some water and try to find something to eat, and to my surprise found Jay sitting on the sofa in the semi-darkness, watching me as I staggered my way into the room.

'Look at the state of you,' he said as I kicked my shoes off and shuffled to the kitchen, clutching at the walls.

'Fuck off, Jay,' I slurred back at him, fairly good-naturedly.

I got to the kitchen, filled a glass with water and drank it all in one go.

'Did you have a good time?' Jay asked.

'Yeah,' I lied. The shock of drinking all the cold water made me gasp and my stomach felt confused.

I stood, swaying, for a while, wondering what the chances were that I would throw up. Deciding I was safe, I opened the fridge and started poking through Jay's packs of lean meat, fish and vegetables hoping for something more palatable.

'You want me to make you something?' Jay asked.

'Yes,' I said, surprised by his generosity, 'please.'

Jay came in and took some eggs out of the fridge, followed by a frying pan from the cupboard and a bottle of vegetable oil. I felt as though something wasn't quite right, but I stood happily enough, watching him blearily as he turned on the hob.

'Thank you, Jay,' I said.

He turned to me and smiled, then he grabbed my hair, and the next thing I knew he was pushing my face down towards the gas burner on the hob. I screamed my lungs out so he put his hand over my mouth and lifted me up a little so as not to burn himself. 'Shut up,' he said, 'just shut up.'

He let go of my mouth and carried on holding me there while I whimpered and started to cry. One of my tears dropped onto the flames and hissed, almost making me scream again.

'Calm down,' Jay said. 'I'm not going to burn you. Just tell me you're sorry.'

Another tear dropped onto the flame, and I started to shake all over. 'Sorry,' I said, 'I'm sorry.' I could feel the heat on my cheek. I was so scared I couldn't even think.

'Say what you're sorry for,' he said. 'Tell me you're sorry for upsetting me. That you're sorry for going out when I told you not to, and that you're sorry you're doing such a crap job with Mark.'

I couldn't gather my thoughts. I opened my mouth to speak, but all that came out were more whimpering noises.

'He should love you by now,' Jay said, giving me a shake, 'but he doesn't, does he? And it's not difficult to see why, looking at you right now. You're a piece of shit.'

Some more of my tears hissed in the flames and I started to make a low moaning sound, which began to turn into the words, 'Please, please.'

'Tell me you're sorry!' Jay said again.

'I... I... I'm sorry,' I said.

He shook me. 'You've already said that!' he yelled. 'Tell me what for. Tell me what you're sorry for.'

'I can't...' I said, 'I can't remember what you said.'

With sudden force I was pulled away from the hob and I thought it was over, but instead Jay turned the kitchen tap on full blast and pushed my face into it until I was gasping and struggling for air.

For a moment I thought maybe he was trying to cool my face

because it had been burned, but then he forced me back down over the burner, the water dripping and hissing so that I started sobbing in terror.

'Has that sobered you up?' he asked. 'Tell me what you're sorry for.'

I wracked my mind. What had he said? My voice trembled as I started the list. 'For going out,' I said, 'and upsetting you... and not doing well enough with Mark.'

Jay turned the hob off and let go of me, and I sank to my knees on the floor.

'Do you do everything he wants?' he asked me.

I nodded.

'Are you sure?' Jay asked.

'Yes,' I said, 'I think so.' I was crying again and I couldn't concentrate. Jay knelt down in front of me.

'You must be doing something wrong,' he said.

'I'm not,' I said, 'I promise.' I couldn't deal with his questions. I was trembling and sobbing and my stomach was churning. My words stumbled over each other and I ended up digging myself a deeper hole. 'I do everything he wants,' I said. 'He doesn't want very much. He's not... he's not like you.'

'What's that supposed to mean?'

'Not...' I said, panicking, 'I just mean...not everything with him is about sex. We just talk, and hang out, and... have fun.'

I covered my face with my hands. My stomach felt really uncomfortable now, and the light in the kitchen was hurting my eyes.

'And we don't have fun?' Jay asked. 'You mean you have more fun with him than you do with me?'

I couldn't answer. I cried into my fingers until Jay pulled them away from my face. He started trying to get his hands under my arms to lift me up, but just as he did my stomach gave in to its churning and gurgling and I threw up, projecting a thick, sweetish smelling stream of liquid that he recoiled from in horror. I bent forward and was sick again and again, while Jay tried to stay out of the way. When it was all gone I slumped back against the cupboard and saw Jay watching me, his face rigid with anger, and I realised that my first stream of vomit had gone all over him.

24

The next morning when I woke up I was still on the kitchen floor, a pillow under my head and a blanket over my body. There was a rumbling sound which I realised was the washing machine, and Jay was kneeling beside me. It was Jay who had woken me up; he was stroking my hair, and for the briefest moment it felt soothing.

'You're awake,' he said, 'welcome back, Flissie.'

I squinted up at him. My eyes felt dry and bloodshot. I couldn't remember why I was on the floor.

'You had a bit too much to drink last night, didn't you?' he said.

'Mm.'

I was starting to remember things. Firstly what he'd done to me with the hob, and I immediately reached up to my cheek to see if it was all right, finding to my relief that my skin felt the same as normal. But then I recalled being sick on him, and I reached up to my temple and found a cut. After I'd been sick he'd slapped me across the face. I must have hit my head on something in the kitchen and been knocked out.

'Right then,' Jay said, taking his hand from my hair. 'Would you like some water?'

He didn't wait for me to answer and filled a glass anyway, holding it out to me.

'Painkillers,' I said, 'and my pills. Please.'

He put the water down on the floor beside me. 'I'll get you painkillers,' he said, 'but I won't give you your pills.' He stood up and opened the kitchen drawer where I kept them, and held them up alongside some vitamin supplements I'd never seen before. 'We're swapping these,' he shook my contraceptives, 'for these.' He indicated the vitamin supplements. 'Things are going to change, Fliss.'

I glanced at the packet of supplements. 'What... what are they?'

He held them closer to me, and I saw that they were for preconception and early pregnancy. I looked up at him but he ignored me, and I watched as he threw my pills in the bin, then he took out one of the vitamins and popped it in my mouth. 'We need to think about the future,' he said. 'I'm giving you a deadline. I want to have finished the plan with Mark by Grace's wedding. After that, we'll move away from here, to start our family where nobody is bothering us.'

'I can't try for a baby with you,' I said. 'I'm still having sex with Mark.'

'You use condoms with Mark, don't you?'

I nodded, though truthfully I hadn't been, not recently.

'Well then, what's the problem?'

Jay sat down next to me on the kitchen floor and stroked my hair again. 'You're so beautiful,' he said, 'when I was getting you out of that awful dress last night I sat and looked at you for such a long time.'

'What?' I said. Then I realised what he was talking about. Under the blanket I wasn't wearing my dress any more; I was in a pair of cotton pyjamas. And I didn't have any underwear on underneath, he'd obviously stripped me naked.

I frowned at him. 'How...' I said, 'how did you get my dress off?' It was so tight I couldn't imagine he'd have been able to pull it over my head very easily.

'I cut it off you with scissors,' he said.

'And then you sat and looked at my body?'

Jay smiled as if it was the most normal thing in the world.

...

Once I'd taken the painkillers and the vitamins, Jay ran me a bath.

'You'll feel better afterwards,' he said, 'and then I'll make you some lunch.'

I thought he'd leave me to it, but instead he sat on the end of the bathtub, watching me.

I tried to smile. 'I... I can take a bath by myself,' I said.

Jay ignored me. 'Flissie, all I'm ever trying to do is to help you, and make you happy.'

I looked up at him and he reached out to touch my face. 'Do you remember the night we met?' he asked.

I closed my eyes briefly. 'You know that I don't,' I said.

'You were so pissed that when you woke up with me in the morning you didn't recognise me. You had to *ask* me whether we'd had sex.'

'It was one week after my parents died.'

Jay carried on as though he hadn't heard. 'You were wearing a dress a bit like the one you wore last night,' he said. 'I remember it well, because I remember pushing it up round your waist and fucking you in that disgusting house I had a room in. We started doing it in the kitchen. One of the other guys who lived there came out of his room and walked right past the doorway while we were at it. He saw us, in fact. And when you noticed him looking, you laughed like it was the funniest thing ever.'

'Why are you saying all this?' I asked him quietly.

'Because I don't want it to happen to you again,' Jay said. 'You're with me now. We're going to have a life together, and I don't want to remember about all that.'

'You don't want to remember meeting me?'

'Fliss, you could easily have woken up this morning in some other guy's bed, not on our kitchen floor. I didn't want you to go out and put yourself in that situation, but you did it anyway.'

'Jay... I... do have some self control. And I didn't do anything wrong the night I met you.'

'I know,' Jay said, 'but you don't have to be like that any more. Don't you see that?'

'Jay, could you... could you please let me finish having my bath by myself?' I asked nicely. 'I've still got a splitting headache, and it's hard to concentrate on talking to you.'

Jay gave me a long look, then he reached down to kiss my forehead. 'Okay,' he said, 'I'll start making you something to eat.'

Once he was out of the room I took a gasp of breath, then another and another, as though I'd been suffocating the whole time he was near me. For a moment I considered getting straight out of the bath and making a run for it, but I quickly decided against it. Jay would almost certainly hear me – for all I knew he might already be standing in the hall, just waiting for me to try something. Besides, where would I go? I could go to Leanne, I supposed, but I didn't want to. I needed time to think it through, to get a plan together. All I could do right now was deal with my more immediate needs.

I pulled the plug out and stood up to turn the shower on, but instead of washing myself I got out of the bath and opened the bathroom cabinet above the basin. I was sure Jay had assumed the packet of contraceptive pills in the kitchen drawer was the only one I had, but that was just the one that was open. I had two unopened packs at the back of the cupboard, and my heart was in my throat as I moved things aside to check they were still there. Sure enough, they were untouched, so I quickly grabbed one and popped a pill into my mouth, swallowing it with some water from the tap. I knew I'd have to move them out of the bathroom to somewhere more secure, but it was far too risky to do it straight away, so I put them back where they were and made sure they were well hidden. I paused for a moment when I'd closed the cupboard again, looking at my face in the mirrored door. There was no sign on my cheek that it had been held over the hob, and I supposed he must not have been holding me as close to it as it had felt. However, the cut on my right temple was very visible, and I looked pale and ill. I carried on looking at myself for a few seconds more, then I got back into the shower.

Once I'd dressed, I was surprised to find Jay making rather an elaborate lunch; a mushroom and leek risotto laced with butter and parmesan.

'I... I thought you didn't do carbs,' I said, 'or... butter.'

'I wanted to treat you,' he said. 'It's what I was going to cook for you last night.'

I sat down at the dining table. I felt nauseous and had no idea how I was going to eat anything. He looked round at me frequently, and I tried to rearrange my face into an expression he might expect, or want to see, though I didn't really know what that was.

'Here,' he said about fifteen minutes later, placing a bowl of steaming risotto in front of me and sitting down at the table with his own portion.

'Jay,' I said quietly, 'I still don't feel very well, I may not be able to—'

'I hope you're hungry,' he said, 'I've made a dessert as well. In fact, that reminds me, I've got us something to drink.'

He went to the fridge and took out a bottle of white wine. He held it up meaningfully and I began to feel frightened. I knew he knew full well I was hungover and that the last thing I wanted was a two course dinner, just as he knew that the thought of a glass of wine was turning my stomach.

'This is... really kind of you, Jay,' I said, 'but how about I just have the food and not the wine?'

He took out two wineglasses, setting one down in front of me and filling it right up, almost to the top.

'I told you, I want to treat you,' he said, 'even after how much you upset me.'

I looked at the wine, then down at my food, and I pushed my chair back and ran to the kitchen where I retched into the sink, though nothing came up. Jay waited patiently until I was done, and I sat down again at the table with him. He picked up his glass and I realised he expected me to do the same.

'Enjoy it,' he said, as I took a sip of the wine. 'Because now we're trying for a baby, you won't be able to have any more for a while.'

Sammie

25

For a little while things were okay between Jay and Sammie as he tried to make up for hurting her by being especially kind and attentive, showering her with affection and compliments until she felt almost overwhelmed. But it couldn't last forever, and things began to go wrong again – with Jay – but before that, with her parents.

It was just a normal evening, and Sammie was surprised when her mum said they wanted to talk to her, and even more surprised when her mum suggested they went to sit in the lounge – something they rarely did as a family. Her parents both sat down on one sofa – together, but quite far apart, while Sammie sprawled out on the other, in a little nest of decorative scatter cushions. 'What did you want to talk to me about?' she asked.

'Today we were looking for a little studio apartment,' her mum said, 'somewhere closer to the business.'

'What for?' Sammie asked.

Her parents exchanged a look. 'Well, it's not really working, both of us trying to drive home every night,' her mum explained, 'so we thought one of us could stay there some of the time during the week.'

Sammie sat up. 'I don't understand,' she said.

'The journey is too long,' her mum said, 'we're both too tired to ever enjoy the new house.'

'Why don't you get jobs round here then?' Sammie asked. Her mum raised an eyebrow, and her dad laughed.

'I'm serious,' Sammie said, 'this was supposed to be a new

start, wasn't it?'

'Yes, sweetheart,' her mum said, 'but it doesn't really work like that.'

Sammie watched the two of them for a while, her anger growing. 'Don't I get any say in this?' she asked. 'I'm not a child.' She stood up. 'In fact, I have plenty of my own stuff going on, if you'd ever bother to ask.'

She stormed out of the room. She thought she heard her mum get up from the sofa, but her dad spoke before her mum could follow her. His voice carried out to Sammie in the hallway, making her freeze and her heart pound with shock. 'Why didn't you just tell her we're separating?' he said. 'She'll figure it out on her own soon enough.'

...

The next day was a Saturday, and in the morning Sammie wandered down into the woods to try to clear her head after what she'd heard her dad say the night before. She'd hoped to hear something from Jay, a nice message from him would be a welcome distraction right now, but she knew he usually slept late on Saturdays – only rolling out of bed just in time to start his shift in the pub kitchen – so she was surprised when she drew near the little clearing where she'd first met Mark and Jay to hear their voices again.

She crept close enough to eavesdrop, and hid herself behind a tree, just in time to hear Jay say something absolutely extraordinary.

'I'm going to ask Sammie to marry me,' he said.

Sammie leant against the tree, and took a few deep breaths. She felt excited and nervous and shocked all at once.

It took Mark a little while to answer, then he said, 'That's the stupidest thing I've ever heard.'

'Why?' Jay said. 'I... I love her.'

'You're too young to even *get* married without your parent's permission,' Mark said, 'and if you somehow did get them to agree, do you really think it would work?'

'Yeah,' Jay said, 'I don't see why it wouldn't. And I know the stuff about getting permission. We wouldn't do that, we'd... run away.'

'Run away where?'

'Scotland,' Jay said, 'I looked it up, and we wouldn't need permission there, not once Sammie is sixteen.'

Sammie crept a tiny bit closer, and she could see the look of disgust on Mark's face, though she quickly hid again before there was a chance he'd look up and see her.

'You wouldn't last a year,' Mark said, 'surely you can see that? What do you even have in common? You don't really even *talk* to each other, do you? You just... have sex.' He said the last two words as though he found them distasteful.

'Yeah,' Jay said, 'that's what couples *do*.'

'It shouldn't be the only thing they do.'

Jay stood up angrily, and Sammie quickly darted away through the trees before either of them could see her.

All weekend she thought about what she'd heard, though when she met up with Jay on Sunday evening he didn't mention anything about it and seemed a bit distracted.

'What's wrong?' Sammie asked.

'I've fallen out with Mark,' he said.

Sammie couldn't help but smile to herself a little. 'Oh,' she said, 'what about?'

'Nothing,' he said, 'just stupid stuff.'

At school on Monday, Mark carried on being distant with both of them, until lunchtime, when they found themselves sitting at one of a cluster of picnic benches in the playground with him, warmed by some early February sunshine. Jay sat with his arm around Sammie's waist underneath her school blazer, while Mark sat opposite them, a look on his face almost of excitement, or anticipation.

'Have you asked her?' Mark said bluntly to Jay.

Jay scowled at him. 'Shut up,' he said.

'Asked me what?' Sammie said innocently.

'Jay was going to ask you to marry him,' Mark said.

Sammie tried to feign surprise, but Jay wasn't paying attention to her, instead he reached across the table and grabbed Mark's arm. 'What the fuck is wrong with you?' he said.

'Jay,' Sammie said, 'Jay, leave him. Is it... is it true?'

Jay let go of Mark and put his arm around her again. 'Yeah,' he said, 'it's true. It was *meant* to be a surprise.'

Mark was rubbing his arm where Jay had been gripping it, but then he stopped and took out his phone. 'There's just one thing,' he said, 'before you make a commitment like that, you should know what Sammie is really like.'

To begin with Sammie didn't understand. It was so long ago she'd sent the photo of herself to Mark that she'd almost forgotten about it. It wasn't until Mark had pushed his phone across the table to Jay and she saw the expression on Jay's face that she said, 'No...', but it was too late.

'You... you *sent* that to him?' Jay asked her.

'By accident,' Sammie said, 'it was an accident. My finger slipped or something—'

'It wasn't an accident,' Mark said. 'She's sent me others. Loads. I get rid of them because I don't want to see it—'

Sammie's mouth dropped open in disbelief at Mark's lie. 'That's not true!' she said. 'I don't send him pictures! I don't... I...' words failed her and she fell silent. She could see Jay trying to make sense of it. 'Please...' she tried again. Jay turned to her. She thought he'd say he believed her, that he knew she wouldn't send photos to Mark, that he could see Mark was making it up, but when he spoke his words crushed her. He gave her a long, hard look and softly, emotionlessly, said, 'You little whore.'

26

Sammie was so upset she couldn't bring herself to stay and explain so she got up from the picnic bench and ran to the toilets. Jay followed her, but he gave up when he saw where she was going and for the rest of the day he ignored her. On the bus home he sat next to Mark instead of her. They were a few rows back, so she couldn't hear exactly what they were saying, but it was clear Jay was angry and Sammie was glad that Mark was getting some grief over what he'd done. She expected Jay to get really mad and for there to be a full blown argument, but when she glanced round at them Mark was talking calmly and Jay appeared to be convinced by whatever was being said. In fact, by the time they drew near Tatchley the two boys seemed like best friends again and far from arguing they had started sniggering together over something. Sammie had the horrible feeling that they were laughing about *her*, and that Mark may have been at work telling Jay more lies, but she couldn't figure out what she should do. In the end she decided she would ignore them, but when they got off the bus and Jay still seemed to be showing Mark something on his phone, Sammie couldn't help but steal another glance at them. She heard Jay say, 'Check this one out,' and she watched Mark's expression as he looked at whatever it was, and then his eyes caught hers, and suddenly she understood.

She made a grab for the phone. 'Don't show him those!' she said. 'What are you doing?'

Jay pushed her out of the way and found another photo, and Mark made a show of admiring it – his appreciation so over-the-top that to her it didn't quite ring true – though Jay seemed satisfied. Sammie made another grab for the phone but Jay dodged out of her way, and the two boys made off towards the woods. Sammie tried to follow them but a car was coming and she had to stop as they dashed across the road ahead of her, but then she ran as fast as she could to catch up. This time she managed to wrestle the phone from Jay's grasp and in her desperation to make him stop what he was doing, she threw it at the ground.

She hadn't really meant to damage it, but when it hit the pavement the screen smashed, and Jay grabbed her. 'What the fuck did you do that for?'

'You were... you were showing him our special pictures!' she looked at Mark, who didn't meet her eyes. She felt ridiculous calling them that in front of him, but that was what she and Jay had always called them to each other. In fact, it was Jay who had first used the name for them, saying that they *were* special, and nothing to be ashamed of or worried about because they were only for him, and no one else would ever know.

'You broke my fucking phone!' Jay said.

'Good!' Sammie snapped back.

For a moment Jay just stared at her, then he bent down and picked it up.

'You're going to pay for this,' he said.

Sammie ignored him and started walking towards the woods, which were a shortcut to her house. She was aware that Mark and Jay were following her, but she walked fast and didn't look back at them.

'Fucking little bitch,' she heard Jay say to Mark.

'Jay, just leave her,' Mark said, 'she's not worth it.'

She heard footsteps close behind her, and before she knew it Jay had caught hold of her and called to Mark to help him.

'Jay, no!' Sammie cried. 'Get off me.'

She realised he was pulling her away from the main path and into the trees. Mark was standing nearby, watching the two of them with a frown.

'Mark, for fuck's sake,' Jay said.

Sammie struggled, and almost managed to get away. She'd taken two steps, when she found herself in Mark's arms. He held her awkwardly, but she couldn't break free, and the two boys pulled her off the path and deeper into the woods.

They didn't take her far. Once they were out of sight of the path Jay stopped and shoved Sammie against a tree.

'I have copies,' he said, 'of the pictures. So don't think you've got rid of them. They're all on my computer.'

'Jay, I'm sorry,' Sammie pleaded. 'I only sent that one picture to Mark. It was a mistake. It was an accident, a stupid accident, and it wasn't like he saw anything in it, not really—'

'So,' Jay said, ignoring her, 'you like guys looking at you, do you?'

'No!' Sammie said. 'Not at all—'

'Why don't you show Mark the rest of you? For real, that is, because he's already seen it all anyway.'

'I don't want to,' she said, 'let me go, Jay.'

Jay leaned in close to her ear. 'Take your clothes off,' he said.

'No,' Sammie moaned.

'Take them off, Sammie. What are you worried about? He thinks you're hot, don't you Mark?'

Sammie looked up at Mark, who shrugged.

'Jay,' Sammie said, forcing herself to sound calm, 'let me go.'

Jay had one arm round her waist, and with his free hand he started pulling at her school shirt. 'No!' Sammie screamed at him. 'Let go of me. Let go of me!'

He wouldn't stop, and he managed to pull her shirt open and yank her skirt and her underwear down over her thighs.

'Stop it!' she said. 'Please, stop.'

'Come on, Mark,' Jay said, gesturing at her exposed private parts. 'She's ready now. I'll hold her, you touch her.'

'No!' Sammie screamed as Mark came towards her. 'No, Jay, no!'

Jay clapped his hand over her mouth. 'Shut up,' he said. 'I'm teaching you a lesson, Sammie. If you show guys pictures of yourself, they'll expect to be able to touch you. That's how it works. And once you've learnt that, you'll know not to do it again.'

He released his hand from her mouth and she started to cry. 'No,' she said, 'Jay, please.'

Mark was in front of her now, and he spoke quietly to Jay. 'I'm not going to touch her,' he said.

Sammie began to sob in relief, but Jay threw her to the ground. 'You hear that?' he said. 'He doesn't even *want* to touch you.'

For a while the two boys looked down at her as she struggled to pull her skirt back up, and she thought perhaps they were shocked by what they'd done. But then Jay turned to Mark. 'Leave me alone with her,' he said.

Mark looked a little scared and Sammie felt his eyes on her.

'Wh... why?' he asked. 'What are you going to—'

'It's between me and Sammie,' Jay said.

Mark hesitated a little longer, then he turned and left them without another word, and Jay knelt down beside her. 'Aren't you going to say anything?'

'I told you,' Sammie said, 'it was an accident! I don't send him *pictures!* He's got it in for us, Jay, it was him who called your mum and made her walk in on us before, I know it was—'

'I asked him about that,' Jay said, 'I asked him ages ago and he swore it wasn't him. Why would he lie? Why would he lie about any of this?'

'I don't know,' Sammie said, 'but he hates me, Jay. He really hates me—'

Jay put his hand on her thigh, and started slipping it up her leg and under her skirt.

'Jay, please, please believe me,' she said. 'I love you. You were going to ask me to marry you—'

'I don't want to marry a slut.'

Sammie started to cry again. 'I'm not a slut,' she said, 'I've never even looked at anyone else. I promise you, Jay, I promise. What can I do to make you believe me?'

Jay tried to push her skirt up but Sammie managed to scramble away, though she'd barely got to her knees before Jay grabbed her from behind. With one arm he held her, and with the other he lifted her skirt and stuffed his hand down her underwear.

'No,' she said, 'no, Jay. Not like this. We can... we can go somewhere, if you want to—'

He began to force his fingers inside her, and she struggled more violently, until he said, 'Sammie, if you don't let me fuck you, I'll put all the pictures of you online.'

27

Afterwards, Jay barely even looked at her. He stood and did his trousers back up, and when she started to try to sit up herself he pushed her back down.

'I don't need to tell you what will happen if you breathe a word about this, do I?' he said.

'The pictures,' Sammie whispered.

Jay nodded and finally met her eyes with his. 'I reckon there would be a lot of guys who'd love to see you doing what you're doing in some of those photos,' he said.

'No,' Sammie said. 'Please, Jay.' She looked at him desperately, and his face changed.

'Why are you looking at me like that?' he said. 'Like I've done something wrong. You're the one who's *cheated!*'

Suddenly he lost it, and kicked her twice in her side and her stomach, until Sammie curled up, gasping and sobbing.

'I loved you,' he shouted at her, 'I wanted to *marry* you, and all the time you were cheating on me. Cheating on me with my *best friend.*'

Sammie tried to speak, to explain that she'd never cheated; that Mark had lied, but she couldn't get the words out.

'I'm not mad at him,' Jay said. 'I wouldn't even be mad at him if he'd had a go. Why shouldn't he, when you make it so easy? But you. *You* should know *better!*'

He scooped up some dirt and leaf mould in his hand, bringing it down against her face and rubbing it over her cheek and across her nose and mouth, pushing so hard that some of it went up her nostrils and between her lips so she could taste and smell it.

Sammie was desperate to explain, but it was too difficult. 'I... I never... I never....' she spluttered uselessly.

Jay took hold of the sapphire necklace that he'd given her, and pulled it until the chain broke and it came away in his hand. 'You never what?' he asked

'I never... cheated.'

Jay watched her silently. 'You want to though,' he said eventually. 'Mark said you want to. He told me you've said you want to fuck him. It's only because *he* doesn't want to that nothing's happened.'

'No,' Sammie said through her tears, 'no.'

Jay leaned towards her and she cowered against the ground expecting to be shouted at again, but then his attention was diverted by the sound of a twig snapping somewhere in the trees.

'What was that?' Jay said. He'd turned white, and he quickly stood up and brushed some mud from his clothes. Then, without a backwards glance at her he made off through the trees, and Sammie carried on lying on the ground, crying uselessly to the empty woods.

...

The next few months were some of the worst of Sammie's life. Mark and Jay both ignored her, and on her sixteenth birthday she ended up at home with her mum, eating a takeaway in front of a stupid romantic comedy. At the end of the film Sammie started to cry, and her mum put her arm around her.

'What is it?' she asked. 'Are you still missing Jay?'

Sammie nodded.

'You really liked him, didn't you?'

Sammie nodded again.

Her mum held her tight for a while. 'Sammie, you shouldn't get in such a state about it,' she said. 'You're only young, before long you'll have forgotten all about him.'

'Have you forgotten all about dad?'

Sammie's mum frowned. 'Why would you say that?'

'Because you've separated, haven't you? That's why he stays in

London nearly all the time. Because that's where he lives now, isn't it?'

'You... you knew?'

'I overheard dad say it.'

'Oh, Sammie. I'm sorry,' her mum said, 'we weren't trying to deceive you, it's just... with your exams and everything, I thought it would be better if we tried—'

'Don't you miss him?' she asked.

'Sammie, things haven't been right between your dad and I for a long time.'

'You mean, since Alfie.'

'Yes,' her mum said, with surprising honesty, 'since Alfie.'

Sammie put her hand very briefly on her stomach, where she could feel the blossoming roundness of her pregnancy hidden away under her baggy cotton hoodie.

'Look,' her mum said, 'do you mind if I just go to bed now, Sammie? I've got a lot on at the moment.'

Sammie shook her head. It had hardly been much of a birthday anyway, it didn't really matter. 'What will happen?' she asked, as her mum got up from the sofa. 'Will we stay living here, just the two of us?'

Her mum seemed to consider how to answer. 'No,' she said at length. 'We're going to stay here until after your exams. Then we'll move back to Kent.' She hesitated, then added, 'that's why I'm so busy right now. I'm trying to find us a house.'

'Oh,' Sammie said, and she frowned.

'You don't mind moving, do you sweetheart?' her mum asked. 'Things haven't exactly worked out here anyway.'

Sammie shrugged, too confused to explain how she felt about it, and her mum left her to go up to bed. Sammie put her hand on her stomach again. She had no idea what she was going to do, but one thing that was for sure was that she didn't know how she'd ever be able to explain to her parents that she was going to have a baby because her ex-boyfriend had attacked her, and she didn't want to move with her mum to Kent.

Felicity

28

After what he did to me on the night of the hen party, Jay watched me like a hawk. Wherever I was, he seemed to be. He stopped going running or to the gym in the evenings, and started fitting it in during the day instead. He took me to work in the morning and picked me up when I finished, and he even refused to let me talk to Mark for a while.

'He's getting worried,' I said after a few days of texts and calls from Mark that I didn't answer. In fact, I only knew Mark was contacting me at all because Jay told me. He'd confiscated my phone, and all my communication with the outside world now had to go through him.

'What do you care?' Jay asked.

'I don't... but... don't you want to carry on with the plan?'

Jay considered it. 'Yeah,' he said, 'but what I find weird is the fact that *you* want to. You only ever did this for me. If you've spent months sleeping with someone you don't even like, shouldn't you want it to stop?'

'Well, perhaps the fact I've spent months doing that means I don't want it to be for nothing,' I told him.

After about a week Jay relented and let me call Mark, but he sat next to me and the conversation was stilted and awkward.

'He wants me to go round,' I said afterwards.

To begin with I thought that Jay would refuse to let me go, but in the end he drove me round and dropped me off a few houses away.

'I'll be right outside,' he said.

'Jay... I... he'll probably want me to stay...'

'Then tell him you can't.'

'Jay—'

He reached across and kissed me, squeezing my thigh with his hand. 'You're a good girl, Flissie,' he said. 'I know you won't let me down.'

...

When Mark opened the door to me he quickly pulled me inside, his face full of concern.

'What's been going on?' he asked urgently. 'Why haven't you been answering my calls?'

'Mark,' I said, 'I—'

'Has he found out about us?'

My mouth dropped open. 'What?' I said.

'Your "flatmate". Jason.'

I was so shocked that I couldn't speak, and I followed Mark down the hallway to the living room in stunned silence. 'I...' I said finally, 'you... you *knew?*'

Mark sat down at the table and I plonked myself down next to him. 'Fliss, I knew all along,' he said. 'I knew he wasn't just your flatmate. You looked shifty when you spoke about him, you were always nervous if we were at your flat, and I've never met him. I'm not stupid. I know when I'm being lied to.'

'Mark, I—'

He reached out and took my hand. 'I don't mind,' he said. 'I mean, I do mind... I'd rather it wasn't like this, but... I don't know. Sometimes people just have relationships with more than one person. If your relationship with him... overlaps... with your relationship with me, I can deal with that. I thought that I'd give you time to figure it out on your own. I thought you'd tell me when you were ready.'

'Mark,' I said, 'all this time, I can't believe...'

Suddenly, I realised he was looking at me closely.

'What?' I said.

He pointed at my forehead. 'How did you get that?' he asked.

'That cut.'

I reached up and touched it. I thought about Jay waiting outside, and before I knew it I was crying, really crying, and I didn't seem able to stop.

29

'Felicity,' Mark said gently, when I'd calmed down just a little. 'Did... did Jason do that to you?'

My instinct was to deny it, but instead I simply nodded against Mark's shoulder.

'Has he done other things to you?'

I nodded again, and Mark stroked my back gently. 'Leave him,' he whispered.

'What?'

'Leave him, and move in here with me.'

I pulled away from him. 'Are you... are you being serious?'

'Yes. I... I love you, Felicity. I've wanted to tell you for so long, but because I knew you were with someone else I... I just...' he gave up explaining. 'Don't even go back to him today,' he said firmly. 'Stay here with me.'

I stared at him. To begin with all I felt was relief, but then reality started flooding in and I realised it was crazy. Mark had no idea who Jason really was, and me staying in Coalton with Mark was impossible.

'I can't,' I said.

'Yes, you can.'

'No,' I said, 'you... you don't understand.'

'Then tell me. You can tell me anything. There's nothing to be scared of. It... it is okay for you to be here at the moment, isn't it?' he asked. 'Is Jason out? Or have you made an excuse that he believes?'

I nodded, and thought again of Jay sitting outside in his van. I rubbed my eyes, scared when I went back out to him he'd notice I'd been crying.

'Okay,' Mark said, 'why don't you... why don't you explain it from the beginning?'

'The beginning?'

'When did... when did all this,' he gestured at my forehead, 'start?'

'He did it last weekend.'

'After Grace's hen night?'

I nodded.

'And he's been making things difficult for you since then?' he asked. 'That's why you haven't been speaking to me?'

'I didn't want to risk talking to you,' I said. 'He... he wants me to have a baby. He's talking about taking me away from Coalton—'

Mark looked horrified. 'Taking you away?' he said. 'When?'

'After Grace's wedding.'

'In two weeks.'

'Yes,' I said quietly.

'Fliss, I wish you'd told me—'

'How could I?' I said. 'I... I don't even know why I'm telling you now.'

Mark was silent for a time. 'We'll figure something out,' he said, 'we'll make sure you're safe before then.'

'Mark, you can't!' I said. 'You have no idea what you're saying. I can't stay in Coalton with you, we'd still have to leave. You'd have to leave everything behind because if he realises I'm with you he'll try to find us.'

'Fliss—'

'I haven't been honest with you about anything,' I said. 'Even my parents. They didn't die in a car crash. My dad killed himself and my mum by setting fire to the house.'

Mark's face went through several emotions, then he said, 'Fliss, I'm so sorry. That's—'

'They were in debt,' I said, not wanting to hear his sympathy, 'massive debt. The house was going to be repossessed. I never even knew about it. Not until after.'

'Fliss—'

'I met Jay—Jason a week later. I think I told him exactly what happened while I was drunk – in any case, he seemed to know the next day, so I must have told him. He helped me... he helped me to forget...'

'Fliss,' Mark said gently, 'you don't have to feel any loyalty to him. Even if he helped you for a while, he's not helping you now.'

'I wanted to help him, too. He was in a bad place, his relationship with his family had broken down, he didn't have anything, not even a proper place to live.'

'You loved him?'

I nodded.

'Do you still love him?'

I hesitated, then I nodded again. I could see no point in denying it.

'I do get it,' Mark said, 'I... when I was still at school, I had a friend. Jay. He was... he was always getting himself in trouble, he was one of these people who seem to want their life to be as difficult and stressful as they can possibly make it.'

My breath caught in my throat. I started to shake, but I held my hands in my lap and hoped it didn't show.

'When he was fifteen, he started going out with this girl. It was... okay to begin with, I guess. But he... he hurt her. She was going to have his baby and she tried to make it work with him, but sometimes... sometimes you just can't make things work. Not with someone like that.'

'What...' I said, my voice almost a whisper. 'What happened to her?'

Mark suddenly became guarded. 'She... she moved away,' he said, 'her parents got divorced, and she moved away with her mum.'

...

I carried on talking with Mark for a while longer, but it was getting late and I was nervous. Jay would be expecting me to make an excuse and go back out to him.

'Mark,' I said, 'I have to go.'

'I'm not comfortable letting you go back to him,' he said, 'please, stay here. He can't do anything to you while you're here with me.'

'Mark, he will,' I said. 'If he... if he knew I was with another man, do you really think he'd sit back and take it?'

'I'm not scared of him,' Mark said.

'Listen,' I said, 'listen to me. For us to be together, you would have to give up everything. We'd have to move somewhere far away from here, and stay hiding for the rest of our lives. I can't do that to you. This is my mess.'

Mark thought about it. 'You should go to the police,' he said.

'Mark, you don't get it. Even if he went to prison, he'd get out again! Then he'd have more reason than ever to come after me.'

'You can't keep running. Not for your whole life.'

'I can,' I said, 'if I need to. There's nothing to keep me here. And... and if I left on my own I don't think he'd be so desperate to find me.'

'When... when exactly do you think he'll try to take you away with him?'

'I don't know,' I said, 'he just said after the wedding. I don't know where he's planning to go, he probably needs time to sort something out—'

'Then we'll have to beat him to it,' Mark said.

'What?'

'Leave it all to me,' Mark said, 'if you're determined to go back today, then go back. Act normally, and I will get something planned.'

'You... you're serious?'

'I told you. I love you, Felicity.'

'I... I love you too,' I said.

30

Jay questioned me at length about what had happened with Mark, but I managed to give him answers that reassured him. I had no idea what Mark would plan in terms of getting me away from "Jason", but I'd asked him not to ever mention about it in any messages to me, and to keep all the plans to himself, because as far as I was concerned the less I knew about it the better and safer for us both. Also, more importantly, I knew any messages from him would be intercepted by Jay.

'I think I might have found us a place,' Jay said when we went to bed that night.

'Oh?'

'A house, in the country,' Jay said, 'away from all the noise and people.'

I tried to smile. 'That sounds... nice,' I said.

'Don't lie to me,' Jay said. 'I know you don't want to go.'

'I do, I just—'

'When you're there, you'll like it,' he told me. 'And it'll be better for when we have a family.'

I thought about my pills. I'd smuggled them into work one day, thrown the boxes away, and hidden the sheets of pills inside a painkiller box instead, which I kept in my handbag.

'Jay, why do you want to have a baby so badly?' I asked him. I couldn't get out of my mind what Mark had said about Sammie being pregnant.

'Why shouldn't I?' he said. 'I love you, and I want to have a family with you.'

'I know, but... why right now? We haven't been together long, why not wait for another few months, at least—'

'Don't you want to have a family with me?' Jay asked, his eyes narrowed.

'Yes,' I said, 'yes, of course I do.'

'Good,' he said. Then he reached across and opened the top drawer of the bedside table. 'I got you something,' he said. He took out a small, smart-looking box and handed it to me, and when I opened it I saw a necklace – a silver chain with a little blue pendant; a sapphire.

'It's lovely,' I said, though I felt strange when I looked at it, as though it was making me half-remember something; something I'd seen before.

The next morning, when Jay went into the bathroom, I remembered the shoe box in the wardrobe that had Sammie's picture in it, and the more I thought about it the more sure I was that I had seen the necklace in the photo he'd shown me. I tried to put it out of my mind but I couldn't, until I had to find out for certain.

I waited until I was sure Jay was otherwise occupied – I heard the toilet flush, the taps running, and when the sound of the shower started and I could be sure he'd be busy for a while, I quickly leapt out of bed and across to the wardrobe.

The box was easy enough to find. Jay had quite a lot of clothes and shoes, but not many other possessions, and the shoe box sat pretty much on its own on the shelf above the rail of clothes. I made a careful mental note of exactly where on the shelf it was, and slid it down gently, placing it on the floor and kneeling in front of it.

I quickly found the picture; Sammie, Mark and Jay standing together in their school uniforms, Jay with his arm around his girlfriend. To begin with I wondered whether I had imagined the necklace, but then I made it out, a little pendant that lay against her striped school tie; a teardrop shaped sapphire dangling from a thin silver chain. My blood ran cold. Although I had no way of knowing for certain, I was convinced that the necklace she was wearing had been bought for her by him, and for a moment I panicked as I thought the one he'd given me was literally the one she'd used to wear; that he'd kept it and passed it on to each new girlfriend as if they were just a long conveyor belt of new, interchangeable Sammies. I looked as closely as I could, though my head was spinning and it was hard to concentrate, but I eventually realised that the two necklaces were not identical. Sammie's necklace contained only a sapphire, while mine had a second stone above it at the point of the teardrop – a little tiny diamond. I quickly dropped the photo back inside the box. It could be a coincidence, but I didn't think so. Jay was obviously still obsessed with Sammie, and when it came to her, I didn't think there would be any *coincidences*.

I was going to put the box back, but a strange impulse made me dig deeper into it, though I had no idea why or what for. To begin with I didn't think anything was any different to when he'd showed me its contents before, until at the bottom of the box I felt something small and plastic. I took hold of it, and when I pulled it out I saw it was a memory stick. In the bathroom, the sound of the shower continued. He'd been in there maybe five minutes, so I knew I had at least ten or more likely fifteen to spare. I went into my old bedroom and grabbed my laptop, and took it back into Jay's room to sit on the floor by the box again. I had no idea what to expect from the memory stick. I supposed it would probably just be more photos, or maybe even old school work or something; I'd kept some rubbish like that, or at least I had done before it got lost in the fire. Even the fact I hadn't seen the memory stick in the box before wasn't that significant. It may well have been in there and I just missed it; I had been more interested in the pictures than if there was anything left inside the box.

My laptop seemed to take an inordinately long time to start. My hands began to shake, and I almost lost my nerve, but I focussed on the sound of the shower, and took some deep breaths. I'd have plenty of warning before Jay came out. Even if he suddenly stopped showering, I'd have ample time to put everything back while he was drying himself – something he did almost as meticulously as washing.

I slid the memory stick into my laptop. There was one folder on it, simply called "pictures". I opened it without any further hesitation, and once I realised what was in it I gasped in horror, and covered my mouth with my hand.

...

The fact that he, and she, had done it in the first place was not so much what shocked me, though the quantity and variety of the pictures took me by surprise. They were poor quality, I guessed from old camera phones, and even without the one or two that showed Sammie's face, I knew that they were of her. Within the main folder called pictures Jay had organised most of the images into several numbered sub-folders. I quickly realised this was a way of grouping them into themes, though I could hardly bring myself to look, and began to feel sick. All I could think about was Sammie's age, and the fact that Jay, despite being a teenager himself at the time, had gone to the effort of taking them off his phone to store on his computer, and had *organised* them. It was like a sort of trophy cabinet, a reminder of what they'd done and what she was willing to do – except that now he wasn't a teenage boy, he was twenty-seven, and I knew he knew he still had them. Jay threw away things when he hadn't used them for a few *weeks* – anything he kept beyond that amount of time was deliberate, and everything he owned he knew about, and he had it for a reason.

I quickly pulled the memory stick out of my laptop and shoved it back underneath the photos, but then I became aware of something else. Whatever was folded up at the bottom of the pile felt like newspaper, and I was sure he'd never shown me any newspaper clippings before. I took hold of it and pulled it from the box. It was folded in half four times, and I opened it out carefully. It was from a local paper, and the headline read: *New appeal for information about missing girl.*

I skimmed the article as quickly as I could. Every few seconds I stopped and made absolutely sure I could still hear Jay in the shower, and then my eyes would drop back down to the words, trying to make sense of it. It said that Sammie had gone missing in the middle of her exams; that she'd left a note for her parents; and that her disappearance happened the day she learned her parents, who had already separated, were getting a divorce. There was only the briefest mention of Jay and Mark, and it was clear that everyone, her parents included, believed her disappearance was as a direct result of her parent's marriage breaking down. The article had been written one year after she went missing, and contained a plea from her parents for anyone who might have seen her to come forward.

I folded the article up and put it back just where I had found it, and slipped the whole box carefully back inside the wardrobe. Then I sat down on the end of the bed and thought about what I'd seen. It hardly surprised me that Jay hadn't told me Sammie had gone missing. There was obviously far more to his relationship with Sammie than he wanted me to know, and I knew I could no longer trust a single word he said. But beyond that, beyond my fear of Jay, my whole nightmarish situation and the revelations about Sammie, something else was scaring and unsettling me, and scaring and unsettling me a great deal. Because only the previous night, Mark had sat there and told me that Sammie's parents had got divorced and she'd moved away with her mum, when he'd lived in the same village as her and couldn't possibly have not known the truth. I turned to my laptop again, though I knew I must have precious few minutes left. I found a missing person database, and quickly typed in all the information I had, praying it would somehow come back saying she'd been found, or maybe that there simply wouldn't be an entry for her at all because she was okay, and it was all some sort of mistake. But there it was, a picture of her face, the date around eleven years ago that she had gone missing, and most damning of all, the information that she was *still* missing. There was no possible way Mark could really think she'd gone to live with her mum. He knew she was missing, he knew she wasn't where he said she was, and he'd lied to me. What I couldn't begin to imagine, was why.

PART 3

Sammie

31

As revision leave started and the exams drew close, Sammie's world became ever more lonely. Although her mum would talk to her sometimes, more often than not she was too busy, or stressed, or tired, so Sammie gave up trying. She missed going round to Jay's for dinner, and chattering away with Jay's mum. She missed the feeling of having somewhere to go when she got back from school – when she had nearly always spent her time with Jay in the past. Most of all, she missed *him*. She missed being hugged and kissed, and having her hand held and being told she was loved. When she'd had him, she'd felt special – she'd had a special person just for her, and she'd been a special person to him, and the isolation she felt without him was a pain that never seemed to get any better.

He spent more of his time with Mark now that he didn't speak to her. The two boys always seemed to be whispering together; sometimes glancing across at her so she had no doubt she was the topic of the conversation – that Mark was at work spreading more of his poison about her. On top of this, Jay would flirt with other girls at school – normally not with any success – though after Sammie's first exam she was horrified to see him walk out holding hands with another girl; someone from his English class, called Kirsty. Sammie followed a few paces behind them, and watched as they sat down together on a bench outside the school gates, and started to kiss.

She was sure that Jay knew she was there, even though she

quickly made her way across to the bus stop and tried to ignore them, but she couldn't help stealing glances. Kirsty was blonde, like her, but that was about where the similarity ended. While Sammie's uniform practically hung from her body, even with the little bump she now had, Kirsty's skirt was strained around her thick thighs, and Sammie found herself looking jealously at Kirsty's chest, which compared to Sammie's, was enormous. Almost as if Jay knew what she was thinking she saw his hand briefly rest on one of Kirsty's boobs, before he moved it down to her thigh.

Suddenly Mark was beside her, and when he spoke, it made her jump.

'Didn't take him long to move on, did it?' he said.

Sammie whipped round and glared at him. 'Fuck off,' she said.

'I'm just saying—'

'I said fuck off!' Sammie screamed. She gave Mark a shove, and with everyone staring at her, including Jay and Kirsty from the other side of the road, she strode off past the bus stop towards town, hot tears in her eyes, and a feeling of fatigue and nausea that she'd experienced a lot over the past few months. Eventually the nausea became so strong that she had to make a dash for some public toilets, and she was sick three times, then she slumped exhausted against the door, and closed her eyes.

The next day, she had another exam, and she gathered her things together shakily and walked to the bus stop in a daze. She didn't seem able to muster any anxiety about the exam; in fact she was more worried about the bus journey, which she knew would make her feel sick. The exam seemed irrelevant to her– all that filled her mind was what she was going to do about the future, and her need to plan her next move. A next move, which, at the moment, she was sure would entail running away.

She wrote nothing on the exam paper. Instead she sat hunched over and lost in her thoughts, until she could finally leave the echoey hall and get some fresh air in the sunshine outside. Mark was walking along behind her, talking with a few other people from their class, who Sammie didn't really know. It had been a Business Studies exam, so Mark had been there but not Jay, who took far fewer subjects than her or Mark did. Mark stopped when they reached the bus stop, but Sammie carried on walking, and before long she heard footsteps behind her.

'Where are you going?' Mark asked.

'What's it to you?'

'You going into town?'

Sammie didn't answer and Mark fell into step with her. In truth she had little idea where she was going or what she was doing, she just didn't feel ready to go home.

'How did you find the exam?' Mark asked.

'I didn't write anything.'

That shocked him. 'You... you didn't *write* anything?' he said.

'No.'

'Why... why not?'

Sammie stopped and faced him. 'Because,' she said, 'I couldn't give a *shit* about the fucking *exam*.'

Mark digested this for a while. 'It's up to you, I guess,' he said in the end.

'Yes it is.'

She carried on walking, but he didn't get the hint that she didn't want his company.

'Leave me alone, Mark,' she said.

'Why? Where are you going?'

Sammie stopped again. 'I'm going to try and figure out what to do about my baby.'

Any hope she had of getting rid of Mark evaporated. He gawped at her, and then he steered her over to the little brick wall at the side of the pavement and sat down with her.

'You... you're *pregnant*?' he said.

'No,' she snapped, 'I just enjoy saying stuff like that.'

'But... but I thought you and Jay weren't really... together... any more? I mean... he's with Kirsty now, isn't he?'

Sammie made a noise of disgust.

'Anyway,' Mark said nastily, 'he doesn't ever talk about you any more.'

Sammie stared down at the ground between her feet. There was a single blade of grass sticking up from a hole in the pavement. She squashed it with her foot.

'Was it fun?' she asked Mark.

'What?' he asked. 'Was what fun?'

'When you made up those lies about me sending you pictures of myself.'

'I... I don't...'

'I hope it was fun for you, Mark. Because my baby won't have a dad because of you doing that.'

'You *did* send me a picture.'

Sammie glared at him, then she looked at the ground again.

'So you're going to keep it?' Mark asked bluntly. 'Because I don't think—'

'Why shouldn't I?' she demanded. 'It's mine. It's nothing to do with you, or Jay, or anyone else.'

She stood up and started walking towards town again, and Mark continued to follow her.

'Sammie,' he said, 'come on, let's go back. The bus will be here in a second.'

'I don't want to go home.'

'What are you going to do, just wander round town on your own for hours?'

'I don't know.'

Mark gently took her arm and Sammie let him, and he steered her back towards the bus stop.

When they got off in Tatchley they went and sat together in the village green, which was empty despite it being a warm day. A few fat ducks were lying lazily in the grass by the pond, and Sammie was grateful when Mark chose a spot underneath a tree, because the heat was beginning to make her feel faint.

'Sammie,' Mark said slowly, 'there's nothing wrong with...

with not wanting the consequences of a bad decision.'

'A bad decision?'

'Well, yeah,' Mark said, 'I mean, this was an accident, wasn't it?'

Sammie closed her eyes for a moment. She'd always tried to be careful with Jay, but the truth was they'd had quite a lot of "accidents". At least, accidents was what they called them to each other, because it was easier to make it sound like nobody was to blame. The truth was that she always wanted to be careful, but Jay had simply made it too difficult; arguing with her, pressuring her, complaining that condoms ruined sex for him. In the end, keeping him happy had seemed more important than keeping herself safe, so she just took the risk. Despite this, her period had always come, and she thought it would be okay. Until the time when finally it didn't, and that was a few weeks after the time in the woods. The time that had made her pregnant.

When she didn't answer, Mark reached out and touched her arm, and she moved away from him.

'Sammie,' he said, 'this *was* an accident?'

She frowned. What was he talking about? Surely he didn't think she *wanted* this.

'I know... I know you're angry with me,' he said gently, 'but I do care. And I understand if... if you did this because you thought it would make Jay love you.'

'What?'

'Having his baby,' Mark said, 'you want him to commit to you, and you were scared he would break up with you—'

'What are you talking about?' Sammie said. 'He loved me. He was going to ask me to *marry* him!'

'*Was.*' Mark said meaningfully. 'Surely you can see that the best thing to do now is to... to get rid of it. It's not fair to make him have a baby he doesn't want.'

Sammie stared at him open-mouthed. 'Jay... Jay doesn't even *know*,' she said, 'are you... are you suggesting I get rid of his baby and don't even *tell* him?'

'I... I'll even come with you,' Mark said, as though he hadn't heard her. 'To the... to the... place.'

'Why the hell would you do that?'

'To help you. To put you right again.'

'Put me right?' Sammie said. 'There's nothing wrong with me!'

'You're not... you're not supposed to use your body the way you have been doing,' Mark said, 'don't you see that?'

Sammie stood up. 'You're crazy,' she said, 'Jay told me you were a weirdo, you and your family. If you're so... if you're all so *religious*, should you even be going round telling girls to get rid of their babies?'

Mark got up too and grabbed her arm. 'I'm not *religious*,' he said, 'but I still think what you've been doing is wrong, and I care about Jay enough that I would do anything to stop him getting trapped into spending his life with a *slut* like you because you've tricked him into it.'

'You're mental,' Sammie said, 'you are actually mental.'

'Tell me I'm wrong,' Mark said. 'Why are you in this state? If it's really not what you want, why are you pregnant?'

Sammie turned to him. 'You really think it's that simple?'

'Yes,' he said. 'You're not stupid, Sammie. Jay might be, but you're not. I know you wouldn't be having a baby unless it was exactly what *you* wanted.'

Sammie tried to walk away.

'Tell me I'm wrong,' he said again. 'You can't, can you? You can't tell me I'm wrong because everything I've said is exactly what you're doing.'

Sammie spun round. 'You want to know why I'm pregnant, Mark?' she said. 'You really want to know?'

'Yes.'

She stared at him, but she couldn't find the words.

'See,' he said, 'you can't deny it. What you're trying to do to trap Jay is disgusting, Sammie. It's dishonest, and it's unfair, and he doesn't deserve it—'

'He raped me,' Sammie said all in a rush, and Mark fell immediately into silence, then he said, 'What?'

'That's how I got pregnant, Mark. It happened because he… because he raped me.'

32

Sammie tried to run back home away from Mark, but he followed her, unable to ignore what she'd said.

'Sammie!' he called after her. 'Sammie, you can't just say that and run away.'

She didn't turn back until she reached her house. Mark had followed her right to her door, and reluctantly she let him inside.

'You're lucky it's me you said that to,' he told her.

'Wh... what?'

Mark took hold of her arm and she began to feel scared. 'Jay didn't *rape* you, Sammie.'

'I... I want you to leave.'

'Jay has only ever done exactly what you want him to.'

'I don't understand,' she said, and Mark's fingers dug more deeply into her arm. 'Mark, you're hurting me,' she said.

'You wanted this,' Mark said, 'it's easy now to say you didn't, but you did. So don't blame Jay for *your* problems.'

'Please,' Sammie said, 'please go.' She felt cold all over. She couldn't understand why Mark was talking like this, where he'd got these ideas from. Was he really so blinded by his friendship with Jay that he'd say anything to make it her fault and not his?

'Before you open your mouth to anyone else, perhaps you should remember what Jay said he'd do if you talk,' Mark said. 'With your pictures.'

Sammie let out a little cry. She remembered the sound of the twig snapping after Jay had hurt her, the way they'd both thought somebody was there.

'You... you *saw?*' She thought about it, remembering how the branch had only snapped right at the end, how Jay had told Mark to go a while before that, and then she said, 'You... you *watched.*'

'Yes,' Mark said, 'I watched you and him together, and you

know what, Sammie? There was not a moment, not one moment, when I thought he was doing anything you didn't deserve.'

Some tears spilt from Sammie's eyes. She tried to pull her arm away, very aware that she was in the house, on her own, with him.

'Mark...' she said, 'Mark, please...'

'He didn't listen to you, did he?' Mark said. 'You told him it was me who made his mum walk in on you, you told him you only sent me the one picture, and he didn't believe you.'

'Mark—'

He squeezed her arm harder. 'When it comes down to it, he'll always believe *me*.'

'Please,' Sammie said, 'let go of me. Please.'

He did as she asked, and she saw him take in her look of fear, the way she backed away from him. 'What?' he said. 'You think *I'm* going to do something to you? *I* have more respect for myself.'

To Sammie's relief he walked away from her, and once he was out of the door Sammie locked it behind him in a panic, then she sank down to the floor and started to cry in massive, terrified sobs.

For the next few hours Sammie lay in bed. At one point she even slept a little, but she had bad dreams and woke up cold and sweating. Then, hesitantly, she picked up her phone and sent a text to Jay.

I need 2 tlk 2 u

He didn't text back for hours, and when he did, his message was cruel.

Got ur message earlier but i was busy fucking kirsty.

Sammie stroked her little bump and took a few deep breaths.

R u and her serious then?

He replied far more quickly this time.

Didn't realise til i got wiv her how crap u really were. I shagged her 4 times earlier. shes not a frigid bitch like u

Sammie threw her phone down in disgust. Then, slowly, she picked it up and read the messages from him again. Something about them just didn't seem right. She could well believe that Jay could have had sex with Kirsty four times in an afternoon, because he'd done the same with her on a few occasions, but it was clearly calculated to hurt her. He was trying to say he'd done the same with Kirsty as he had with her – that what they'd done wasn't special. In fact, in his disgusting, lurid messages Sammie began to see another meaning – that he wasn't interested in Kirsty at all, and that his only interest was in making Sammie jealous. And Sammie realised something else. If that was true, and she played things right, perhaps she could get him to understand about Mark's lies, and get him to want her again, and her little baby might be able to have a dad.

33

The next day all three of them had a Maths exam, and afterwards Jay made a great show of making out with Kirsty, but Sammie ignored them. Even when he came up to her and Mark and said he was going into town with Kirsty, Sammie just shrugged and let them go off together.

When she got home, she sat on her bed and put her hand on her stomach. 'He still loves me, baby,' she told her little bump, 'and he'll love you too, you'll see.'

She took her school uniform off and got changed into a loose t-shirt that hid her bump, and her short denim skirt. She waited a little while, hoping it would give Jay enough time to get home, and then she set out to go and see him.

'Did you have a nice time with Kirsty?' she asked when he opened the door.

'What's it to you?'

Sammie stepped inside and Jay let her, but she felt overwhelmed, and had no idea how to tell him about the baby.

'Sammie,' Jay said, 'what do you want?'

'Can we... can we talk?'

'I've got nothing to say.'

'Well, I have something I'd like to say to you,' she told him. 'Could we... could we go upstairs? And talk in your room?'

She was worried he'd refuse, but without a word he turned and led the way upstairs, and she followed him. When she went inside, she was surprised to see her necklace was out on his bedside table, as though he'd been looking at it.

'I... I miss my necklace,' she said, pointing at it. 'I still reach up to touch it sometimes, then I remember it's not there any more.'

Jay opened a drawer and dropped the necklace into it. 'You

can't have it back,' he said.

'I know,' Sammie said, 'it's broken, anyway, isn't it?'

'I was going to fix it,' Jay said, 'and give it to Kirsty.'

Sammie felt a pain in her chest and swallowed hard. 'You… you don't really like her though, do you?'

'She's all right.'

Sammie took a few deep breaths. She could tell Jay was impatient.

'There… there isn't any easy way of saying this,' she told him, 'so I'm just going to try to say it.'

Jay waited without encouraging her.

'Jay… I… I'm…' she gave up, and her eyes stung with tears. She sat down on his bed and lifted her t-shirt up to show him her bump, but he stared at it uncomprehending. 'It… it's a… it's a baby, Jay,' she said, 'I'm pregnant.'

She didn't even see his reaction because she started to cry. She let her t-shirt fall back down over her stomach and cried into her lap. He didn't do anything for so long she began to think all was lost, and that she'd misjudged the texts he'd sent her. Perhaps he had never been meaning to make her jealous; perhaps he had only been trying to hurt her because he hated her now. She put a hand on her stomach and tried to calm down. Then, to her astonishment and relief, Jay sat down next to her and gently put his hand over the back of hers, and the flood of emotions she felt made her cry even harder.

'Was it… was it from that time… in the woods?' Jay asked her quietly.

She nodded, and Jay took his hand away and put his arms around her instead. 'I'm so sorry,' he said, 'I didn't mean to hurt you. You know I didn't mean to hurt you, don't you?'

Sammie nodded again.

'The thought of you sending pictures to Mark, going behind my back like that. I've never been so angry, Sammie. I don't ever want to be as angry as that again.'

'Mark… lied,' she said.

'Sammie, please, just tell me the truth.'

'I am.'

Jay let go of her and looked down at her tummy. 'Why didn't you tell me before?' he said. 'You must have known for... for months.'

'Three months,' Sammie said, 'roughly.'

'I wanted to speak to you,' he said. 'I've missed you. But Mark... Mark said you weren't right for me and that I should forget about you.'

'Mark doesn't want us to be together,' Sammie said, 'yesterday... yesterday I had an exam with him. I accidentally... let it slip to him that I'm pregnant, and he thought I shouldn't even tell you. He said I should get rid of it. He even offered to come with me, he was so determined I should do it.'

'Are you... are you sure? Is that really what he said?'

'Yes,' Sammie said, 'he told me that I'm a slut and that I'm no good for you. He even accused me of getting pregnant on purpose.'

Jay's face grew hard and Sammie could see that finally he believed her. 'He's been going on at me for months,' he said, 'saying stuff about you. I thought... I thought he was trying to look out for me.'

'He isn't,' Sammie said. 'He just... he just hates me. I never sent him pictures, Jay. I don't even *like* him, I don't want him to see my body.'

'I... I was going to let him touch you,' Jay said softly.

'It's all right,' Sammie said. 'I understand. I do.'

'No, I... I hurt you. I really hurt you.'

'Jay, it... it's okay,' Sammie said with difficulty. 'I... I forgive you.'

Jay stared at her. 'I'll kill him,' he said.

'Jay, no,'

'I will,' he said, 'I'll fucking kill him.'

Sammie grabbed his hand. 'Listen to me,' she said, 'forget about him. We know now. We both know what he's done, and we're not going to let him hurt us any more.'

'You think we should let him get away with it?'

'No, I think… I think we should just leave. Let's run away, like you wanted to before. We can leave and get married. I… I have some savings. My parents set up an account for me, it's supposed to be for me to use for university and maybe putting towards a house one day. If you still wanted to run away and have a wedding, I could take all the money.'

'How much money?' Jay asked.

'Tens of thousands of pounds.'

Jay's eyes widened. 'Fuck me,' he said.

'We could use it to get somewhere to live,' Sammie said, 'and it could tide us over until we got jobs. We wouldn't have to worry.'

'I don't care whether you have any money,' Jay said, 'when I was thinking of asking you to marry me, I would have gone anywhere with you, even if we had to sleep on the street.'

'You… you mean it?'

'Yes,' Jay said, 'Sammie, I love you. That… that's why I got so angry. You know that, don't you? The thought of losing you made me so crazy I didn't know what I was doing.'

'Then let's go,' Sammie said urgently. 'Tomorrow.'

'Tomorrow?'

'Why not? All we need to do is pack. We can do that, can't we?'

'I… yeah,' Jay said, 'yeah, we can do that.' He smiled at her. 'I can't believe you're going to have my baby,' he said.

'You're not… you're not upset?'

'No,' Jay said, 'I'm not upset at all. I think it's amazing. And Sammie…'

'Yeah?'

'I never had sex with Kirsty.'

34

They made arrangements to meet late morning the next day. They would go into town and Sammie would withdraw all her savings – or as much of them as she could – then they would get on a train. Sammie started to pack as soon as she got home. It was hard work thinking about what she needed to take because her mind felt woolly and foggy, she was exhausted in a way she'd never been before and there was a churning in her stomach that was nagging and constant. By about seven in the evening she thought she was ready. She'd packed some clothes and toiletries, her passport and other documents she thought she might need in the future, and a couple of sentimental bits and bobs – a picture of Alfie and a card he'd made her, and a bracelet her parents had given her on her twelfth birthday, not long before Alfie had died. She hid the bags inside her wardrobe so her mum wouldn't see them, and then sat down to write a note to her parents. She struggled to begin with, but in the end kept it very simple.

> *To mum and dad,*
> *I've left home because I think I will be happier away from here. If you care about me, please let me live my life the way I want to without trying to find me.*
> *Sammie.*

She barely slept that night. She text Jay, who said that he couldn't sleep either, but that he would take care of everything from now on, so she mustn't worry. She fell into an exhausted doze around dawn, only to wake up again when her mum left for work. She got up and made herself breakfast, then she had a quick shower and dressed. There was still a while to go before she needed to leave to meet Jay, and she wasn't sure what to do with herself, so she lay on her bed, her hands on her stomach – on the baby.

When there was a knock on the door, she assumed it would be Jay. She rushed downstairs to answer it, but to her surprise it was Mark, and she noticed that he had a cut on his nose, like someone had hit him. She realised immediately it must have been Jay, and she tried to shut the door in his face but he put his foot in the way.

'You pleased with yourself?' he said.

'What?'

'Getting Jay to come round yesterday and do this to me.'

'I didn't ask him to,' Sammie said, 'and I want you to leave.'

'Jay told me what you're planning to do today,' he said.

Sammie was surprised Jay had told him, but she tried not to let it show.

'It's got nothing to do with you, Mark. There's nothing you can do to stop us, just leave us alone.'

Mark gave the door a shove, and before she knew it he was inside.

'This is what you want, is it?' he asked. 'To have a baby when you're sixteen, and have everyone looking at you and talking about you?'

'Lots of girls have babies when they're my age.'

'Yeah,' Mark said, 'and what do you think people call them?'

'I don't care what people call me.'

'Fine,' Mark said, 'and what about what Jay did to you in the woods? You know that the next time you make him angry he'll do it again, and again, and again.'

'He won't.'

'Really? So he's never done anything like that any other time? He's never hurt you before?'

Sammie hesitated as she remembered Jay smashing her head into the tiles in her bathroom for no reason other than a bad mood.

'He doesn't mean to,' she said, 'he loves me.'

Mark watched her for a while. 'You really are going to leave with him?' he said.

'Yes.'

He nodded slowly. 'Okay,' he said, 'if you want to spend the rest of your life getting beaten up then that's up to you.'

'Can you leave now,' Sammie said, 'if you've said what you came here to say?'

'No,' Mark said, 'I'm not done yet. I knew you'd have your heart set on leaving. And I'll let you. But first you have to do one thing for me.'

...

Sammie laughed, though nervously. 'What do you mean, you'll "let" me?' she said. 'How the hell are you going to stop me?'

'I'll call your parents.'

Sammie was silent for a while. 'You wouldn't,' she said. 'And... you don't even have their numbers.'

'I do,' he said, 'my mum has your mum's mobile number, and anyone can get hold of the number for your dad's company. I'll call Jay's mum as well. I'll say I just found out what you've planned, and I'm worried about you. And I'll tell them you're pregnant, too.'

Sammie made her way over to the dining table and sat down. She felt faint, and her head was pounding again. 'No,' she said, 'you can't do this to me, Mark. I *have* to go away with him. I can't tell my parents what has happened, I need... I need to go.'

'I'm not just going to let you leave with him Sammie.'

Sammie slammed her hand against the table. 'What do you *want?*' she said. 'Tell me. What do you want from me?'

Mark looked at her meaningfully and after a few seconds Sammie understood. 'No,' she said, 'no. Not *that*. Are you being serious? Are you seriously asking me to... to *fuck* you?'

'No,' he snapped, 'you think I want to do *that* with *you?*'

'What... what do you want, then?'

Mark stepped closer to her and whispered in her ear.

'No,' she said, 'I'm not doing that either. I'm not having any kind of sex with you, Mark, and you can't ask me to! What's wrong with you? Do you… do you really think— '

'I thought you wanted to be with Jay,' Mark said, 'I thought you wanted your *baby* to have a dad.'

Sammie stood up. 'I'm going to call Jay,' she said, 'when he finds out what you're asking me to do—'

Mark caught her arm. 'Fine,' he said, 'call him if you want. But I'll still call your parents and his mum, and they'll stop you leaving. It won't achieve anything.'

'Jay'll kill you.'

'Jay's mad with me anyway. It makes no difference.'

'Mark, I'm not—'

'It's simple, Sammie. If you want to go and be with Jay, then you'll do what I'm asking, and I'll never bother you again. He never has to find out what you did.'

Sammie stared at Mark for a moment, and she realised he really was serious. She waited in the hope he would change his mind, then, reluctantly, she made her way towards the door out to the hallway and Mark stood up to follow her.

35

Mark seemed nervous as she led him upstairs to her bedroom, and at one point she caught sight of his hands, which were trembling, but she didn't comment on it.

Once they were in her room, he sat on the end of her bed and looked at her expectantly. 'Mark,' she said, with quiet desperation, 'please don't make me do this. I'm sorry if you've felt shut out since I came here, and I know you're angry with me, but I never meant to take Jay away from you.'

'I didn't come upstairs with you to talk,' he said.

Sammie sat down beside him, 'No,' she said, 'I know you didn't. Mark, listen to me. I know… I mean, I'm sure you feel like you want to start doing… sex things as soon as you can. Especially… especially with Jay going on about what me and him have done together. But don't you want it to be with someone special? Don't you want it to be with somebody who *wants* to be with you, not someone who… who has to?'

'It's my choice,' Mark said, 'and I'm choosing to do this with you now, like this.'

'Mark—'

'Take… take your clothes off, Sammie.'

He was shaking so badly now that Sammie reached out and touched his hand. Even though she hated him, part of her was beginning to pity him. Perhaps all the awful things he'd said to her after she told him she was pregnant really were just ignorance. If he really didn't know much about sex, or if his parents had given him strange information, perhaps it wasn't entirely his fault. 'I'm not going to do it,' she said, 'you know that. Just… let me and Jay go. Don't try to stop us.'

'Do what I asked, Sammie.'

'No.'

To her surprise, Mark took his phone out and called a number, and she heard someone answer at the other end. 'I'd like to speak to Mrs Kilburn,' Mark said, 'it's about her son, Jay.'

'No!' Sammie said. She grabbed the phone out of his hand and ended the call. 'You can't do this! You can't—'

'Then make it so I don't have to.'

'Mark, I... I'm *pregnant*—'

'Sammie, just do what I asked.'

Sammie waited a little while in case he changed his mind, but he clearly wasn't going to. Slowly, she took hold of the hem of her t-shirt and lifted it over her head. Mark wasn't really even looking at her, but she carried on with the instructions he'd given her in the kitchen, taking off the rest of her clothes until she stood in front of him naked. She thought at one point she saw his eyes flick over her bump, but he said nothing about it.

'Do you... do you want to stay sitting like that?' Sammie asked him. 'Or you can lie down on the bed if—'

'I'm fine like this.'

Sammie nodded and knelt down in front of him while he undid his jeans. She settled herself between his thighs and looked up at him one more time in the hope he'd change his mind, but he ignored her.

'Mark,' she said, 'please—'

Gently, he placed his hand on the back of her head and pushed it into his lap.

Sammie kept her eyes closed as much as possible. In a way it was easy enough to do the thing Mark wanted – she'd done it for Jay so many times, and if she closed her eyes she could pretend she was just doing it for him again. The couple of times she did look up Mark didn't seem happy, or excited, and she began to worry how long it was going to go on for if he wasn't even enjoying it. At one stage he reached down and touched her bare back and Sammie shivered, but she soon realised that wasn't the only thing he was doing. He'd touched her back to distract her, what he had really been doing was taking his phone from his jeans pocket, and she understood when she looked up, when she saw him holding the phone and realised she'd been tricked.

She stood up and immediately tried to grab the phone from his hand. 'No!' she said. 'What have you done? Mark—'

He managed to keep it out of her reach for a few more seconds, and then he simply handed it to her. Sammie looked at the image of herself on the screen. He'd caught her just as she started looking up, her eyes beginning to widen in shock, but there was no mistaking what her mouth was in the middle of doing. Then the phone popped up with the information that a message had been successfully sent. To Jay.

'No!' Sammie screamed. She threw the phone at Mark and then hit him, but he scrambled out of her way while fumbling to do his jeans back up. 'What have you done?' she said again. 'What have you *done*?'

Felicity

36

The next couple of weeks as I waited for Grace's wedding were hell. Jay insisted that I quit my job so I did, and spent my days with him in the van as he went round doing his deliveries. He watched my every movement. He expected us to continue trying for a baby, and not wanting to arouse suspicion I went along with it, and hoped my pills were well enough hidden that he wouldn't stumble across them and realise my deception. I went to see Mark a couple more times because Jay still wanted me to continue the plan, and he would wait outside – far enough away from the flat that Mark wouldn't spot him but close enough that I had to behave. I knew he was scared I'd make a run for it.

Mark told me very little about what he was planning for us, except that to say he thought he could get a transfer to a different office, and that everything was in hand. I trusted him – or at least I had little choice but to trust him – and said I would somehow get away from "Jason" when I got back from Grace's wedding, so he should be packed and ready to leave by then.

...

I couldn't bring myself to put much care into my appearance for the wedding. I wore a plain pale grey dress, only the lightest makeup and ran a comb through my hair and nothing more. At the last minute I grabbed a fuchsia pink scarf to place around my shoulders and give at least a small nod to what was supposed to be a happy day.

The hotel where Grace had her wedding was lovely. Not too

flashy or grand, but stylish, with sweeping lawns all around. Through the ceremony Jay sat by my side completely unmoved, while the sight of Grace in her simple ivory dress looking so obviously happy threw the mess of my life into stark contrast. I knew I wouldn't be able to see any of my friends again. Once I was gone, I'd be gone.

I was still thinking about this as we all spilled outside onto the lawn, and when Jay and I were offered glasses of champagne I took one without thinking twice, only for Jay to snatch it out of my hand. 'What the hell are you doing?' he hissed at me.

'What?' I said, genuinely not understanding.

'We're trying for a baby. What's wrong with you?'

He said it quietly enough that nobody could hear his words, but people had certainly seen us. A little way away Leanne and my other friends were watching from their circle. I'd barely spoken a word to them since we arrived. I understood that somehow I had made myself unwelcome. They'd put up with me for the hen party but communications from my friends had completely dried up since, and now I was on the outside.

'Sorry, Jay,' I mumbled. 'I forgot.'

He put my glass of champagne down on a table and found me an orange juice instead. I felt it made it obvious to everybody that I was either pregnant or trying to be and I realised that was probably partly what he intended.

The day passed uneventfully up until after we'd finished eating, in the early evening. There was a little bit of spare time where people were milling around and chatting, and having had several drinks Jay had struck up a conversation with some of the other guests, but he kept stealing glances at me. I saw all of my friends sat on some sofas the other side of the bar and I tried to summon up the courage to talk to them. I bought myself a rum and coke, thinking that appearance-wise at least it could pass for a soft drink, and I was about to make my way over to Leanne and the others when Jay appeared at my side.

'What is that?' he asked, clearly meaning my drink.

I tried to ignore him, but at that second it seemed my friends thought of something better to do, and without having noticed that I was trying to come and see them, they stood up en masse and disappeared outside. I turned to Jay. 'It's just a coke,' I said.

He took it out of my hand and had a sip himself.

'There's alcohol in that,' he said. He slammed it down on the bar, and I looked around but nobody seemed to have noticed. 'Do you think I'm stupid or something?' he asked me quietly.

'No,' I said.

'Then why are you drinking?'

I couldn't answer, and he took hold of my hand, gripping it very hard. I walked with him out of the bar and up the stairs to our hotel room, where he slammed the door behind me.

'I'll ask you again. Why are you drinking?' he said slowly.

'Because it's my friend's wedding,' I said, 'I just wanted to enjoy myself—'

'By getting pissed when you might be pregnant?' he shouted at me. 'What the fuck is wrong with you?'

'It was just one drink—'

He grabbed me and shook me. 'What kind of attitude is that?' he said.

'I'm sorry,' I said, 'but I don't think I'm pregnant yet, I'm sure it's okay—'

Jay looked at me for a very, very long time.

'Where are they?' he asked eventually.

'What?'

'Your pills!' he said. 'Your fucking pills. You're still taking them, aren't you?'

'You threw them away,' I said, 'I don't have any—'

'You're lying,' he said, 'I can see it in your face.'

He went to my overnight bag and started pulling things out of it, throwing my clothes and toiletries all over the floor.

'Jay!' I said. 'I don't have any pills!' Subconsciously, I clutched my handbag close to me, and he noticed immediately, snatching it from my hand and emptying it out onto the bed. Without hesitation he picked up the painkiller box that my pills were hidden inside.

'They're painkillers,' I said, 'I've been getting headaches—'

He opened the box and pulled out a sheet of contraceptive pills. 'They label painkillers with days of the week now, do they?' he said.

'Jay—'

Before I could get away he grabbed me and pushed me face first onto the bed. 'You lying fucking bitch,' he hissed into my ear. 'You let me think we were trying for a baby.'

'I'm sorry!' I cried, but he pushed my face into the duvet, muffling my voice and making it hard for me to breathe. With the hand that wasn't on the back of my head he lifted my dress and I made a little squealing noise in my throat.

'Jay,' I cried into the duvet with what little breath I had, 'I'm sorry.'

'Shut up!'

'I didn't feel... ready... to have—'

'I said shut up!' Jay said.

He let go of me briefly and I heard him undoing his trousers, so I tried to scramble away from him, but before I could get anywhere I was pressed against the bed again with both his hands around my throat. He squeezed harder and harder, until with terror I realised I couldn't draw breath and he was choking me. I tried to reach behind me to stop him but I couldn't seem to hurt him enough to make him release his grip. I felt him lean down close to me, his lips by my ear, and the words somehow got through to me while I clawed at his arms uselessly with my nails. 'Let me do it,' he said. 'Let me do it, and I won't hurt you.'

He still had his hands round my neck making it impossible for me to speak, so the only way I could show I agreed was to try to open my legs. The weight of his body was on me and he didn't realise straight away what I was doing, but finally he understood and let go of my throat, and I lay gasping against the duvet. I was still struggling for air as he pulled my knickers down over my thighs, and somewhere downstairs in the hotel I thought I heard music begin to play. Grace and her new husband were having their first dance.

37

Before we rejoined the party Jay looped my pink scarf around my neck to hide the marks he'd made and used his thumb to wipe a little stray makeup from under my eyes.

'You look beautiful, Fliss,' he said.

I smoothed down my dress with trembling fingers, and he took one of my hands in his. 'I love you,' he said.

I didn't answer and he continued to wait, his eyes fixed on the side of my face. I knew what he wanted me to say. 'I love you too,' I mumbled.

Downstairs we discovered a room next to the bar had been opened up for dancing. I wanted to sit down because my legs felt weak, but Jay insisted that we dance and held me pressed up against him, arms firmly around my waist. In the dim light and chaotic surroundings it was easy enough to close my eyes and let the odd tear spill out. After a few minutes Jay decided he wanted to kiss me and I went along with it, not even protesting when he decided to tastelessly leave one of his hands resting on my bum. It was getting late and most of the guests were drunk, but I hated the thought of how we'd look – how I was just letting Jay have his hands all over me like that. I told him I wanted to go for a wee but he followed me to the toilets and waited just outside the door.

'What's wrong with you?' he asked when I came out a good fifteen or twenty minutes later.

'Nothing's wrong,' I said unconvincingly, 'I feel a bit tired, that's all.'

With a quick glance around to check we weren't being observed he pulled me further down the corridor, away from where there might be people going back and forth and he pressed me against the wall.

'I've got a little surprise for you, Fliss,' he said.

I didn't answer, and he carried on. 'I was going to take you away to our new home tomorrow,' he said, 'but now I'm thinking, why wait?' He leaned close to me, 'I'm going to take you there tonight. Right now. Although actually, first, I think it's about time we ended our plan with Mark.'

...

It was about a two and a half hour drive back to Coalton, and when we got to the flat Jay started packing some bags. By the time he was done it was about two a.m.

'We won't take much,' he said, 'we'll buy everything we need when we get there.'

'Where...' I whispered, 'where are we going?'

'You'll like it,' he said.

He kept me by his side as he packed, and followed close beside me as we walked out to his van. My heart was pounding, but at the same time I kept reminding myself that he was taking me to Mark, and that was my chance to get away. Once I got to Mark's I could try to explain what was happening, and maybe the two of us could make a run for it. Even with Jay parked outside in his van, we had the element of surprise on our side – perhaps we could run out to Mark's car and get away without Jay catching us. I kept this thought in my mind as Jay drove us over there. There was no question of me failing. Whatever happened, I *had* to get away with Mark.

Outside Mark's house I sat quietly by Jay's side in the van as he outlined what he wanted me to do.

'Take your phone,' he said, holding it out to me, 'and call me just before you get inside so I can listen. I want to hear you tell him it's over. I want you to say you never cared for him, that you've been sleeping with someone else, and I want to hear his reaction.'

I nodded, but I felt afraid. Within seconds of me entering Mark's flat I knew the conversation wouldn't go as Jay expected.

'If you do this right, everything will be okay,' he said. He touched my hair. 'The house I've found… it's a bit of a mess but it's in a beautiful place in the countryside. I know you'll love it.'

I took my phone from him.

'Flissie,' he said, 'don't even think about using this to call anyone except me.'

I nodded again, and he lifted my chin with his hand.

'You're everything to me, Fliss,' he said.

I swallowed painfully.

'I'll see you in a few minutes,' he told me.

I called him as I walked up to Mark's front door, and slipped the phone back in my pocket with the call still connected. Mark took a little while to answer, and when he did his hair was all sticking up and he was wearing shorts and a scruffy t-shirt that was obviously what he'd had on in bed.

'Fliss,' he said, immediately alert, 'what is it, what's going—'

I quickly put my finger over my lips, and thankfully he took the hint and shut up. I brushed past him down the hall to his living room, where I noticed a few bags were packed and ready to go.

'I have something to tell you,' I said.

I looked round at him and he was frowning. He looked like he was about to speak, and I shook my head.

Once we were in the living room, I picked up a pen from the coffee table and Mark seemed to understand what I needed and grabbed an electric bill from a pile of post, turning it over so I could write on the back of it.

Jason is listening, I wrote. *Play along.*

'Mark,' I said, 'I… I don't want to see you any more.'

Mark sat down next to me. I could see from his face that he had no idea how to react or what to do.

'I… I don't understand,' he said eventually.

I took a few deep breaths. I knew we were making such a mess of the conversation that Jay probably already suspected, so I quickly took out my phone, ended the call and spoke very quickly to Mark.

'That was him on the phone,' I said, 'he was listening. I was supposed to split up with you, so now he already knows something is wrong. He is outside in his van. We need to leave.'

38

We had little choice but to make a dash for it out of the front door and to Mark's car. There was no other way out of the flat apart from through a window, and even if we did that we'd have to climb over a fence out of the garden and God knows what we'd do then. Jay was parked a reasonable distance from the flat, whereas Mark's car was right outside – we could get to it in seconds.

I'd never run so fast in my life as I did from Mark's front door round to the passenger side of his car, but then I found myself standing helplessly pulling at the handle, waiting for him to unlock it and let me in.

'Mark!' I screamed. 'Mark, open the car, open the car!'

But he didn't. He was stood, completely still, by the driver's side. The key in his hand was held out towards the lock, but he was staring at something down the pavement. 'Mark!' I screamed again. 'Mark, we've got to go!'

I was nearly hysterical. I couldn't understand what was wrong with him, and I yanked helplessly at the handle while he stood there, transfixed by something. Finally, I looked round towards whatever it was that had drawn his attention, and I realised immediately what the problem was. There on the pavement, not more than ten metres from us, was Jay.

'Mark,' I said, almost sobbing, 'Mark, please. We have to go—'

'Jay,' Mark said in wonder.

'Yes. It's Jay,' I said. 'I'll explain, I'll explain everything, please, please…'

Mark lowered his hand and the car keys. 'He… he followed me here,' he said. 'He followed me to Coalton. He found me.' He started to move away from the car, and took a step towards Jay. 'No!' I said. 'We have to go! Now!'

Mark walked towards Jay as though he was in a trance. Then, abruptly, he stopped and turned to me. 'What's he doing here?' he asked. 'How do you know him?'

I stared at him. 'He... *he's* Jason!' I said.

'He... what?'

'Jason *is* Jay,' I said. 'It was... it was all a plan, he wanted me to hurt you...' I couldn't think how to explain and I gave up. Mark looked from me back to Jay. 'Jay,' he said, 'is that... is that true?'

Jay looked levelly at Mark for a while, but he didn't answer him. Then he made a dash towards me.

...

Mark was so overwhelmed by the whole thing that he made no move to stop Jay. He watched as I tried to run but Jay grabbed me and put his hand over my mouth. 'I'm taking her now,' he said to Mark.

'I... I don't... understand,' Mark said.

'She's mine,' Jay said, 'and I'm taking her.'

Everything that was happening was too much for Mark to take in. He watched silently as Jay began to drag me towards the van, and although I screamed against Jay's hand Mark seemed paralysed with shock and confusion for so long that I was almost in the van before he did anything.

'You... you can't take her,' Mark said finally. 'She doesn't want to go with you.'

'She doesn't know what she wants,' Jay said.

'Jay,' Mark said gently, 'I think she does. Let her go.'

'What, so *you* can have her?'

Mark stared at Jay and then he nodded. 'I understand,' he said, 'I understand why you're doing this. But Felicity... Felicity isn't Sammie.'

At this, Jay flipped. He threw me towards the van, and I hit it and fell to the ground. 'You think I don't know that!' he yelled at

Mark. 'Look at her! Does she look like Sammie to you?' He grabbed Mark and made him look at me, as I struggled to pull myself to my feet. 'Look at her!' he said again. 'She's a piece of crap.'

He kicked me just as I was getting to my knees and I fell again.

'That's the best I can do now,' he told Mark, '*this*,' he aimed another kick at me, 'is the best that I can get.'

As if this admission suddenly unlocked a whole new well of hatred for me Jay started to kick me repeatedly, in my stomach, my chest, my hips. Things began to go fuzzy, but I heard Mark shout at Jay to stop. 'You're killing her!' he said desperately.

'Good,' I heard Jay say, seemingly from a great distance. I felt another blow and Mark grabbed hold of Jay to try to stop him. Just before I passed out I heard one more thing; Jay's voice, harsh and cold. 'Let me take her,' he said, 'let me take her, or I will kill her right here in front of you.'

...

I woke some indeterminate amount of time later. At first I thought I'd gone blind, because everything was black. Then I realised there were strange sounds; rumbling, like an engine, and I was pressed up with bags and boxes all around me, bouncing against a hard floor. I moaned loudly in my throat, as I couldn't open my mouth. It was covered with something that felt like tape. Somewhere nearby I could hear the fuzzy sounds of a radio, and there was no response to my moan. I tried to move my arms but I couldn't, and after several attempts I realised they were joined together at the wrists, and the same was true of my ankles. I was just trying to process this and what it meant but I didn't get very far before I fell unconscious again. The only thing I did manage to understand was that I was in the back of Jay's van, and we were on our way to our new home.

PART 4

Felicity

10 MONTHS LATER

39

When Jay got back from work, he was in a good mood. He was often in a good mood these days, and as usual he came straight upstairs to the bedroom, where I sat up in bed waiting.

'You'll never guess what I saw on the way home,' he announced.

'What?'

'It was this fucking *massive* bird,' he said. He held his hands out to emphasise its size. 'It was just swooping across the fields, I've never seen anything like it.'

He sat down on the bed and I smiled at him. 'What sort of bird was it?'

'God knows,' he said, 'it was awesome though.'

I shuffled closer to him. I found it funny how much he seemed to like being back in the countryside. He always seemed like somebody who would prefer the cleaner and less muddy life of a city. 'Jay, I need some new clothes,' I said.

He looked at me. 'Yeah,' he agreed, 'you're getting pretty big. I'll pick some up for you tomorrow.'

He put his hand on my bump, and then he lay down beside me so that his head was near it and just looked at it for a while.

'We should probably start getting some stuff for the baby, as well,' I said.

'I'll go shopping at the weekend.'

He stroked my bump gently and then he closed his eyes. I let him rest for a moment. I knew he enjoyed these first few minutes of getting home and being close to me and the baby.

'Jay,' I said, 'I'd like to be involved in choosing the clothes and the baby things.'

He thought about it. 'Okay,' he said, 'after dinner I'll get my laptop and we can pick out some things together, then I'll go and buy it when I get a chance.'

He sat up beside me. 'Felicity, you are happy aren't you?' he asked. 'I give you everything you need? You must tell me whenever you want anything.'

'I just did.'

'Yeah,' he said, 'but I mean anything. I don't want you to be sad. I never did this to make you miserable.'

'I know.'

He kissed me on the forehead and stood up. 'I'll make you some dinner,' he said.

When he came back upstairs a little while later he gave me a bowl of chicken and vegetable stir fry and sat beside me in the bed with his own portion. We ate together quietly, and then he sat with me while I looked at clothes and baby things on his laptop.

'I like this,' he said, after a few minutes.

'You like what?'

'This,' he said, 'us looking at stuff together. It's nice.'

'Well, we need to start getting things sorted,' I said, 'it's only a couple of months until the baby will be here.'

I put the laptop down. 'Jay, can we talk about what happens when the baby comes?'

'No,' he said, his mood immediately darkening. 'We've had this conversation.'

'Jay—'

'No,' he said.

He took the laptop away from me and went downstairs with our bowls from dinner balanced on top of it. 'I'll clear up,' he said, 'and then we'll get you washed and ready for bed.'

I waited patiently for him to come back. Getting bathed was a palaver. First of all he had to undo the chain that looped through the set of handcuffs to release my left wrist from the headboard in the bedroom. Then I would take all of my clothes off and he'd lead me to the bathroom where he'd watch me brush my teeth and then I'd get in the bath and kneel while he washed me with the shower attachment. Some days, and today was apparently one of those days, he would run me a bath so I could have a more relaxing experience. I lay in the bubbles for a while, and then I decided I would have to try talking to him again. 'Jay,' I said.

'Mm?'

'We have to discuss what happens when the baby is due —'

'No, we don't,' he said. 'I told you earlier. Just leave it Fliss.'

He picked up a bottle of shampoo and handed it to me. 'Give your hair a wash,' he said.

I did as he asked, and then he rinsed it clean for me. 'How have you felt today?' he asked me. 'You were having some pains this morning, weren't you?'

I put my hand on my bump. 'They were just little twinges,' I said, 'they stopped not long after you left for work.'

'Good.' He looked me over. 'I'll do your eyebrows,' he said.

He got some tweezers, and I closed my eyes as he started plucking at the hairs. He'd looked up on the internet how to do it, as he didn't trust me with any sharp objects, but apparently he couldn't bear for me to look un-groomed either.

Strangely enough, as I lay with him gently tweezing my eyebrow hairs, I realised he liked doing it. I could tell he was fairly calm and relaxed, concentrating on his task.

'Jay,' I said quietly, 'are *you* happy?'

He stopped tweezing and I opened my eyes. 'Do you really like living like this, with me?' I asked.

Jay lowered the tweezers back towards my face. 'Yes,' he said, 'I told you that earlier, didn't I?'

'I know, but... isn't it a lot of hard work?'

I knew already that it was. Every morning he had to get up, get himself ready for work, make me breakfast, and bring some food up for me to eat for lunch later on, then untie me and supervise me while I changed out of my nightwear into some clean clothes, tie me back up again, do a full shift of deliveries, then come home and do the cooking, cleaning, housework, and supervise me as I got washed, sort out the bucket on the bedroom floor that served as my bathroom, then go to bed and start out all over again the next day. Added to that, he still sometimes went out running, and he was trying to do up the house.

Jay didn't really speak about our practical or financial situation, but I understood that he wasn't being charged much rent for the house we lived in because it was in such a poor state of repair. The landlord was apparently hoping we'd do the place up in exchange for paying him so little, though he never checked whether any work was being carried out and was apparently quite happy to ignore us and leave us to it. I wasn't even sure whether he was aware I existed; for all I knew Jay may have told him he intended to live in the house alone. In any case, some evenings, and at the weekend, Jay would makes attempts at DIY – some more successful than others. It was rare I was allowed to venture anywhere except the upstairs bedroom and bathroom, but I had been downstairs on a few occasions under close supervision and seen the woodchip walls in the lounge, the brown seventies tiles in the kitchen and the general air of tired decrepitude, and I knew it got Jay down.

Jay didn't seem like he was going to answer my question, so I asked him again. 'Don't you get tired?' I asked. 'Of how much you have to do all the time?'

'Yes,' he said, 'I get tired.'

'Don't you... don't you sometimes wish—'

Jay threw the tweezers down on the floor. 'Don't even say it!' he said. 'Don't you even say it.'

'Say what?'

Jay eyed me suspiciously. 'You were going to ask me if I

wished it wasn't like this, or that it didn't have to be this way.'

'Was I?'

'You know this isn't what I want, but you don't give me any choice.'

'I know,' I said, 'I know, I'm sorry... I just... I worry how exhausted you might get.'

'Don't worry about that,' Jay said, 'I *want* to look after you. I'll always look after you.'

40

The next day was a Saturday, and Jay worked in the morning before arriving home mid afternoon with groceries, and on this occasion, some clothes for me and a few of the baby things I'd chosen; a flat-packed cot and some curtains and other bits for the nursery. He came upstairs and showed me everything and then he stroked my hair and gave me a quick kiss. 'I've had an idea,' he said.

'Okay.'

'I'm going to untie you, and we're going to spend the rest of the weekend decorating the nursery together.'

I stared at him. 'Really?'

'I thought about what you said. I want to have a relationship with you again. It's going to be very hard for me to trust you, but we can start making some little steps.'

He undid my wrist and smiled at me. 'Come on, then,' he said, 'let's go.'

I followed him out of the bedroom and into the nursery next door, where he slept on a mattress on the floor. He had stopped sleeping with me once I became pregnant, saying that he didn't want to stress me and the baby out. I wondered sometimes what he did for sex now, because I didn't believe he could ever be content dealing with his needs himself. On a few occasions I had heard him go out somewhere in the middle of the night, and the fact that when he came home he always had a shower made me not want to wonder about it any more, because I had a suspicion about what he was doing, and I didn't really want to think about it.

I helped him carry his "bed" out of the room, and he put down a large pot of creamy white paint along with a couple of rollers.

'We need to wash the walls first,' I said, touching the existing grotty blue paintwork. 'Like you did in the main bedroom.'

Jay scowled. I was the one who'd had to explain to him how to go about decorating the main bedroom, as he had no clue about any of it.

'It's fine,' I said, 'just go and get the sugar soap and some cloths. And sandpaper.'

I knew what the problem was. Those things were in a different room and he didn't want to leave me unsupervised, yet he also didn't want to go back on his promise to let me help him. In the end his caution won out and he put me back in the main bedroom and locked it from the outside, like he did when he was at work.

When he came back up I could see his mood was beginning to take a turn for the worse, but he let me out and we started work on the walls in the nursery.

'I wish...' he said, after a while, 'I wish I could trust you.'

'You can,' I said.

'I know what you're doing,' he said, 'you'll leave the second you get an opportunity. You're just playing a long game and waiting until I give you enough freedom that you won't have to fight me.'

'We're never going to have a relationship if you believe that,' I said. I tried to keep my voice light, but inside I could have screamed. It was exactly what I was trying to do.

'I guess we'll never have a relationship, then,' he said.

...

Despite what he said, he relaxed a little as the day went on. He still kept a close eye on me, but he stayed calm and even let me come downstairs for dinner, which to my surprise was pizza, although true to form he put a big bowl of salad down on the table to go with it. I helped myself to some while he sorted out drinks for us both, giving me a glass of apple juice and himself some mineral water from a bottle in the fridge.

'Maybe you should think about trying to get a job working with food,' I told him, 'isn't that what you wanted to do, when you were younger?'

He sat down at the table. 'That was a long time ago,' he said. 'I thought I might try to get an HGV license.'

I put my slice of pizza down. 'You want to be a lorry driver?' Jay carried on eating, ignoring me for a while. 'Jay?' I said.

'I don't know,' he said, 'maybe. I need to earn more money.'

'Will you earn more money doing that?'

He shrugged.

'Jay,' I said slowly, 'wouldn't driving a lorry mean you had to go away overnight?'

'Probably.'

'Then, how will you look after me?'

'I don't know,' he said, 'I'd figure it out.'

I munched through my pizza quietly.

'You know what I wanted to do, when I was younger?' I said.

'No,' Jay replied, but he looked interested. 'Didn't you always want to make jewellery?'

'No,' I said, 'not always. Before that I wanted to be a blacksmith.'

Jay frowned.

'Yeah, exactly,' I said, 'that's the response I got when I told the career advisor who came to the school once. Actually, I think she laughed. I mean, how many blacksmiths do you think there are nowadays?'

'None?' Jay suggested.

'Well, there are some,' I said, 'but it was never very realistic.'

Jay considered what I'd said for a moment. 'What's your point?' he asked.

'I don't know,' I said, 'I don't have a point. I'm just... talking.'

We fell into silence until we'd almost finished eating. 'Fliss,' Jay said finally, 'The only reason I'm talking about changing job is so I can look after you and the baby better. That's all I think about. You know that, don't you? Since you got pregnant, it drew a line under everything that happened before. I've forgiven you for everything you did.'

I found suddenly that I couldn't swallow, as I remembered how angry he'd been that I was going to run away with Mark. I'd thought he would never stop punishing me for it.

'Jay, can I ask you something?' I said.

'Of course you can.'

'When he... when he saw you again... his reaction was strange. Mark, I mean.'

'We don't mention that man's name in this house,' Jay said flatly.

'I know, but... Jay...he seemed... it was like he seemed *pleased* in a way, to see you.'

Jay shrugged. 'He's a weirdo,' he said.

'Yeah, but—'

'Let's not talk about it any more.'

After dinner we did a little more painting, and instead of Jay washing me in the bath like he usually did I had a shower on my own while he hovered on the landing outside. We curled up in bed together and watched a bit of TV, then Jay attached me to the headboard again for the night.

'I'll see you in the morning,' he said.

'Jay,' I said.

'Yeah?'

'Why don't you stay in here tonight and sleep with me?'

Jay thought about it for a long time. 'I'm not sure it's a good idea,' he said.

'You could just sleep here, couldn't you?' I asked. 'I mean, no sex, we could just be in here together.'

'Why?'

'Because I'd like to try it. And besides, the nursery smells of paint, you can't sleep in there.'

Jay stood up.

'Jay, please,' I said. 'Can't we try?'

'Yes,' he said, 'that's what I'm doing.'

'Why are you going then?'

'Fliss,' he said, 'calm down. I'm coming back. Just let me

brush my teeth.'

41

I lay awake half the night by Jay's side, but the problem was he did too. I knew he was scared that if he fell asleep I'd find some way to attack him, although how he thought I'd detach myself from the bed I had no idea. I knew full well he wouldn't be stupid enough to have the handcuff keys with him in bed or even in the room, and if I knew how else to release myself I'd have done it a long time ago. In the early days I'd spent hours trying to think of ways to get out of the handcuff, chain, headboard arrangement, but it had proved futile. Jay had even attached the legs of the bed to the wall with heavy metal fixings, so I couldn't move or drag it across the floor. I'd tried calling out when I heard the postman come to the door, but as far as I could tell he never heard me, and we didn't get much in the way of post anyway. I understood from rare occasions when I had looked out of windows that the house was deep in the countryside. There were no neighbouring houses, and on one side we were hidden by woods, while to the other were rolling fields. There were a couple of buildings dotting these fields in the distance, but they were too far away to be of any use to me.

We carried on with the nursery the next day, and had almost finished painting by mid-afternoon. Jay brought mugs of tea upstairs and we sat on the floor with them, talking about our progress on the room, and what we'd do next. Then I decided that after the failure of him sleeping in the same bed with me that I'd try something more radical.

'I want to have sex with you,' I said bluntly.

Jay smiled. 'No, you don't,' he said.

'I do. It's been months, Jay. I still have feelings.'

Jay slammed his mug of tea down on the floor and glared at me. 'You really think I don't understand what you're trying to do,' he said.

'I'm trying to have sex with my boyfriend.'

Jay stood up and picked up the paintbrush he was using for the fiddly bits around the door frame.

'If you need sex, Felicity, you're more than welcome to go in the bedroom and take care of it on your own. Or do it right in here in front of me if you want. But don't treat me like an idiot.'

He started painting the thin strip of wall between the door frame and the ceiling, and I stood up.

'How are you ever going to know if you can trust me if you never let me show you how I feel?' I said. 'Isn't it possible that I might want you? Have you ever even thought about that?'

He watched me for a long time. Then his face changed. He threw his paintbrush down, making a spatter of white droplets across the floor. 'You want me to have sex with you, do you?' he said.

'Yes.'

He took hold of my arm and dragged me into the bedroom, where he pushed me onto the bed and laid down next to me. He kissed me briefly, so hard it was almost painful, then he leant down to my ear. 'Have you heard me go out at night, Fliss?' he asked me.

'Ye...yes,' I said.

'Do you know where I go?'

'I don't want... I don't *need* to know.'

His hand moved to the top of my jeans and no matter how hard I tried to stop it, my body stiffened.

'You don't want me,' he said.

'I do! I'm nervous, that's all—'

'I *pay* for it,' Jay hissed in my ear, 'that's where I go.'

'It doesn't matter,' I said, 'I don't mind—'

Jay thrust his hand down my jeans and my body betrayed me again, reacting so strongly to the touch of his fingers that a kind of convulsion of horror went through my waist and my hips and Jay took his hand away.

'Don't treat me like this,' Jay said, 'don't fucking lie to me, you stupid, little, *bitch!*'

He was kneeling next to me on the bed now, shouting down into my face, and I couldn't help but start to cry.

'How gullible do you think I am?' he said. 'Do you think I'm stupid?'

'No,' I moaned.

'You think I don't know that you're trying to run away with the baby, with *my* baby—'

'I'm not,' I said, 'I'm not, I swear—'

'You're lying!' he said. 'Admit it. Admit it to me.'

He slapped me. 'Admit it,' he said. He slapped me again, and again, and again, until finally I snapped.

'Fine!' I cried. 'I was trying to leave! But what choice do I have? What are you offering our baby? I am scared, Jay! What's going to happen if I go into labour and you're not here? What's going to happen when the baby's born and I can't even get out the house if I need to take it to the doctor? Women *die* giving birth, Jay, and babies can die, and I've never even seen a doctor or a midwife, let alone had a scan, and I don't want to live trapped in a room for the rest of my life with a child who's never even been outside! What happens when it's supposed to go to school and we've never registered the birth? What happens when it starts asking why mummy is locked up like a prisoner, and where daddy goes in the middle of the night? Do you want your child to realise one day what you did, that you locked me up in the house, forced me to have a baby and then got your kicks by going out to have sex with prostitutes?'

Jay stared down at me, then he grabbed my wrist and wrenched it back towards the headboard, cuffing me straight to it rather than using the chain that allowed me greater movement.

'How dare you talk to me like that?' he said. 'When I do *everything* for you—'

'Well I don't want you to!' I screamed. 'I hate you! I hate it here, and I don't want my baby anywhere near you. You're a pathetic, weak, *sick* man—'

'Sick?' Jay said. 'How am I sick? When I care for you, and

cook for you, and fucking *wash* you—'

'Because you keep me here like a prisoner!' I shouted. 'And… and do you know what else? I know what you have inside that shoebox!'

Jay's face went white.

'What?' he whispered.

'I know that Sammie is missing,' I said, 'and I know that you hurt her, and I know that she was pregnant!'

He was still staring at me in disbelief. 'Mark told me some of it,' I said, 'and I discovered the rest myself. The newspaper article, and those pictures. Of Sammie.'

I could see the shock on his face. 'That's right,' I said. 'I found them, and I looked at them. It's *disgusting* Jay. *You're* disgusting. That what keeps you warm at night, is it? Does it make you feel like a man, looking at pictures of an underage teenage girl—'

Jay hit me again, but this time everything went black.

42

For the next couple of weeks or so Jay and I reached an unstable truce. He stayed suspicious of me, unsurprisingly since I'd made it crystal clear how little I wanted to be with him, and he punished me in small ways; taking my books and magazines away or hiding the remote control so I couldn't watch my little TV, or not giving me enough food, so that when he got home I was starving and he could make me beg for something to eat. For four days in a row he didn't bathe me or let me change my clothes, until I think I began to look and smell bad enough that he was forced to act. If I irritated or provoked him in even the smallest most unintentional way he'd slap me, and sometimes he'd put my dinner on the floor, so I had to eat it like a dog.

Gradually, I began to realise that this room I had spent all these long months in really would be where I gave birth, and where I started caring for my baby. Why we'd even bothered painting and furnishing a nursery, I could only guess. It was just a stupid dream; some idea of Jay's that everything would be okay. I could see that in reality I'd be locked in the bedroom indefinitely, with the baby in its cot by my side, and these four walls would be my whole world.

As the days went on I kept trying to think of ways to save myself. I knew my best option was not so much escape, which was difficult and dangerous, but instead to call for help.

As far as I knew there were two devices I potentially had access to that I could use to contact the outside world – Jay's laptop and Jay's phone. The phone he took with him whenever he left the house and the laptop he hid somewhere. When he spent time with me upstairs his phone was generally not in his pocket – where presumably he thought I might steal it – instead he left it downstairs, knowing perhaps that my chances of getting free from my handcuffs, running downstairs, and calling somebody before he stopped me were basically zero. He'd also told me on several occasions that there was no phone signal inside the house, and sure enough he had gone outside to make calls on several occasions, though whether this was really to get signal or to avoid being overheard I couldn't be sure. Inside the house, his phone or laptop would automatically connect to the internet assuming the router was on, and Jay regularly used the internet, albeit not usually in my presence. Events like looking for clothes and baby things online together were few and far between, and he never took his eyes off me for a second when they did happen.

I was trying to imagine what sort of scenario I could create that would involve me either stealing one of these devices or him accidentally leaving them in the room with me, when fate intervened and delivered an opportunity, so unexpectedly I almost didn't see it before it was too late.

It was one night that I had been sleeping badly. The baby was restless, I felt hot and panicky and uncomfortable, and the anxieties I already had about the birth made me start imagining things were wrong. I called out to Jay, and he came and sat with me, holding my hand and trying to soothe me.

'You're okay, Fliss,' he said, 'you're okay.'

He used his phone to check on my symptoms, asking me questions and reassuring me when the website gave him answers. I fell into an exhausted sleep near dawn, and soon after he went to have a shower before work, and though he left the room, his phone didn't. It was still on the bedside table, and I woke up because it made the little chiming sound that alerted him he had an email.

I very nearly went straight back to sleep. I was exhausted and I didn't immediately grasp the significance of the sound, but something in my mind made the connection and I sat bolt upright, looking around the room until my eyes suddenly came to rest on the bedside table, and when I saw the phone really was there my breath caught in my throat. I had to blink several times to reassure myself I wasn't seeing things.

It was easy to reach across and grab it. It felt bizarre in my hands; the first time I'd held a phone since he brought me to the house. I felt absurdly guilty, and my cheeks began to grow hot. Now I had it, I didn't know what to do with it. I sat stupidly, gripping the thing in my hand, my mind completely blank. I could hear the shower, but it wasn't a loud shower and there was no extractor fan in the bathroom that would obscure any sounds I made. If I phoned somebody and started talking, there was every chance he would hear me, and in any case I saw he had been telling the truth. The phone had no signal. My only hope was to get in touch with someone online.

My hands were shaking as I logged in to my email account and I could immediately see Mark had contacted me, and contacted me a lot. There were hundreds of messages from him, far too many to read. In the bathroom, the sound of the shower stopped. I had five minutes, tops, before Jay came in to get dressed, perhaps far less. I tried to think. This was my only chance, but the pressure meant I couldn't gather my thoughts. What the hell should I say? I took a slow, deep breath. I had no time to write an elaborate message, I just needed Mark to know where I was. I opened up a map online, my heart in my throat as I waited for it to load. Every second I thought I'd hear Jay's footsteps, but then I could make out the sound of the bathroom tap, so he must still be in there doing something. The map finished loading, and to my relief I didn't even need to do anything to trigger it to tell me where I was, it was showing my location automatically, and there on the map was a big, round marker. I didn't have time to investigate more fully. The area around us was pretty blank, I could see that much; few roads, no close towns. That was about what I had worked out myself about our location, and from that point of view at least the map looked accurate.

With fumbling fingers I tried to figure out how I could send the location to Mark, but my mind wouldn't work properly. I didn't know if I could send him the address of the page I was on

– would that contain my location? I pressed desperately on the marker hovering over our house on the map, and somehow I managed to bring up a little window that showed some coordinates. I took a deep breath, trying clumsily to highlight them while my stomach churned and my vision seemed simultaneously both heightened and blurred. The tap in the bathroom turned off, and I heard Jay moving around. Any second I thought I'd hear the bathroom door open. Maybe he was messing around with his hair. I hoped that was it, because that could buy me another five or even ten minutes. Somehow, impossibly, I managed to copy the coordinates to the clipboard and open up my emails again. I hit reply on the most recent email from Mark and pasted the coordinates into the message. I wanted to write something, but then I heard Jay moving around again and I lost my nerve. I hit send with no additional information. I heard the handle turning on the bathroom door and my heart started pounding so hard I thought I would pass out. I did my best to make sure neither the email nor the maps page were still open on his phone, practically threw it back down on the bedside table, and curled up into a ball under the covers, my eyes tightly closed.

'Fliss?' Jay said when he came in. He could obviously tell something wasn't right, because some concern crept into his voice as he said, 'Fliss, are you okay?'

He made his way over to me and put his hand on my forehead, and I pretended that I had only just woken up. 'You're all hot and clammy,' he told me. 'Do you want me to stay off work to keep an eye on you?'

I shook my head. 'I'm just tired,' I said in my best sleepy voice.

'Are you sure?' he said. 'You don't want me to stay a bit longer?'

'I want to go to sleep.'

'Okay,' he said, 'I'll bring up some food for you, and then I'll try to get home early.'

He stood up to go, but then his eyes fell on his phone. He

glanced across at me, but I pretended not to notice, so he just scooped it up in his hand. But then he did, and said, a very strange thing. He touched the sapphire necklace around my neck – which he insisted I wore all the time – and bent down to kiss my forehead. Then, with his lips hovering just above my skin, he said, 'I love you, Sammie.'

'Jay?' I whispered, frightened.

'It's okay, Sammie,' he said, 'everything is going to be okay. Everything I do is for you. For you and our baby. Just like you wanted.'

Sammie

43

'You need to leave,' Mark said to Sammie.

'That's what I'm trying to do! I'm trying to leave with Jay.'

Mark held up the phone to her so she was forced to look again at the picture he'd just sent to Jay.

'I mean alone,' he said. 'You've got no choice, Sammie. Surely you can see that it's impossible for you to be with Jay now. Once he's seen my message—'

'I have to go and see him. I have to explain.'

'Sammie,' Mark said softly, 'how are you going to explain?'

Sammie's eyes filled with tears. 'How could you do this to me?' she asked him. 'How could you do this, Mark? I... I'm *pregnant—*'

'And now you've cheated on him,' Mark said, 'with me. You can't expect him to support you now.'

Sammie shook her head. 'What's wrong with you?' she said, 'You... you're... you're *evil.*'

Mark stood up. 'I'm going home,' he said, 'and if you know what's good for you, you'll get your bags and leave. *You've* made it so that you can't stay here. Don't blame me.'

Sammie let him leave and sat down on the bed. There was still another hour before her and Jay were supposed to be catching the bus into town. Perhaps in that time she could talk him round. No matter what Mark said, there had to be a way of getting Jay to understand that Mark had tricked her, and she owed it to herself and the baby to try.

She was terrified as she walked to Jay's house. Her legs were shaking, and she had to stop and rest with her hand against a tree at one point, taking deep breaths to try to calm herself. When she got to Jay's house, it was a long time before he came down to answer the door, and when he did, he looked her up and down and simply said, 'Come upstairs.'

She followed him, not sure whether to start explaining straight away or to wait until he brought the picture up himself. Once inside his room he closed the door, then he picked up his phone and showed her the picture of herself with Mark.

'Jay,' Sammie said, 'Jay... I...'

He slapped her across the face. 'You fucking little slut,' he said.

Sammie could taste blood. She lifted her hand to her mouth, and when she lowered it again her fingertips were red.

'He says that's not the first time,' Jay told her. 'He says he's fucked you, too. He says he did you earlier, right before you sucked him off.'

'No,' Sammie said, 'no, that's not true. He's lying again—'

Jay grabbed her and thrust the phone in front of her face. 'This,' he said, 'is *this* a lie?'

'No! It was a trick, he made me—'

'He made you? He made you give him a blowjob?'

'Yes,' Sammie sobbed.

'How? I don't see him holding you and stuffing it down your throat.'

'I came round to explain,' she said quietly. 'He said he was going to stop us leaving unless I did it—'

Jay caught hold of her hair. 'I don't believe you!' he said.

I know,' Sammie said, as calmly as she could, 'but you have to listen to me—'

Jay twisted his hand in her hair. 'I'm done with that!' he said, 'I'm done with fucking *listening!*'

He used the hand in her hair to give her a shove so hard it sent her sprawling against his desk and she stumbled to her knees.

'Jay,' she said, 'it's not what—'

He walked over to her and she looked up at him. 'Your mouth,' he said, touching her lip with his finger, 'I've *kissed* your mouth. Would you have let me kiss you today? Straight after you'd been doing *that*,' he pointed at his phone.

'No!' Sammie said. 'Yes... I... I don't know—'

He hit her and her face smacked against the corner of the desk, catching her nose. A few drops of blood splashed into her lap, and she could feel it trickling over her lips.

'Jay...' she said, but she could feel herself starting to grey out. He grabbed her by her hair again and forced her to look up at him.

'How many times?' he asked her. 'How many times have you done things like this with him?'

'Not...' Sammie said, '...none.'

He threw her down onto the carpet and for a moment Sammie thought it would be over and he'd leave her alone, until she felt a blow that caught her in her thigh and she realised he was kicking her.

'No,' Sammie said, as she realised he was going to do it again. 'Jay, you can't! You can't. The baby—'

He stopped, just staring at her. But then they heard a noise from the hallway and Jay's eyes snapped towards his bedroom door. 'What was that?'

He rushed to the door and opened it, and as he looked out Sammie heard the unmistakable sound of the front door slamming closed.

'That was my mum,' Jay said, horrified, 'that was my *mum*!' He stared at her, open-mouthed. 'What if she heard?' he said.

'Jay—'

'You stupid bitch,' he yelled, aiming another kick at her, then another. 'What the fuck am I going to say to her?'

Sammie gasped for breath. His foot had caught her first in her ribcage, then in her stomach. Jay looked at her, and then he realised something. 'You've got blood on the carpet!' he said. He pulled her up and she lolled against the door. She could see the blood from her nose had dribbled all down her top as well as onto the floor.

Jay walked over to the window and Sammie heard a car door.

'Why was she even here?' Jay asked. 'She never said she'd come home in the morning.'

Jay slammed his hand against the window pane and Sammie let out a little gasp. Then she closed her eyes and lost consciousness.

When she came round she was on the floor. Whether she had slid back down to the floor herself or Jay had put her there she wasn't sure, but there was a thick pile of tissues underneath her face to stop her bleeding on the carpet.

'You're awake,' Jay said when he noticed her eyes were open. She thought she could hear relief in his voice, but it wasn't echoed in his words. 'Now you can get out,' he said.

'I'm not... leaving,' Sammie said, 'I'm not leaving... until you understand.'

'I got another message from Mark,' he said. He passed the phone down to her, and Sammie read what Mark had said.

Im sorry i had 2 send u that photo. Its been goin on for weeks, i felt too guilty 2 keep lying so i had 2 show u what sammies really like.

'No,' Sammie said, 'that's not true!'

Jay snatched the phone out of her hand and Sammie rested her head against the door. 'I don't feel well,' she said quietly. She held her hand out to Jay, though she knew he wouldn't help her. 'Please,' she said.

'Is it mine?' Jay asked. 'The baby. Or do you not know?'

'Of course it's yours! Jay, I've never been with anyone except you—'

'Really?' Jay said. 'And if you hadn't been caught out by the photo today, would you also sit there and tell me that *nothing* had ever happened between you and Mark?'

'No... I... I don't know.'

She held her hand out for a second time, and Jay looked

down at it.

'What do you want?' he said.

'I don't... I don't feel well. Please. The baby....'

There was silence for a while. 'Please,' Sammie said again, 'please Jay. Just listen to me.'

'I don't want to listen to you. I want you to get out.'

Sammie carefully pulled herself up until she could sit on the bed beside him. She noticed for the first time since she'd got there that there were a couple of bags packed and waiting in front of Jay's wardrobe, and the knowledge that he'd been ready to run away with her gave her the strength to carry on trying to persuade him.

'Jay, I promise you, Mark made me do it. I know it sounds stupid, but he said he'd stop us... why do you think your mum suddenly turned up here?' she said. 'Mark called her work when I was with him earlier, he didn't speak to her because I stopped him, but whoever he spoke to must have told her someone phoned and—'

'Just get out, Sammie.'

'No,' she said, 'you have to listen. We're going to have a child together. I know... I know things have gone wrong between us, but the baby happened because we *love* each other, Jay. This baby, *our* baby. It's made out of love.' A tear spilt from her eye as she remembered how it had actually been made, and she pushed the thought aside.

Jay grabbed her hair and pushed her down onto the bed, holding her face pressed against the duvet. 'How stupid are you?' he yelled at her. 'I don't have to love a girl to get her pregnant. I don't even have to know her name! That's how *special* it is.'

'Let go of me. Let go of me, Jay.'

He carried on holding her hair. 'Why *should* I believe it's mine?' he said. 'Why should I take your word for it? It could be anyone's!'

'No,' Sammie said. 'I told you, I've only had sex with you, it can only be yours. I know it's a lot to take in, but soon... soon you'll come to—'

Jay twisted his hand in her hair and Sammie had to choke back tears. 'Come to what?' he said. 'Come to *love* it?'

'Yes,' Sammie said, 'because it's yours. It's your little son, or daughter.'

Jay leant down very close to her. 'Listen to me,' he said, 'that thing inside you; it's nothing to do with me. It's trash, Sammie. It's not wanted, it's not loved, and if it isn't already dead from what I've done to you, I want you to go and get rid of it. Do you understand?'

Sammie didn't answer and Jay twisted his hand so hard that her hair started to pull loose from her scalp. 'Do you?' he said again.

Sammie nodded.

'You better do,' he told her, 'because I don't want *it*, and I certainly don't want *you*.'

Felicity

44

Once Jay had left for work I waited anxiously. I was sure that if Mark had seen the email and left straight away he would arrive in enough time to help me, but I had no way of knowing if he'd got the email, or whether he'd understood it if he had.

The hours dragged, and I began to feel genuinely ill. My pulse raced uncontrollably, and I felt sweaty and frightened and nauseous. When I heard a car door outside I nearly jumped out of my skin, even though it was what I'd been waiting for. There was a knock on the front door, though I could only just hear it from where I lay locked in the bedroom. I called out, but it was no good. I knew from experience trying to call out to the postman that my voice didn't carry well to the outside.

There was another knock on the door, then silence, and I began to worry it wasn't Mark. It seemed almost too much to hope for, after all. I braced myself for the sound of the car door again, but instead, frighteningly loud, came the sound of smashing glass downstairs, so that I screamed in shock.

'Felicity?' a voice called out. 'Felicity? Are you in here?' It was still a little muffled, but the words and the voice were unmistakable.

'Mark!' I shouted. 'I'm upstairs.'

When he finally drew back the bolt on the outside of the bedroom door and came inside, it was as though I was in a dream – he really had got my message, and he really had come. For the briefest moment all I saw in his face was relief, then his eyes fell to my bump, and then to the handcuffs and the loop of silver chain that was attaching me to the bed.

'No,' he said, his eyes back on the bump again, 'oh no. No. No...'

He took a few stumbling steps towards me and I reached my hand out to him.

'This is all my fault,' he said when he reached me. 'This is all my fault.'

I pulled him down onto the bed beside me where he sat with his head in his hands. 'Help me, Mark,' I said calmly.

'I...' he said into his hands, 'I can't...'

'Mark,' I said, 'for God's sake, we need to be quick. Jay knows he accidentally left his phone in here with me this morning, he's probably already suspicious.'

Mark lowered his hands from his face, but he seemed transfixed by the sight of my body, staring at my bump as though he'd never seen anything like it before.

'Did he... did he do that by forcing you?' he asked.

'Mark—'

'Did he?' Mark asked again.

'Mark,' I said, as calmly as I could, 'we can talk about this another time. You need to get me out of here. Now.'

Slowly, as though he was in a daze, Mark got up and came to look at the handcuffs and the chain that attached me to the bed. 'Where does he keep the key?' he asked.

'He keeps it with him,' I said, 'I don't think there's a spare one in the house.'

Mark took hold of the metal bar of the headboard and tested its strength, then he did the same with the chain.

'They're strong,' I said, 'I've tried.'

Mark stood up and started pacing. 'Does Jay have any tools?' he asked finally. 'Anything that can get through metal?'

'I don't know. Not that I know of. There's a garage outside but I don't think there's much in there, just some old stuff that belongs to our landlord—'

Mark looked again at my wrist and the headboard. 'I don't know how to get you out,' he said. 'I don't know what to do... I don't know what to do.'

'Then call the police!' I said. 'Or have you already?'

Mark stared at me as though I was talking nonsense. 'The police,' I said, 'you must have called them when Jay took me. Say that you've found where I am and…'

I trailed off at Mark's expression. I could see he'd never called the police.

'Mark,' I said slowly, 'you did… you did get the police to look for me when Jay took me, didn't you?'

Sammie

45

Sammie checked carefully up and down the street before she left Jay's house, because she didn't want anyone to see the state she was in. She held her hand up to her nose, which thankfully had stopped bleeding, and dashed down the road as fast as she could considering how unwell she felt, and towards the quieter lane that led to her own house. When she heard someone call out her name she froze in horror, and when she turned she saw it was Mark.

'Leave me alone,' she said, though he wasn't close enough to hear, 'leave me alone, leave me alone.'

She started to run, but she stumbled as she left the pavement to turn down the little lane, and she fell against a hedge, scratching her arm on some brambles. Mark caught up with her and pulled her hand away from her face so he could see what damage Jay had done.

'Why didn't you leave?' he said. 'Why didn't you leave like I told you to?'

Sammie pushed Mark away from her and carried on walking towards her house. 'Don't follow me,' she said. 'Please. *Please* just... let me be.'

He ignored her and followed her down the lane and up the driveway to her house, right to the kitchen door.

'What do you want?' Sammie turned and yelled at him, her voice startlingly loud on the still summer afternoon. 'What else could you possibly want? Do you... do you want to finish what we started doing earlier, is that it? Is that it, Mark?'

He stayed standing silently behind her, and on a crazy whim

she thrust her hand into his crotch, cupping him through his jeans and he jumped back, almost in fright.

'I don't think you even could,' she said, 'you weren't even properly *hard* earlier.'

Mark was still just watching her.

'Is *that* why you hate me so much?' she said quietly. 'Do you hate all girls, because you want to stop being a virgin but you can't because you can't even *get it up*?'

Mark took a step towards her, and Sammie tried to move away, sagging against the kitchen door in exhaustion. Her head was pounding, and she really didn't feel well at all.

'I can get it up,' Mark told her. 'Just not when I'm looking at you.'

Sammie fumbled in her jeans pocket for her house keys. She needed to go and lie down, but she didn't want Mark to see how ill she felt.

'You think you're so special,' Mark went on, 'but you're not. I never thought you were. And I'm not going to let Jay be hurt any more by a girl like you.'

'This isn't about Jay, is it?' she said. 'In fact, I don't believe it's even about me. It's about the fact that me and Jay have *sex*, and you're jealous. Do you think I haven't noticed how you watch us, the way you were looking at those pictures of me he showed you?'

Sammie managed to open the door and she went inside the house. Mark followed her and she let him, because she didn't have the energy to get him to leave. She made her way up the stairs to her bedroom and Mark stood there beside her. He didn't seem able to leave her alone.

'What?' she said. 'What is it, Mark? What do you *want?*'

He didn't answer.

'You know what,' Sammie said, pulling her t-shirt over her head, 'if you want sex *that* much, why don't you just do me, Mark? Or don't you have it in you?' She took her bra off, though Mark's eyes didn't move to her breasts, they were fixed on her stomach where there were huge, angry, pinky-red bruises.

'He...' Mark said, 'he...'

'Yes,' Sammie said, 'he beat me.' She started to undo her jeans. 'Why aren't you happy? Isn't this what you want?'

She pushed her jeans down and stepped out of them, her eyes fixed on Mark, and she was about to do the same with her underwear when she saw Mark's face fill with horror. He pointed towards her and said, 'Your... your legs...'

Sammie looked down, and saw what he meant. There were smears of blood on the inside of her thighs, and she felt between her legs, where she discovered that her knickers were wet. When she took her hand away her fingers were covered in blood. 'No,' she said, 'no, no, no, no.'

Mark was backing away from her. He looked terrified, his face white and sickly.

'Help,' Sammie said, 'help me...'

Mark looked at her one second longer. Then he turned and ran from the room.

Felicity

46

Mark sat down beside me again, and I stared at him in horror. 'Mark,' I said, 'Mark, you did tell the police Jay had taken me, didn't you?'

When Mark spoke, he was looking down at his lap, and wouldn't meet my eye. 'He can't go to prison,' he said quietly.

'What?'

'He can't,' Mark said, 'it would... it would make him worse. They...' he looked at me. 'Can you imagine what he'd be like in prison?' he asked me. 'They'd... they'd destroy him. He can't go through that.'

I couldn't answer, and I began to feel afraid.

'Look,' Mark said, 'Jay doesn't mean to do these things. I... I'll help you get out, and I want... I want to be with you, but I don't want Jay to get in trouble.'

'You... you what?' I said softly.

'I love you, Felicity,' Mark said, 'and you love me too, don't you? I want you, and the baby—'

'I don't love *you*!' I said. 'I love the Mark I knew back in Coalton, who made my jewellery website and cooked ridiculous amounts of food to try to impress me, and who was kind to me, and who was normal! I loved the Mark who was upset when he found out I'd been hurt, who told me I should go to the police—'

'I'm still the same person.'

'No,' I said, 'no, you're not. As soon as this involved Jay, it's like... it's like you're somebody else.'

Mark was silent for a while. Then I realised he was staring at something; the sapphire necklace Jay had given to me. 'That necklace,' he said. 'It's just like hers.'

'What?' I said, although I already understood.

'You know what this is about, don't you?' he said. 'He's trying to make you into her. He's trying to make you into Sammie.'

My blood ran cold as I remembered how Jay had called me by her name, but I said nothing to Mark.

'After you'd gone, I remembered how you said you told Jay about what happened to your parents the night you met him. And I thought about the way you look, even the way you act sometimes.'

'What are you talking about?'

'Sammie looked a bit like you,' Mark said, 'and her parents, they weren't dead, but... they weren't exactly *there*. I think Jay saw something in you, and maybe not straight away, but at some point he decided to make the life with you that he'd once promised her.'

'He promised her this?' I said, showing him my handcuffed wrist.

'No,' Mark said. 'It obviously went wrong. You decided you didn't want to be with him, but I think by then he couldn't stop.'

'If he wants to be with *Sammie* so much,' I exploded, 'why didn't he put all his effort into finding her, instead of messing around with you and me? I know she's missing, but it's not like he knows she's dead, so why didn't he...' I stopped talking, as another realisation hit me. 'No,' I said, 'no... she's not.' I could already see in Mark's face that what I suspected was true. 'She's not,' I said again, 'she... she's not dead. Is she?'

Mark was silent for a while, and then he nodded. 'Yes,' he said, 'she's dead. Jay... Jay killed her.'

Sammie

47

Once Mark had left Sammie sank down to her knees and held her stomach. 'It's okay,' she whispered, 'it's okay, baby. Just hold on… hold on.' She picked up her phone, not sure what to do, and found herself calling her mum.

Her mum's voice sounded funny on the end of the phone.

'This isn't really a good time,' she told Sammie.

Sammie closed her eyes, pressing the phone too hard against her ear and trying not to cry. 'Mum, I… I really need—'

'Everything is such a bloody mess,' her mum said suddenly, taking Sammie aback with the emotion in her voice.

'Mum, what's… what's happened?'

Her mum made a little noise that might have been a sob. 'I'm sorry darling,' she said, 'you don't need all this right now. How was your exam? History, wasn't it?'

Sammie's mind went blank. Her mum thought she'd had an exam today. That's why she thought Sammie was calling.

'Mum, I need—'

'It's your dad and me,' her mum said, 'I know you're in the middle of your exams right now but I'm sure you realised this was coming after you found out about the separation. We… we're getting a divorce.'

'Oh,' Sammie said. Inside her head, things began to seem unreal. She felt a bit like she was floating, and then a wave of painful cramps in her stomach made her gasp, though her mum didn't notice. She was talking about the practical arrangements, about the move to Kent, about Sammie going to college, and then she said, 'You know, I think this will all work out for the best.'

'What?' Sammie said.

'I mean, nothing's really been right for years, has it? Everything will get better now.'

'No!' Sammie said, crying. 'Nothing is better now. Everything is... everything is *fucking shit*.'

Her mum was stunned into silence.

'Sammie!' she said eventually. 'Don't you dare talk to me like—'

'I hate you!' Sammie shouted. 'I never wanted to move to this stupid place anyway, *you* made me, and you have no idea what it's been like for me, what I've been through, and now you're telling me things will be better, like you know what's better for me! You have *no* idea what's better for me! You don't even know who I am. As far as you're concerned I'm dead, aren't I? I'm dead like Alfie.'

'Sam—' Sammie cut off her mum's voice by flinging her phone at the wall, where it broke in two and fell to the floor in a clatter of plastic.

She tried to gather her thoughts, but before she could get anywhere she heard the sound of the back door opening again. She thought it must be Mark, and she was so relieved he'd returned that she cried out, 'Mark, you came back! I'm upstairs, come and help me.'

She got unsteadily to her feet, wrapped a dressing gown around her body, and made it out onto the landing. She couldn't see or hear Mark coming, so she started making her way down the stairs to find him, clutching at the banister.

'Mark—' she began to say again as she reached the kitchen and stepped inside. But then words failed her as the person who'd just let themselves into the house locked eyes with her, and instead of Mark, she found herself looking at Jay.

'Sorry I'm not who you were expecting,' he said.

'Jay,' Sammie said.

'Why was he here?' Jay asked her. 'I saw him leaving.'

Sammie pulled her dressing gown more tightly around her body, but she saw Jay take in her bare legs, and the fact she didn't have a top on. He strode across to her. 'Why were you calling out to him to help you?' he asked, taking her arm. 'Was that why he was here? Were you... were you telling *him* he had to help you with the baby?'

'No,' Sammie said, 'Jay, please, just leave me alone. I won't bother you any more—'

'You really don't know whose the baby is, do you?' Jay said.

'Jay—'

He gripped her arm more tightly, '*Do you?*' he said.

Sammie wrenched her arm away from him and ran out into the hall, but Jay followed her. 'Was that what you were doing just then? Trying to persuade him to look after the baby, now that I've said I don't want it?' He paused a second, then said, 'Is that why you don't have any clothes on? Were you going to sleep with him again to try to get him to help you?'

'No,' Sammie said, 'no, Jay. I've never... I've never slept with him. I told you—'

Jay grabbed her and threw her towards the stairs and Sammie stumbled, falling to her knees as he stood over her.

'I came here to tell you I'd give you another chance,' he said, 'I thought about what you told me, and I came to talk, and try to work things out. But then I found you were here with *him!*'

Sammie closed her eyes. This couldn't be happening.

'Jay...' she said helplessly, 'I—'

He dragged her to her feet again. 'You're what?' he said. 'You're sorry?'

'I am sorry.'

He looked her up and down. Her dressing gown was coming undone, and she wrapped it back around to cover her chest. 'You're disgusting, Sammie,' he said, 'you really are a slag.'

He began to walk away from her, and Sammie followed him.

'You never give me a chance!' she said. 'You just want to believe the worst of me—'

'Because it's true!' Jay said. 'Mark told me what you're really like. He told me you're no good, and I've given you chance after chance. You almost persuaded me he was lying to me. He's my best friend, Sammie. You tried to make out like he was deceiving me, making stuff up about you, when all the time it was *you*—'

'What do you want me to say?' Sammie cried. 'It's like you want it to be true. Is that what you want to hear, Jay? Do you want me to tell you I don't know who the baby's father is? Do you want me to tell you I'll do it with anyone, that I've done it with Mark, and half the boys at school, that in fact so many guys have had a go that I don't even *know* how many I've been with? That all this time I've just been laughing at you? Is that... is that what you *want me to say*?'

Jay looked at her for a moment. Just a moment. Then an expression came over his face that was extraordinary. She had no time to understand what was going to happen; no time to take it back, find the right words to sort it out. His hands were around her throat, pushing her back against the wall, pressing her windpipe; crushing it. She tried to push him away from her, to fight him. She thought for a second that perhaps he was just scaring her and he'd stop, but he didn't. He carried on watching her, squeezing while she choked for air, until everything started greying out.

The last thing Sammie thought was that she wished she had her parents. She wished her mum and dad would walk through the door, see what was going on, and save her. Even if Mark came back she'd be glad, because she was sure no matter how much he hated her that he wouldn't let Jay do this. But all there was was Jay, and she realised that's all there would ever be, now. Nobody would save her. Nobody would come. She was alone.

Felicity

48

'And you...' I said to Mark, 'you *knew*. All along, you knew he'd killed her.'

'It was an accident.'

I closed my eyes. Why had I contacted Mark? I'd known there was something strange about the fact he'd said Sammie had gone to live with her mum when he knew she was missing, and I'd known there was something strange between him and Jay.

'He did it because he thought she was sleeping with me,' Mark said. 'She was pregnant with his baby, and the thought of her being with me was too much for him. He just... he just lost control. It wasn't his fault.'

'Where...' I said, 'where is she? Where is her... body?'

'She's safe,' Mark said, 'we took care of her. For a while I thought we'd get caught, but... Sammie had written a goodbye note to her parents. We left it out for her mum to find and we got rid of the bags she'd packed along with her body. Nobody ever questioned it.'

'Where is she?' I asked again. 'Where is she Mark?'

'Just down the road,' Mark said. 'In the woods.'

'You... you... she's... she's *down the road?*'

'You didn't know!' Mark said, amazed. 'This house. This house is just outside Tatchley.'

...

'Mark,' I said, after a long, shocked silence, 'why? Why did you... help him?'

'It was... it was like some crazy... reflex,' he said. 'Something terrible had happened and I wanted to make it go away. I just did it. I barely thought. I still dream about it sometimes. It was really hard work, and Jay barely helped. He wouldn't touch her, so I had to do everything. I wrapped her up in a sleeping bag I found in her room; one of those ones that go up over your head, with the drawstrings. I did it up so that all you could see was her nose, and a little of her hair that managed to escape. When I rolled her body into the grave we dug in the woods she fell on her back. I didn't want to touch her again to turn her over, so when I first started covering her with earth I had to throw it onto that little opening to her face. I told myself it wasn't real, and we were just playing a game.'

He paused and looked at me, but I couldn't speak so he carried on.

'I thought the police would find us,' he said, 'I thought me and Jay would both get arrested. For years I thought they would come, but they just... *don't*. And everyone around me wanted me to carry on doing normal things. They wanted me to finish my exams, go to university, get a job. I sleepwalked through everything. Then one day it felt like it couldn't really have happened, like I must have imagined it all, because my life was just... normal. But Jay went to pieces. He *suffered*, Felicity. People don't understand him. His mum... his mum figured out what had happened. Not... not *exactly* what happened, but she knew Jay had something to do with Sammie going missing. She'd overheard an argument between Jay and Sammie, and I think there were other things too. She ignored it for a few years, but then it got too much for her and she threw Jay out. As if *that* was going to help him.' He added violently.

'Mark,' I said slowly, when he seemed to have said all he was going to say, 'please will you just help me get away? I won't go to the police about you or Jay, or any of this. I swear. Just please, get me out of here. I don't want my baby to be born here—'

'Fliss, I'll let you go,' Mark said. 'I'm not... I'm not going to *leave* you here.'

'Okay,' I said, 'okay. Thank you. Thank you, Mark.'

'I'll go and look in the garage for some tools,' he said calmly, as though the past few minutes hadn't even happened, 'I'm sure there will be something that can—'

There was a sound, and we both froze.

Keys in the front door.

Jay was home.

...

He came straight upstairs. There was no question of him knowing Mark was there. He'd have seen Mark's car outside, but apart from that he was home too early. He'd said he'd come home a little early and check on me after I'd been unwell in the night, but it was only lunchtime now. He must have realised what I'd done with his phone, and he'd probably been planning what he'd do ever since.

When he found us in the bedroom, Jay didn't even look at Mark or comment on his presence. He was holding a container in his hand; the sort you'd carry chemicals in, or fuel, and I didn't understand what it meant until without a second thought he opened it and started sloshing it over my body. I tried to dodge out of the way but I couldn't get very far from the bed, and though I threw myself onto the floor my left arm was still stretched up towards the headboard, and petrol dripped from my hair and soaked into my clothes.

Mark hurled himself at Jay to try to stop him, but Jay shoved him aside and took out a box of matches.

'Jay,' Mark said slowly, 'don't do this.'

Jay still ignored him, stepping over to where I lay crouched and shaking on the floor, and he stood over me.

'I really thought we could make this work, Flissie,' he said.

'We can,' I sobbed, 'just don't hurt me, please don't hurt me.'

'Jay,' Mark said firmly. 'You don't have to do this.'

'Don't I?' he said, turning to him. 'Why, what do you suggest I do? Let her go so she can be with you? So that *you* can bring up *my* baby? So that you can take her away from me, just like you did with Sammie?'

Mark spoke very calmly. 'I never took Sammie away from you,' he said, 'I've told you that over and over. I didn't love Sammie.'

Jay pointed at me. 'What about her?' he asked. 'Do you love *her*?'

'I love Felicity,' Mark said, 'but Felicity isn't Sammie. Look at her, Jay. Look how scared she is.'

Jay looked at me, and smiled. Slowly, he slid open the box of matches.

'I'm the one you're really angry at,' Mark said, 'not her. She's going to have your baby. You don't want to hurt her.'

Ignoring him, Jay selected a match, and held it against the strip on the side of the box.

'Sammie didn't enjoy it,' Mark said desperately, and Jay turned to him. 'What me and her did together – she didn't like it. She only did it because she was scared, and alone. And Felicity only ever started having sex with me because she was trying to make you happy. That's how much she cares for you, Jay. For *you*. Not me.'

Jay considered this. 'Why would you say that?' he asked finally. 'Why would anyone ever say that, unless they were saying anything they could think of to save somebody's life?'

Without further hesitation, he swiped the match against the side of the box, and it burst into flame.

49

I screamed, and he faltered. Only for a second, but it gave Mark enough time to come up behind him and simply blow out the flame, and snatch the box of matches from his hand. Jay didn't even try to stop him. He fell to his knees on the floor by my side, and he started to cry.

I watched him in astonishment for a while, taking great gulps of air and thanking God that I was still alive, while to my even greater astonishment, Mark knelt down beside Jay and put his arms around him.

'It's all right,' Mark said, stroking Jay's back. 'We're going to sort this out. It's all right.'

'Why did you do it?' Jay asked shakily. 'Why did you do it to me?'

'I don't know,' Mark said, 'I'm sorry, Jay. I'm so sorry.'

They stayed kneeling together like that for a long time, until Mark let go of Jay and talked to him slowly, gently.

'Where are the keys, Jay?'

'What keys?'

'For Felicity. We need to let her go.'

Without resistance, Jay reached into his pocket, and handed Mark his key ring, on which the small handcuff key dangled. Mark stood up and set me free, while Jay stayed on the floor with his face in his hands.

'Go and wash the petrol off,' Mark told me, 'I'll deal with Jay.'

I ran into the bathroom, stripping my clothes off on the bathmat and shaking as I cleaned myself with water so hot it burned. I shampooed my hair three times and sluiced the petrol from my skin. It became too much to stay stood up so I dropped to my knees in the bath and tried to take slow, calming breaths. Instead I just started to retch, and I felt like I was going to collapse. I was still in this state when Mark knocked on the door and then came in to check on me.

'It's over,' he said, reaching across to turn the shower off. 'Jay's not going to hurt you any more.'

'What do you mean?'

'I've talked to him. He's going to leave you alone.'

'And you *believe* him?'

Mark handed me a towel, then he sat on the edge of the bath while I stood up and dried myself.

'Felicity, you remember I told you where we are.'

'Yes.'

'I'm going to take Jay to Sammie's grave now. I'm going to try to help him say goodbye to her properly.'

I didn't answer, and Mark continued. 'I... I want you to come with us.'

'No,' I said, 'why would I...'

'Let me look after you,' Mark said. 'Not forever, if you don't want to, but you can stay with me until you get yourself sorted.' He reached out to my face. 'I... I really do love you, you know,' he said.

I looked at him, and then I nodded.

I stepped out of the bath, feeling strange and hollow. Mark went back into the bedroom, but I thought twice about following. I needed some clean clothes and that's where they were, but I didn't want to see Jay. I didn't want to put myself at any further risk from him. Tentatively, I left the bathroom and peeked around the bedroom door, where I saw Mark helping Jay unsteadily to his feet. He seemed dazed. He let Mark lead him out of the room straight past me, so I went inside and found myself something to wear. They were waiting by the door as I came downstairs, and I followed after them as they left, amazed at what an odd pair they looked – Mark encouraging Jay along like he was a child.

For the whole journey I followed several paces behind them, my hand on my bump. At one point Mark stopped and came to speak to me. 'It'll be over soon, Felicity,' he said. 'After this, I'll take you away from here.'

I nodded, and when he started walking again I continued to follow them. I felt like a sort of strange, dazed, shuffling creature, blinking in the sunlight. Jay didn't look at me once.

We didn't stop again until we were in a little clearing in the thick of the woods, way off the well-trodden paths, and though to me it didn't look much different to anywhere else, it was clear from the look on both men's faces that we'd arrived, though how they each reacted was in stark contrast. While Mark looked solemn, and serious, but still self-contained, Jay went to pieces. His face turned a sickly white and his steps slowed to the point where it looked like it was an intense physical effort to make his body move. He was visibly shaking. I didn't think I'd ever seen anybody in such a state of horror. He dropped to his knees in front of a big dead tree trunk, furry with moss and draped in mustard yellow fungus.

'Is that...' I whispered to Mark, 'is that where... she...'

Mark nodded.

Jay placed one hand flat on the earth in front of him, and for a second I thought he really was going to say goodbye. But then he was suddenly on his feet.

'Why did you bring me here?' he asked Mark.

Mark stepped towards him. 'Jay,' he said softly, 'it's over. You need to accept she's gone, and let Felicity go.'

Jay looked at me. 'She means nothing to me,' he said, 'you're welcome to her.'

Mark tried to touch Jay's arm but he stepped away from him. 'She means nothing to me,' he said again, 'she never did. None of them... none of them ever do.'

'Jay,' Mark said, 'let's... let's say goodbye to Sammie now. We can do it together.'

Mark helped Jay to kneel down on the ground again, and he was about to speak but before he could get any words out Jay began to cry.

'You... you wouldn't even let me dress her,' Jay said. 'You

wouldn't even let her have her dressing gown on. She... she wouldn't have wanted to be almost *naked*. And the *blood*, the blood, on her legs...'

Mark glanced round at me, then turned back to Jay. 'There was no time,' Mark said quietly, 'it was too difficult to get her in the sleeping bag with a dressing gown on—'

'Didn't you care?' Jay said. 'Don't you care that she... that she's cold? That the... that the baby—'

'Listen to me,' Mark said harshly, 'she's gone. You killed her, Jay. She's dead. She doesn't feel cold, she doesn't feel anything.' His voice softened a little. 'But she's at peace now.'

Jay began to cry more heavily, and Mark sat with him for a while, but he showed no signs of stopping, so Mark got to his feet and came back over to me.

'Let's leave him be,' he said quietly.

...

Mark led me away from the sound of Jay's sobs and into the trees.

'I know it's a shock,' Mark said, 'are you okay?'

'Yes,' I said, untruthfully.

'Here,' Mark said, 'let's rest here a moment. You look tired.'

I nodded, and leant against a tree, while Mark took his jacket off and laid it on the ground.

'Sit down,' he said.

I did as he asked, and he sat beside me and put his hand briefly over mine. 'I'm sorry, Felicity,' he said. 'You didn't deserve all this.'

'You have to tell the police,' I said. 'I know... I know you'd get in trouble too, but all you did was hide the body, you didn't *hurt* her, and if you come clean now, I'm sure they—'

'I can't, Felicity.'

'But don't you think Sammie's parents deserve to know the truth?'

Mark watched me for a while, then he reached his hand towards my face, and brushed some hair out of my eye. 'I do love you, you know,' he said, 'in a way, at least.'

I frowned. 'What are you—'

Before I could finish my sentence, Mark's hand was over my mouth and he was pinching my nostrils closed. I struggled against him and made noises in my throat, but he pushed me down onto the ground and knelt over me, continuing to stop me breathing. My feet scrabbled uselessly in the dirt, and I grabbed his arms to try to push him away from me, but he simply stared down at me, pressing my mouth and nose as hard as he could, his face completely empty of emotion.

50

All of a sudden, Mark was being pulled away from me, and I saw Jay's face, contorted with anger and confusion.

'What the fuck are you doing?' he shouted at Mark, while I lay gasping for breath.

'She was... she would have told—'

'She's pregnant with my child!' Jay said. 'You were going to kill her—'

'So were you!' Mark said. 'You were going to *burn* her.'

Jay stepped up close to Mark. 'That's different,' he said, 'she's *my* girlfriend. I can do what the fuck I want with her, but she is nothing to do with you.'

Mark looked down at me. 'You said you didn't want her,' he said. 'You said she was nothing to you.'

'And why do you think I have to say that?' Jay said.

'I... I don't—'

'Because of *you!* Because as soon as something is important to me, you'll want to take it.'

'That's not true,' Mark said, 'I care about you. I don't want to take things from you.'

'No!' Jay said. 'You knew I loved Sammie and you took her away from me. You took her away from me *deliberately* because you wanted her for yourself, when you already had everything I ever wanted. A family, friends—'

'No—'

'Why did you have to do that to me?' Jay shouted. 'Why did you have to decide that you loved her too?' His eyes were fixed on Mark, and I started to get up from the ground but then I stopped, scared. If either of them saw me I knew they wouldn't let me get away.

Mark seemed like he wanted to speak but couldn't bring

himself to, and Jay gave him a shove.

'Why?' he shouted at him again. 'Why did you do it to me? Why did you have to love her?'

'I didn't love her!' Mark shouted back. 'I wasn't in love with her; I was in love with *you*!'

...

The words hung in the air. Jay stood, rigid with disbelief, staring at Mark. He stayed this way so long that Mark took a step towards him. Jay still didn't move, and slowly Mark began to reach out his hand towards Jay's face. Jay remained frozen with incomprehension right up to the second that Mark's fingers brushed his cheek, then he twisted away from him. 'What?' he said. 'You... what?'

'I loved you, Jay,' Mark said, 'I *still* love you.'

Jay staggered back several paces from Mark. 'No,' he said, 'no, you don't.'

'I do,' Mark said. 'I did it all for you, Jay. Everything—'

'Why... why did you... why did you sleep with her then? With Sammie—'

Mark smiled. 'I never slept with her.'

'You told... you told me—'

'Because she wasn't a nice girl, Jay. You weren't even *interested* in girls before she came along—'

'Yes, I was,' Jay said, 'of course I was—'

'You didn't talk about them.'

'No,' Jay said, 'because you weren't interested in hearing about them—' he stopped and stared at Mark. 'And now I know why,' he said, and he looked disgusted.

'It wasn't your fault,' Mark said, 'any of it. She *corrupted* you. And me. I had to show you what she was like. She didn't love you properly Jay, not like I did, but you were so obsessed with her I had to prove it. I had to stop you making a mistake that would ruin your life. I mean, what did she ever do for you? Was she the one who was there for you year after year after year, through all the stuff with your mum and dad, all the times you got in fights at school? Was she the one who saw you crying sometimes, because you felt so alone and you thought nobody was there for you? *I* was the one who was there, and I was the one who was still there, after her, to try to pick up the pieces.'

'You... you did all of it,' Jay said, 'you lied about her sending pictures, you tricked... you *tricked* her...'

'Yes, and it didn't take much to get you to believe me, did it? All I had to do was say the right few words here and there, sow a few seeds of doubt, and it was like you *wanted* her to be betraying you.'

'She was *pregnant!* She needed me—'

'She needed attention,' Mark spat, 'that's all she wanted. She wanted boys to look at her. She wanted them to want her. If she wanted respect, she should have kept her clothes on for once—'

Jay gave Mark a shove.

'I loved her!' Jay said. 'I loved her more than anything.'

'No. You beat her. You beat her, and you were cruel to her, and you *raped* her, Jay. That's how she told me she got pregnant, she said you raped her.'

'No,' Jay said, 'no. She said... she never said that.'

'Well it's what she said to me. She was scared of you. That's the truth.'

'No,' Jay said, 'she knew I never meant it. She wasn't scared of me—'

'Yes, she was. She couldn't make you happy, and she knew it. They never can, Jay, because they don't get you. None of them do.'

'None of who?'

'Girls. Women. That's why things could never work with Sammie. They'll never work with any of them.'

Mark reached out to Jay again. 'Jay, you tried to kill Sammie,' he said, 'that's how much you—' Mark realised what he'd said and stopped in horror, though it took Jay a second to absorb it.

'Tried?' Jay said at last.

'Jay... I...'

I watched Jay's face as he understood. 'You,' he said, '*you* killed her?'

Suddenly, Mark's self − assurance disappeared and he backed away. 'Jay,' he said, 'Jay, I—'

Jay lunged at him.

Mark

51

Mark had made it barely halfway home before he got the phone call from Jay, who was frantic, hysterical. It was difficult to make out the words.

'Calm down,' he said, already turning back towards Sammie's house, 'you did what?'

He ran there in a daze. He dashed around the side of the house, into the back garden and to the door into the kitchen, which was still ajar. The house was much as he had left it, except that Jay was sitting in the middle of the kitchen floor, crying.

'I didn't mean to,' he said.

Mark knelt down beside him. 'What?' he said. 'What have you done?'

'I... I... I hurt her... and she... she won't wake... wake up.'

Mark's blood ran cold. He put his hand on Jay's shoulder. 'Is she... is she dead?' he asked, surprised how calm his voice was.

'I tried... I tried to... save her, but I don't know how to do it. She wasn't moving, and then I saw... I saw all this... this *blood*, between... between her... between her *legs*—' he started to cry too heavily to continue talking.

'Okay,' Mark said, 'okay. It's all right, Jay, calm down.'

He tried to put his arms around him but Jay pushed him away. 'It's your fault!' he said. 'Because you've been sleeping with her...'

Jay started to cry even harder, and Mark realised Jay had something in one of his hands. He tried to prise his fingers open, but it wasn't easy.

'Her necklace,' Mark said, when he finally saw the little blue pendant.

'I fixed it for her,' Jay said through his tears. 'I found a new chain. I was going to tell her we could still... we could still go... but then she was here with you...'

'Where is she?' Mark asked him. 'Where's her... body?'

Jay pointed towards the door out to the hallway, which was closed.

'Okay,' Mark said. He stood up and tried to pull Jay up too. 'Come with me,' he said, 'we'll check whether there's anything we can do to help her.'

'No,' Jay moaned, 'no.'

Mark knelt back down and this time when Mark held him, Jay didn't protest. 'Listen to me,' Mark said into his hair, 'I'm going to make this right.'

'I... I killed her!' Jay said. 'I've killed the... the baby—'

'Listen,' Mark said more firmly. 'This is going to be all right. I won't let anything happen to you.'

'To... to me?'

'She's got injuries all over her,' Mark said, 'on her face, and her body. I've seen them. And when I left her she was already losing her baby. It's not your fault, Jay. I know that it was an accident, but the thing is, other people aren't going to see it that way. You'll end up in prison.'

'No!' Jay said. 'I can't... I can't go to—'

'You won't have to,' Mark said, 'not if you do everything I say. But first we need to go and... to go and look at her. Do you understand?'

'I can't,' Jay said, 'I can't.'

'You can,' Mark said. 'And you can give her the necklace. You can put it on her.'

'You,' Jay said, holding the necklace out to Mark. 'You... do it.'

Mark took it and held Jay close to him. 'You're not a bad person,' he told him. 'You made a mistake. I know that.'

Jay sobbed into Mark's t-shirt and Mark stroked his cheek. 'It's all right,' he said, 'it's all right. You trust me, don't you?

Haven't I always been here for you?'

Mark waited a moment, then he felt Jay nod. 'I look after you, don't I?' he said. 'We look after each other.'

He felt Jay nod again and he gently pushed him away. 'I'm going to go and look at Sammie now,' he said. 'It's going to be okay. Tell me you know it's going to be okay.'

'Okay,' Jay said.

'And you trust me.'

'Yes,' Jay said, 'I trust you.'

Slowly, Mark stood up. He felt frightened to go and look at Sammie's body on his own, but there was no way Jay was going to get up from the floor and he knew he had no choice. He opened the door out to the hallway and stepped through, closing it behind him with a soft click, and when he saw Sammie he almost cried out.

She wasn't dead. She was on her knees gasping for breath, the sound so loud he couldn't believe they hadn't heard it, though Jay's sobs were echoing through the house. But that wasn't what horrified him so much as the blood, which was worse than when he'd seen it earlier – it was still mainly on her legs, but there was some in a little pool on the floor which had been smeared around. When she saw Mark, Sammie held her hand out in a weak, desperate gesture. Mark took a step towards her and knelt by her side.

He thought he was going to help her. Up until the last second he thought he was going to help her. Even when he watched himself place his own hand around her throat he didn't quite realise what he was doing, though she struggled and grabbed weakly at his arm. He continued to squeeze long after she stopped moving and he thought to himself that Jay had probably let go far too quickly – he'd probably got scared. When Mark finally let go his hand was shaking, and her body slumped down to the floor so that she was lying on her side in front of him. He carefully held her wrist and checked for a pulse, and put his fingers up to her nose to see if he could feel any breath. There was nothing. In the kitchen Jay was still crying, and Mark looked down at Sammie. Her dressing gown was undone and he could see all of her body, and though she was a mess and part of him didn't want to look, he found he couldn't tear his eyes away from her, not for a long time. Finally, he pulled the gown closed around her, and swept her hair back from her face, before taking the necklace that Jay had given him and fastening it round her neck. Then he took in the sight of her face, tracing his finger down her cheek to her lips, pressing her bottom lip for a moment, pulling it down so her little white teeth became visible, then he let go so that it fell slackly back into place. His whole body was shaking. He felt scared of her, in a way, but strangely excited too.

He'd felt a little like this once before, when they'd been in the woods, and he'd pretended to leave but had really hidden in the trees to watch Jay rape her. He'd known that what was happening to her was wrong, and that it was happening in part because he had told lies about her, but he'd been both frightened and exhilarated by it, and hadn't been able to stop looking. He had even imagined himself in Jay's place, doing to her as Jay was doing, because she was a slut, the worst kind of slut, and no amount of suffering could ever be enough for her. She'd *spoilt* Jay, turning his head and making him obsessed with her by what she did in bed with him. Mark had found himself wanting to make her understand that, wishing that *he* could hurt her with sex, hurt her as much as he possibly could. He could remember those moments in the woods so clearly now as he looked down at Sammie's lifeless body on the floor in front of him. He could remember how she'd been on her back on the ground, her legs splayed awkwardly, skirt pushed up and her school shirt hanging open. Her head had been turned away from where he'd been standing so he hadn't been able to see her face but she must have been in pain, her whole body moving with the force of what Jay was doing to her. It had made Mark feel sick, briefly. But the longer he'd stood there in the woods the more he'd felt hot, and flustered, and uncomfortable. His cheeks had started burning, and the urge he'd usually managed to fight for the last two or three years had started to nag at him again, and nag him worse than ever. He remembered how his eyes had stung with tears, but the feeling when he had finally gripped himself in his hand had been so intense that he could almost have cried out. Within what seemed like mere seconds it was over, but the force of his orgasm had made him stumble backwards, snapping the twig and making Jay look round and say, 'What was that?' Then, even though he'd felt dizzy and his head had been spinning, he'd had to run away through the trees, before he was found.

Slowly, with the memory of that afternoon still filling his mind, he bent down over Sammie's body, bringing his mouth close to her ear. Could he really bring himself to say it – the words that had suddenly popped into his mind? It would be sick and appalling to speak them, but at the same time he wanted to so badly that he felt giddy. He looked over her face again; her delicate skin, her eyelids fringed with lashes of the lightest, feathery gold. He'd never looked at her so closely before. Not even when she had been doing the sex thing for him had he looked at her as closely as he was now, and he realised that she *was* beautiful in her way. When she'd been alive and with Jay, he'd never noticed it before. All he'd felt was hate for her. Hate, and a kind of fascination, because Jay was having all of his first sexual experiences with *her,* when Mark had always hoped, and wished, that they would be with him.

Finally, the words could stay inside him no longer, and with a stab of wild, forbidden joy, he whispered, 'I won.'

He stayed just a moment longer, then he gathered himself together and got to his feet. He opened the door into the kitchen, and Jay looked up at him with a desperate, stricken hope in his eyes.

Mark shook his head. 'She... she's dead,' he said, 'I'm sorry, Jay. There's nothing we can do. You... you've killed her. But don't worry, I'm going to help you sort it out. I'll help you sort everything out.'

Felicity

52

I watched what happened next in silence, my hand on my bump, trying to gather the courage to get away. Jay had Mark on the floor in seconds, and punched him two, three times. How Mark could still be able to speak after this I had no idea, but even I could make out his words, said with a horrifying calmness. 'You can... you can hit me if it makes you feel better,' he said, 'but I did it for you. She wasn't right—'

Jay raised his fist again. 'And *you* are?' he said.

'I know,' Mark said, 'I know this isn't... this isn't what you think you want. But I could make you so happy, Jay. Haven't I proved how far I'd go for you? I... I love you. I'll always love you.'

Jay lowered his fist. 'If you *love* me so much,' he said, 'why didn't you let me stay with you when I came to you for help back when you were at uni? Why did you kick me out on the fucking *street*?'

'It was... too painful,' Mark said, 'I realised you didn't... that you didn't feel for me like I did for you. And I thought you never would. But then... then I discovered you followed me to Coalton. You sent Felicity to me. And I understood then that you're just scared, Jay. You do feel it, you just don't want to admit it, and I get it—'

'I came to Coalton because I hate you,' Jay said. 'I don't *love* you. I never even *liked* you that much. You just... hung around me all the time, pretending like we were best friends, and all you wanted... all you wanted was to... to have some *grubby* little fumble with me.'

'It wasn't like that!' Mark said. 'You needed me. We needed each other. You thought I had this big, happy family, but it wasn't like that! I wasn't myself with them! I had to be somebody else, somebody I wasn't. You thought you had... the... the *monopoly* on feeling like nobody wanted you. You acted like you were the only person who ever got laughed at, and ridiculed. You would never believe anyone loved you or liked you even when they said they did. The only person you ever trusted and wanted to spend time with was me, but then *she* came along—'

'What did you think?' Jay said. 'That I'd carry on wanting to... to play stupid games in the woods with *you,* when I had a girl like Sammie?'

'We have a bond,' Mark said, 'you can't deny it any more. You came to Coalton to find me again. You can't forget about me any more than I can forget about you.'

'What?' Jay said. 'You think I wanted to find you so I could... so I could what? So we could *fuck*? Is that what you really think? Do you think I want you to... to *kill* my girlfriends—'

'I'd do it all over again,' Mark said, 'I've never felt I've had a... *connection* with anyone except you. If you would just admit you love me too I'd be better than anyone else you've ever been with. I'd be better even than *her*... than Sammie. I would do anything... *anything* for you.'

Jay watched Mark in silent, horrified disgust for a moment. Then he drew back his fist again.

53

Jay carried on kicking and punching Mark long after he must have known that he was dead. I was too scared to move, thinking that if I reminded Jay I was there his rage might turn to me, so I sat and listened to the awful, thick sound of the blows punctuated by the rustle of the wind in the leaves, and the faraway rumble of traffic that just about carried through the trees.

When Mark had been reduced to nothing more than a motionless heap on the ground, Jay dropped to his knees by the body and started to cry.

I was still so afraid that my body seemed frozen, but I forced myself to move. Slowly, I got to my knees, and using a tree trunk to steady myself I made it to my feet, fearing every second that Jay would turn and see me. I waited one more moment, taking in the sight of Jay hunched over the body on the ground, then I took a silent step away into the trees, then another and another, only taking my eyes off him for a split second each time. When I was sure I was far enough away, and Jay was showing no signs of even being aware of my presence, I turned my back on him, and made out something of a narrow path through the trees in the distance. I took a deep breath, fixed my eyes on the path, and without so much as a backward glance at Jay, I ran.

Found You

Book Two in the chilling NO ESCAPE psychological thriller series

She escaped. But he's coming to get her.

After her imprisonment at the brutal hands of her ex, Jay, Felicity is slowly putting her life back together. She's got a new name, a new hairstyle, and even a new partner: strong, supportive Scott, whose down-to-earth nature makes him the perfect stepfather to little Leo. Though the nightmares still haunt her, she's starting to feel that her struggles are over; that she may, finally, be safe.

But Jay is still out there somewhere.

And Felicity can't shake the feeling she's being watched.

Never Let Her Go

Book Three in the chilling NO ESCAPE psychological thriller series

All he wants is his family...

After escaping her ordeal at the hands of her obsessive ex, Jay, Felicity thought she was safe, building a new life with Scott and son Leo in a seaside town. Little does she know that Jay has tracked her down and wormed his way into the confidence of Vicky, a woman from Scott's past who has her own very sharp axe to grind...

In the gripping final book of the No Escape trilogy, Jay's obsession with Felicity pushes him to ever more desperate lengths to get her back. Felicity soon discovers that he'll stop at nothing, and history begins to repeat itself as she finds herself terrified, alone, and at Jay's mercy once again. Can she escape him before it's too late, or will she be destroyed by his determination to never let her go?

Get all the news about my upcoming books!

If you liked Anything For Him and you're keen to read more of my books in the future, I invite you to join the LK Chapman Reading Group. I send only occasional emails with information about new releases, offers and giveaways - no spam. You will also be able to download a free copy of my short story about a one night stand gone wrong, 'Worth Pursuing' (a prequel to Anything for Him that's now available exclusively to Reading Group subscribers) when you sign up!

Visit my website, www.lkchapman.com or any of my social media pages to sign up to the reading group.

Thank you so much for supporting me by buying my book, it means a lot to me, and I hope you enjoyed reading Anything For Him.

Help and support for issues covered in Anything For Him

UK
Refuge
Support for those who have experienced violence and abuse
www.refuge.org.uk
Call 0808 2000 247

Respect Phoneline
Help for people who inflict violence
Call 0808 802 4040 or visit www.respectphoneline.org.uk

US
The National Domestic Violence Hotline
www.thehotline.org
Or call 1-800-799-SAFE (7233)

Other books by LK Chapman

No Escape Series

Worth Pursuing (short story)

Anything for Him

Found You

Never Let Her Go

Psychological thrillers/suspense

The Stories She Tells

Sci-fi thrillers

Networked

Too Good for this World (short story)

Acknowledgements

A huge thank you to Shaun Smith for his vital feedback on the story, and to Carol Barber and Ben Smith for their ongoing help and enthusiasm for both this book and my previous novel.

For their support through the process of writing Anything for Him I would also like to thank my parents, and for his contributions and encouragement through every stage of the novel, thank you to my husband, Ashley. I couldn't have done it without you.

About the author

Louise Katherine Chapman was born in Somerset, UK in 1986. She studied Psychology at the University of Southampton before working as a psychologist developing personality questionnaires. She published her first novel, science-fiction thriller *Networked*, in 2014.

LK Chapman lives in Somerset, with her husband and young family.

You can find out more about LK Chapman by visiting her website **www.lkchapman.com**.

Connect with LK Chapman

Keep up to date with the latest news and new releases from LK Chapman:

Twitter: **@LK_Chapman**

Facebook: **www.facebook.com/lkchapmanbooks**

Subscribe to the LK Chapman newsletter by visiting **www.lkchapman.com**

The Stories She Tells
A psychological page-turner by LK Chapman

A heartbreaking secret. A lifetime of lies.

When Michael decides to track down ex-girlfriend Rae, who disappeared ten years ago while pregnant with his baby, he knows it could change his life forever. His search for her takes unexpected turns as he unearths multiple changes of identity and a childhood she tried to pretend never happened, but nothing could prepare him for what awaits when he finally finds her.

Rae appears to be happily married with a brand new baby daughter. But she is cagey about what happened to Michael's child, and starts to say alarming things: that her husband is trying to force her to give up her new baby for adoption, that he's attempting to undermine the bond between her and her child, and deliberately making her doubt her own sanity.

As Michael is drawn in deeper to her disturbing claims, he begins to doubt the truth of what she is saying. But is she really making it all up, or is there a shocking and heartbreaking secret at the root of the stories she tells?